CREATED

JANICE BOEKHOFF

WILDBLUE PRESS

WildBluePress.com

CREATED published by:
WILDBLUE PRESS
P.O. Box 102440
Denver, Colorado 80250

ISBN 978-1-947290-03-7 Trade Paperback
ISBN 978-1-947290-02-0 eBook
ISBN 978-1-960332-79-0 Hardback

Interior Formatting and Cover Design by Elijah Toten, www.totencreative.com

For Jenna

*May your curious spirit lead you to many amazing
discoveries of truth.*

CHAPTER ONE

"Pick up the pace, Tanol. If you cost me a hot meal, I'll smash your face." Christian looked over his shoulder, giving Tanol a piercing glare.

Tanol rolled his eyes. As if he would be scared. Christian was six inches shorter with more ego than muscles, unless you counted the muscles in his mouth. "Relax, we have plenty of time to get to the village and back before dinner."

Christian deepened his scowling eyebrows before turning around and plunging ahead through the dense trees. The rain forest closed them in on them on all sides like a green blanket draped over the sun.

"This is stupid anyway." Christian threw a fist into the air without turning around. "Why can't Manuel send a villager with the money? I hate being an errand boy every week."

"It's the jungle version of customer service." Tanol snorted out a laugh. More like Manuel paid their boss extra to keep his spotless reputation in the village. Tanol and Christian had to pick up the money, but they wouldn't get to keep much of it. Their boss took all the extra cash. Even so, Tanol wouldn't complain. The last guy who did was forced to hike twenty miles out of the jungle on his own.

The dense foliage thinned out, and they pushed into a small clearing with a few downed trees at the center—an island of open space within the sea of tangled jungle. A perfect place to rest, but Tanol didn't bother to ask.

Christian seemed too tense to rest. A few feet into the clearing, when Christian abruptly halted, Tanol almost ran into his back. Instinctively, Tanol lifted his gun and aimed, then lowered it back into the strap slung over his shoulder. A black tapir, one of the most elusive animals in the forest, stood on the other side of the clearing, using its short, twisting trunk to pull tender leaves off a bush. The tapir's left ear lifted straight up, then turned to the side. Had it heard their approach? It didn't really matter. They had plenty of tapir back at camp. Plus, he didn't want to carry it to the village and back.

The tapir shifted on its feet. Twisting its head away from them, it sniffed the air and held its ear erect toward an area off to their right. Was there someone else in the jungle?

The tapir's back legs tensed, ready to flee. Tanol furrowed his brow and turned to look where the animal was focused.

Several branches bounced up and down. Leaves rustled in a muted crackle. Something big was in there. Tanol grabbed his weapon again, aiming it at the trees.

A second ticked by. Then, two. Tanol had just relaxed the muscles in his shoulders when a brown shape broke through the branches, leaves spiraling out in a green tornado. It ran at the tapir with more speed than Tanol could track. He couldn't have shot it even if he wanted to.

The tapir leaped over a downed tree, darting for the shelter of the brush, but at the edge of the clearing, the brown mass slammed into it. The tapir fell onto its side, its lungs heaving, its legs flailing.

Tanol's mouth dropped open as he stared at the brown shape. It was some kind of animal, but what? Long snout, sharp teeth, stringy feathers, almost the size of a man, but formed like a large lizard. In the ten years he'd hunted in this cloud forest, he'd never seen anything like it.

The strange animal arched its back and snarled as it hovered over the fallen animal. The tapir continued to beat its legs in the air, trying to roll over onto its back. The creature put one foot on the tapir's neck to stop it from squirming. Then, as quick as a striking snake, the creature drew back a set of sharp claws on its foot and slashed into the hide along the tapir's ribs. Strips of skin and blood slid down the tapir's belly.

The creature opened its snout, exposing long, sharp teeth. Two more slashes with the claws ripped open the entire underside of the tapir. With a loud grunt, the creature buried its snout in the tapir's stomach.

Tanol's heart raced. This thing was vicious...and incredible. Their boss had to see it. Surely, it was worth something.

Christian poked him hard in the side with an elbow. Tanol didn't respond. He didn't want the creature to notice them. Not after seeing it rip and tear the tapir apart.

Christian tapped on the strap of the gun that Tanol had slung over his shoulder. Tanol leaned down to whisper in Christian's ear. "It's not a tranquilizer gun."

"Why not?"

Tanol shrugged. "We weren't hunting specimens. I only brought a gun for protection."

"Idiot." The harsh whisper was too loud.

The creature swung its head around to face them. Lifting its snout, it sniffed the air in huffing gusts of breath. Blood sprayed from the corner of its mouth. It stared at them like a sniper assessing a target.

Tanol stood still, holding his breath, trying to silently communicate with the creature. *Everything is fine. Just go back to your meal.*

Christian nervously shuffled his feet.

No, don't move.

Christian took a tiny step backward. The movement

set the creature off. Its lips curled back. It dug its back feet in, gave a low growl, then charged.

Tanol ran for the cover of the jungle, plunging into the safety of the dark canopy. Tiny branches slashed at him, but he didn't care. He wouldn't run far—just long enough to gain a few seconds to turn and take aim. He didn't want to kill it, but he would if necessary. Darting to the right, he ducked behind a large tree, pulled the gun off his shoulder, and spun around. But there was nothing to aim at.

The creature had chased them off, presumably to return to its kill. He took a large gulp of air and lowered the weapon.

From behind another tree, Christian appeared. He crept over to Tanol and grabbed for the gun. Tanol circled it out of his reach.

Christian pointed at the clearing, and then at the gun. He wanted to shoot the creature, probably just because it had attacked them, but that wasn't the smart thing to do.

With a wild lunge, Christian grabbed the gun and tried to pull it from Tanol. "We need to kill it."

Tanol shook his head and held tight to the weapon. Their boss would disagree. This creature was worth much more alive.

CHAPTER TWO

Dinosaurs held him captive. Not in the I've-loved-dinosaurs-since-I-was-a-kid sense, although of course he had, but in the dinosaurs-pay-my-bills sense. Paleontology Professor Travis Perego had sacrificed his life to the long dead creatures. He'd spent countless hours memorizing anatomy and forms, and even more hours at dusty dig sites brushing dirt from entombed bones.

He'd done it gladly, with no thought of career or advancement, simply for the sake of passion. Recently, though, his burning quest for knowledge had morphed into a smoldering mass of confusion.

Travis gathered the papers from the pop quiz he'd given to his Evolution of Dinosaurs class. He tapped them on one end to make a neat pile, then glanced around at the empty seats of the small lecture hall. Fifteen minutes ago, almost every seat held an eager student soaking up facts about the ancient reptiles. He had played the part of the engaging, confident professor. Not one student knew of his struggle.

"Professor Perego?"

He turned around at the quiet word to see a former student standing in the doorway. "Harmony, how's your semester going?"

Harmony tried to push a strand of brown hair behind one ear, but the too-short lock wouldn't stay. She tugged on it again, finally holding it against the side of her head. "It's been, uh ... strange."

He leaned against the edge of the desk. "How so?"

She took a few steps into the room. "Maybe we could talk about that later. Right now, I need some help. Can you give me some information about raptor to bird evolution?"

Travis changed his position on the desk and folded his arms across his chest. "Care to be a bit more specific?"

"I need to know about the evolution of flightless birds."

"Okay, but why not ask Dr. Tiernay?" Harmony worked as a graduate assistant in Dr. Tiernay's biology lab. Surely, he had access to that information.

"He's out of town." She shifted on her feet. "I'm doing research for a project."

"Your graduate research?"

She nodded without elaborating.

He peered at her, noting the dark circles under her eyes and the fidgety way she rubbed her hands together. Not like her. As an undergraduate, Harmony had been a student in his Evolution of Dinosaurs class. Although she'd decided to pursue biology, instead of paleontology, they'd kept in contact through their mutual interest in dinosaurs. Every time a new skeleton was discovered, he'd send her an email and they'd debate the name. Often, she'd come up with funny alternative ones, like *Scarfasaurus* for a dinosaur that looked to be wearing an elaborate headdress. He knew her to be a confident, carefree person, but right now she looked uncomfortable, like she'd swallowed a handful of rocks.

"Is everything okay?" he asked.

She shook her head and seemed to consider her next words. "I think I'm in some trouble."

He pushed off the desk and took a step toward her. "What kind of trouble?"

"I might have helped Dr. Tiernay do something unethical."

Whoa. Was she serious? "Let's go to my office."

They made their way out of the classroom and down two hallways to a quiet part of the building. A dozen small offices lined the north wall. They walked down the hall to his, the last one on the right.

As he opened the office door, he breathed in the comforting smell of old books mingled with the earthy scent of bones which had long ago turned to stone. Corinne, his teaching assistant, spun in her chair, a long blond braid swinging behind her like a rope.

Travis gestured between the two young women. "Corinne, this is Harmony. She's a grad student who used to be in my Dino class."

Corinne nodded and smiled, then turned back to the desk against the far wall. She grabbed resumed her work of making changes to the digital version of a handout.

Travis and Harmony walked through a doorway, with no door attached, to his inner office. He sat at the large mahogany desk that was as wide as the office and tucked up against the far wall. Sunlight from a brilliant spring day shone through the floor-to-ceiling windows, transforming hundreds of dust particles into a shimmering curtain.

"Have a seat." He pointed at the old desk chair across from him. "Do you want to tell me what you've been doing for Dr. Tiernay?"

She sat, holding herself stiff on the edge of the chair. "For about a year, I've modified embryos for him. Depending on how the results turn out, the work is supposed to be part of my doctoral thesis. I think that's all I can say right now."

Travis ran a hand through his hair. Despite her earlier admission, he couldn't imagine Harmony being involved in anything unethical. And James Tiernay was a well-respected biologist in the field of molecular genetics. How could either of them be involved in something questionable?

He rolled his chair backward to the filing cabinet and pulled open a drawer, looking for the file labeled Evolution of Dinosaurs. It contained handouts he'd used last spring, the same ones Corinne was revising for this class. He grabbed one that showed an intricate evolutionary tree starting at *Deinonychus*, a fast bipedal dinosaur, and branching out until it ended with modern birds.

"Here's what you're looking for." He swiveled in the chair to see her staring at a different paper on the corner of his desk. Instead of an evolutionary tree, this sheet had a list of several dinosaur ancestors with question marks between the ancestors and their descendants. The question marks were the result of hours of his unsanctioned research.

She tapped the paper. "What's this?"

"Something else I'm working on." He grabbed the paper, quickly sliding it under a stack of books, then gave her the handout on bird evolution.

She took the paper with two fingers, her skepticism showing on her face. "Thanks."

He refused to explain further. His personal research was none of her business. "There are references at the bottom. If you need more information, you can look up those articles in the university's database."

She looked at him for a minute, quietly studying him.

He sensed her hesitation to leave. "Are you sure you don't want to tell me what's going on? Maybe I could help."

She lowered her head and picked at teal blue nail polish, most of which had already flaked off. When she spoke, she kept her head down, and he had to lean closer to hear the quiet words. "I think he created something."

"You mean Dr. Tiernay?"

She looked up, her gray eyes reflecting a determination as hard as steel. Her voice grew stronger. "A few days ago, a friend of mine, Bob, told me about something that happened while he was at work. He's a janitor. After it happened, a couple of security guards came to his apartment to threaten him. He was freaked out."

"Okay. Back up. What happened?"

Her fingers kept working at the nail polish. "Bob was emptying the trash in the basement when the door to Dr. Tiernay's lab flew open. The one down in the basement of Kepler Hall. I've been down there, but not inside the lab." She took a deep breath before continuing. "So, the lab door opened, and Bob turned around. Something big ran into him and knocked him down. When he got back up, he was face to face with Dr. Tiernay who was holding a tranquilizer gun. Dr. Tiernay shot at something over Bob's shoulder. As he turned around, he saw the side profile of a strange creature falling to the floor."

"A strange creature?"

She nodded. Her lips parted as if she wanted to stay something more, but again she hesitated.

"What did this creature look like?" he asked.

"Bob described it as wide in the rear end with a fat tail, but skinny legs. It had a thick neck and a long snout. He also said the skin felt rough where it bumped into him."

"What color was the skin?"

"Brown and green together."

"Like camouflage?"

"I think that's what he meant." Her eyes widened. "Oh, and it had a thick ridge of furry stuff going down its back. His words, not mine."

Travis stretched out in his chair, having a hard time believing he was having a conversation about a mysterious creature on campus. If this had come from a different student, he would have recommended counseling. But then again, this was Bob's story. Maybe

Bob needed counseling. "So the dart hits the creature. It goes down. Then what?"

"Bob said Charles came out to help Dr. Tiernay, and they started to drag it back to the lab. Oh, Charles is Dr. Tiernay's other lab assistant. Bob knows him from Vertebrate Biology class."

"Did they get the creature back into the lab?"

"Bob didn't know. Dr. Tiernay yelled at him to leave, so he did."

"Bob left without finishing his shift?"

"Yeah. He said he didn't want to be anywhere near that thing. He tried to forget about it, but then, a couple of days later, these men came to his apartment. They didn't have uniforms, but said they were campus security. They told him not to talk about what happened or he'd lose his scholarship."

Travis tapped his foot on the floor as he thought about the story. This could be a prank. Perhaps Bob wanted to get a little attention from Harmony. But that didn't explain why Harmony, an intelligent, level-headed girl would believe him. Unless ... "You think Dr. Tiernay grew this creature from the embryos you modified. Is that the unethical part you were talking about?"

She hung her head. "Yes. I wanted to ask Dr. Tiernay about it, but he's gone."

"Gone where?"

"I don't know. I think Charles knows, but he won't tell me."

Travis leaned forward and put his elbows on the desk. This was the weirdest thing he had ever heard, but technically it was possible to grow modified embryos. Most of the time they didn't live much past the initial stages of development. But Tiernay was a brilliant researcher. Maybe he had found a way. And depending on what he did, Harmony could be right about it being unethical. "If Dr. Tiernay did what you suspect, how could we find out?"

She gave him a relieved smile. "I don't know if Bob will talk to you. He didn't want me to tell anyone else. He's the first in his family to go to college and can't afford to lose his scholarship."

"It won't hurt to try. Let's meet up after my next class and we'll visit Bob together."

***

Travis paced in front of the Evolution of Dinosaurs class, thumbs hooked in the front pockets of his jeans. Harmony's words cycled through his mind on a continuous loop. *I think the professor created something.* Was she right or was this Bob's idea of a classic practical joke?

His curiosity threatened to derail him. All eyes were riveted on him, waiting for him to continue his train of thought. He set his gaze on the seats in the middle of the group and let his natural teaching instinct take over. For forty-five minutes, the students scribbled down his every word as if words alone could recreate the gigantic beasts in their minds. Dinosaur junkies. He understood it—that longing to see what you never could, the fascination with the unknown. What did they really look like? What did their skin feel like? How intelligent were they? The questions were endless.

As he talked, he flipped through several slides. "The *Saurischian* dinosaurs are closely related in form to the *Ornithschian* dinosaurs. The main difference in the two groups is the shape of their pelvic bone. The *Saurischian* dinosaurs had pelvic bones similar to lizards, so they're called lizard-hipped, and the *Ornithschian* dinosaurs had pelvic bones like birds and ... you guessed it, they're called bird-hipped dinosaurs."

A hand shot up in the third row. He pointed at the young man in a plaid shirt who needed a shave. "Then the *Ornithschian* dinosaurs gave rise to modern birds?"

Travis paced the length of the floor before answering. "Actually, no definitive evidence exists to prove the ancestry of dinosaurs to birds, but most paleontologists believe the smaller raptor dinosaurs like *Velociraptor* and *Oviraptor* gave rise to modern birds. Those dinosaurs were part of the *Saurischian*, or lizard-hipped, dinosaurs."

The young man tilted his head. "Birds didn't evolve from the bird-hipped dinosaurs?"

"Not according to current evolutionary thinking."

"Weird." The guy scratched at his stubble. "How long ago did the *Sauri* ... The lizard-hipped dinos live?"

Travis stopped pacing. "It's not known for sure, but sometime during the Triassic and Jurassic periods."

"Okay, but can you give me a few dates so I know which dinosaurs lived together?"

Travis pointed at the slide, projected like a mural on the wall—a jungle scene packed with dinosaurs. Dinosaurs in the wild would never have congregated so close to one another, but the students liked the "Jurassic Park" feel of it. "We'll discuss habitats in detail next week. Specific dates are not important because these periods covered many years." The young man furrowed his brow and opened his mouth to say more, but Travis glanced at his watch. "Actually I think that's all the time we have for today. Read chapters six and seven for Friday. Class dismissed."

Travis turned off the projector. For a few minutes, the rustling of papers and backpacks filled the air, then students filed out both doors, their chattering voices receding down the hall. He closed the computer program. When he looked up, the scruffy young man stood before him.

"Professor, why aren't we going to study dates?"

His question, probably innocent and curious, made Travis's pulse pound. He straightened and ran a hand through his hair. "Scientists disagree on exact dates for the time periods surrounding the dinosaurs."

"So you're not going to share them at all?"

"Not when there is disparity among the experts. I'll focus on the relationships between the animals. If you're concerned with dates, you should take Professor Dornan's Paleostratigraphy class."

The young man tilted his head. Travis didn't blame him for being confused, in fact his refusal to discuss dates stemmed from his own confusion.

The young man shrugged and walked away with a curt, "If you say so."

The sing-song tone of his phone saved Travis from dwelling on the conversation. He checked his watch. He could talk on his way to the cafeteria to meet Harmony. He threw his laptop into the computer bag and answered his cell phone as he headed out the door. "Hello?"

"Hi. Oh, hold on a sec. Eddie, stop telling your sister she's not as smart as you. She's only in first grade. Sorry, Trav. How are you?"

He smiled at his sister's loud voice. Trudy always had trouble with volume control. "I'm hanging in there."

"That doesn't sound great."

"I'm all right. It's just that something weird got thrown at me today, but I don't know for sure what's going on, so I'd better not talk about it yet."

"Okay. How's the research going?"

"Interesting, although I may have to stop for a while."

"Why?"

He breathed in the cool spring air as he stepped outside and made his way toward the quad. Shafts of sunlight sliced across the majestic columned buildings and manicured walkway, creating a facade of peace and serenity, typical of a college campus, but rarely found in the real world. "The dean seems to be watching my every move. If what I'm researching gets back to him, he'll lose confidence in my ability to teach."

"But as a researcher..." He imagined her putting air quotes around the last word. "Wouldn't he want you to do research?"

Travis lowered his voice. "Yes, but not about God creating the world."

"Why not?"

"Because it goes against evolution."

Trudy huffed out a breath. "You can get in trouble for that?"

"Yeah." He rubbed a hand across his face. "It's kind of my job to teach *evolution*."

"I guess, but it's supposed to be a theory."

He gave a humorless laugh. "Not in geological circles. Evolution is fact."

A whining cry came through the phone. "Sorry, one more sec. Eddie, I told you, she doesn't know long division, and it doesn't make you smarter, only older. If you can't talk nice, then you can go to your room. Okay, now he should finally stop pestering her." The children's voices in the background faded. "The dean can tell you what to teach in your classes?"

"Sort of. He can't dictate what I teach, but I don't have tenure, so he can fire me, instead."

Trudy's voice softened, and her words came slowly. "Maybe you should think about whether this profession is worth it."

He pushed through the outside door and into the open green space of the quad. He squinted against the bright sunshine. "Paleontology is all I've ever wanted to do."

"But when you became a Christian, you made a commitment to a certain set of beliefs. How can you teach evolution when the Bible says God created everything?"

She paused, and for a second, he thought she might break out into scolding the kids again. "If it helps, I'd say the same thing if you were an actor in adult movies."

"Seriously?" He gripped the phone tighter. She was trying to make him laugh, but nothing seemed funny today. "There are intelligent Christians who believe there's not a conflict with evolution."

"And do you still think that? What about all the gaps in the tree?"

This religion thing was new to him. He couldn't just dismiss a lifetime of believing in evolution so easily. "Maybe missing specimens?"

"You know better."

"Come on, Tru. This is my job."

A few minutes later, he said he need to go and hung up. It was pointless to argue with her. She couldn't understand. All the research papers, the doctoral dissertation, the hot desert summers spent with only bones for company. If evolution proved false, then his career—and his life—had been wasted.

CHAPTER THREE

The main cafeteria at Grant Commonwealth University overflowed with students looking for a late lunch or perhaps an early dinner. Travis weaved his way around the lines and into the seating area. After a quick scan of students, he found Harmony in a quiet corner staring out the window at the river that ran through campus. The straight river, really a wide canal between two lakes, didn't have an official name, but everyone called it Big Green for the pea green color it turned after a rain. Big Green lived up to its nickname today as it raged past carrying muddy water from the rain that fell last night.

Travis laid his computer bag on the ground, draped his sport coat over one chair, then sat in the chair across from her. His legs didn't fit underneath the small table, so he scooted the chair back until he could rest one foot on top of his knee. No one took special notice of them. In his jeans, and without the sport coat, most students assumed he was one of them. Blending in had its advantages.

"Before we go see Bob, I have a few more questions for you."

Harmony shifted in her seat, but she met his eyes and waited for him to speak.

"First of all, I know of Dr. Tiernay's personal reputation, which makes me wonder why you agreed to work for him in the first place?"

She huffed out a sigh. "Let me tell you, he lived up to that reputation. The yelling, the insults, calling me stupid...He was awful to work with. I put up with it because he promised the research would be groundbreaking." She traced the outline of a scratch embedded in the fake wood of the table. "In our first meeting, he made sure I knew the work was completely confidential, and then..." She pressed her lips together. "Then, he asked me an odd question. 'Can you turn back the clock on evolution?' I didn't know what he meant."

Travis sat up straight, dropping his foot to the floor. "How could he do that?"

She put up a hand, signaling for him to let her finish. "He gave me a lengthy lesson on the growth of embryos—how in a developing embryo, there's no central governing region and growth comes through a cascade of reactions directed by the genes themselves. This growth is separated into phases with each new phase triggered by the end of the phase before it. He said evolution would have left a clear trail through those phases."

"A trail?"

"Yes, like a breadcrumb trail running through the DNA of an organism. Over generations the accumulated changes in DNA would lead to physical changes. As evolution progressed, it would have left a clear path—non-functional remnants of DNA, inactive genetic markers, those kinds of things. So, the professor wanted to follow that path in reverse to retrace the steps of evolution."

Travis's mouth dropped open, and he leaned forward. Never mind that it sounded impossible, the idea of rewinding evolution was fascinating. "You mean inside the embryo?"

She nodded. "We were changing the developmental instructions of the embryos."

"To create what?"

"An ancestral stage of evolution."

That sounded more like a quote from a professor,

probably Dr. Tiernay. Travis looked out the window at the river channel. The flow of the water constant and clear, unstoppable in one direction as it cut into the landscape. Was DNA like that? Did it have a clear progression over time? A pathway defined by tiny evolutionary changes? And, unlike the river, could that path be reversed?

"I modified genes for months," Harmony continued. "Some of them, Dr. Tiernay wanted disabled, others, which he thought had already been disabled, he wanted me to turn back on. Later, he taught me how to use restriction enzymes and viral vectors to copy genes and paste them to other genes. Then, a few months ago, he wanted me to start splicing genes from other animal species into specific areas of the DNA strand." She ran a hand through her hair, each piece falling forward as soon as she released it. "At the end of every day, I handed my work over to Dr. Tiernay and, as far as I knew, none of the embryos grew past the blastocyst stage."

"Did he tell you he would destroy the embryos?"

"Looking back on it, he didn't tell me much of anything. He left me instructions, I did my work, and put the embryos in the refrigerator. The next day, they'd be gone. He kept saying the time would come for me to know more, but I rarely saw him. He spent all of his time in the basement lab."

"You didn't ask him how the research was going?"

She twisted her lips to the side and glared at Travis. "Of course, I did, but he blew off my questions. He would tell me to be patient, that I would understand everything eventually. Then, Bob came to me with his story." She leaned back in her chair and pressed her hands under her chin, a gesture that instantly transformed her from budding researcher to scared kid. "When Dr. Tiernay disappeared, I knew something was wrong."

"Maybe he's just taking some personal time."

"Uh, no. Dr. Tiernay doesn't have a personal life.

He's never missed a day of work in the year I've worked for him. If I came in on a Saturday, he'd be here. The man has no life."

"And you're convinced the research has something to do with what Bob saw?"

Her voice barely rose above a whisper, but her tone held conviction. "I think the professor grew an animal from these embryos instead of destroying them."

Could Tiernay have done it? The man was known to be brilliant, but this would have been reckless and irresponsible. It was anyone's guess what kind of creature would grow after all of the genetic manipulation.

"I'm in a lot of trouble, aren't I?" Moisture welled up in Harmony's eyes.

His gut wrenched at her distress, then hardened with anger at Tiernay. Whatever he'd done, he shouldn't have pulled a sweet kid like Harmony into this mess. Travis didn't know if he could reassure her. The ethics of the situation were sketchy at best. The university had a strict no-cloning policy, but that might not apply here. And then it hit him—the reason Harmony had come to him, the lineage she had asked for, Bob's story. "What type of embryos did you modify?"

She bit her lip and avoided his gaze, turning to stare out at the river instead. She answered without looking at him. "Rhea."

Understanding swept over him in a cold rush. He let his head fall back until he stared at the maze of panels on the ceiling. The rhea was a flightless bird, similar to an ostrich. Tiernay wasn't trying to turn back the evolutionary clock on just any animal—he was trying to reverse-engineer a dinosaur.

But had he done it? The answer to that question held implications for all of science. Travis snapped his head back to look at Harmony. They had to find out the truth. "Let's go see Bob."

She nodded slowly. Her expression said she had to follow through with this, but would rather not. Silently, she followed him out of the cafeteria.

At the Green Hill apartments, they stopped at the mailbox directory. The building had the worn brick exterior typical of apartments in a college town. And yet, the landscaping was well maintained with dark mulch and daffodils just starting to bloom. The directory listed apartment 309 as Robert Turpin Jr.'s residence. Travis took the lead up the metal and concrete stairs to the third floor. Harmony followed behind without a word. She hadn't spoken since their conversation in the cafeteria, as if she'd given this whole situation completely over to him. He felt the weight of it pressing down, but refused to worry. This could still be a prank. An immature college kid's attempt to impress a girl.

Apartment 309's brown door displayed a poster of a rock star he didn't recognize. It must have been put up recently. No way it would have survived the winter, even in the sheltered part of the open stairway. He knocked on the spiked hair of the rocker.

After a minute with no answer, he knocked again.

Still no answer.

He looked over at Harmony. "You okay with waiting for him?"

"Yeah, I don't have anything going on tonight."

Normally at this time of the early evening, he'd be pounding the pavement. Jogging preserved his sanity in the "publish or perish" world of academia. But a good run would have to wait until they got some answers. He leaned against the opposite wall, and Harmony stood next to him. "Do you think Bob's telling the truth?"

Harmony shrugged. "He seemed scared to me."

"You said Bob mentioned a student named Charles was helping Dr. Tiernay. Would Charles keep this kind of secret for him?"

"Probably. Charles plays any angle he can to get ahead."

They waited only a few minutes before a young man walked down the hall and stopped at apartment 309. He put a key in the lock.

Travis looked at Harmony, but she shook her head. Not Bob. Travis pushed himself off the wall. "Excuse me."

The guy turned around. "Yeah?"

"Do you know Bob?"

"I'm his roommate, Drew. Why?"

"My name is Professor Perego. I have a few questions for Bob."

The guy's eyes opened a little wider, and he looked Travis up and down, his eyes focusing on the sport coat draped over Travis's arm. "Professor of what?"

"Paleontology."

"I don't think Bob is taking any paleontology classes this semester."

"It's not about a class. It's about ... something else."

Drew ran a hand through his greasy hair. "You're here about that thing, aren't you?"

"What thing?"

"The creature."

Travis closed the distance between them. "What do you know about it?"

Drew backed up into the door. "Only what he told me. I promised I wouldn't tell anyone else because he might get in trouble." He turned the knob and pushed open the door. "You can come in and wait. He should be back soon. Just so you know, I don't think he'll talk to you."

They walked into the foyer of an apartment that, while organized on the surface, looked in need of a deep cleaning. Still, it wasn't the worst bachelor pad Travis had seen.

Drew motioned to a torn, brown leather couch. Travis sat on one end, placed his backpack on the floor and laid his coat on top. Harmony sat on the other end of the short couch. Drew tossed his backpack into a chair and went to the kitchen. Leaning through the part of the wall that opened to the main room, he said, "I'm heading to the bathroom, but if you want to see what that thing looked like, Bob drew a picture. It's on the desk over there." He pointed across the room.

Travis stood and moved to the desk. On it lay an upside-down piece of paper. He flipped it over. The hand-drawn image took his breath away. He drew it closer, holding it just inches from his face. A running two-legged dinosaur, a theropod, with a ridge of feathers snaking down its back. Amazement and trepidation warred within him. The idea of this thing running through a campus building was frightening, and yet incredible.

He passed the paper to Harmony. She held it at arm's length as she looked at it. Swallowing hard, she passed it back to him. He returned it to the face-down position on the desk.

A gruff shout came from a room at the back of the apartment. They both turned to look, but couldn't see anything beyond the curve of the hallway. Another shout came, the words garbled.

"Stay here," Travis told Harmony.

He hurried around the curve, stopping behind Drew in the doorway of a bedroom. "This is my room." Drew yelled and bent over, hanging his head between his knees, where he continued to mumble, "This is my room."

Travis peered over his head. On the bed, a young man in jeans and a blue sweatshirt lay on his back. He was staring at the ceiling with unblinking eyes. On his left arm, the sleeve had been pushed up. An elastic tie wrapped around his arm like a snake, and a needle stuck out from the crook of his elbow.

"What's going on?" Travis felt Harmony pressing from behind to see around him. He tried to block her, but she stuck her head under his arm. She gasped, then screamed. "Bob!"

CHAPTER FOUR

Volcanologist Lenaia Talavera revved the four-wheeler to get more traction on the steep, rarely-used dirt trail through the rain forest. The humid air closed in around her like a warm cocoon, steamy with a touch of sweltering. Too hot for her long hair. She slowed the machine, pulled an elastic tie off her wrist, and swept her hair into a draping ponytail. Then, she grabbed the wheel again with both hands and hit the gas pedal.

After a few miles, the trail grew steeper and the dirt mixed with crumbly lava rock. She pressed on. As she continued her ascent, the rocks turned to boulders, and the trees thinned out.

When she broke through the tree line into the open air, she stopped the vehicle to gaze up at the dark, 5,400-foot-high peak of the Arenal Volcano. A deep, teal sky framed the majestic peak. Misty white tendrils of cloud and steam wrapped around the cone in circles, as if God was reaching down to grasp the mountain and test the warmth of the stones.

Hello, gorgeous.

She savored the postcard-perfect sight for a few moments before starting the ATV again and steering it at an angle up the slope. The small vehicle bravely charged the incline, but less than half a mile later, her wheels started to slip. She floored the gas pedal and zig-zagged, but still couldn't get traction on the rock encrusted slope. Time for a walk.

Slipping her backpack off, she dug through it,

looking for the map of the most recent seismic data. She sifted through the pages of background information sent by Adriana Soto from OVSICORI, the Costa Rican Volcanic and Seismic Observatory. Most of the information Lenaia had already memorized. The Arenal Volcano, once thought to be dormant, sprang back to life in 1968, killing more than eighty people. The mountain had exploded regularly until a few years ago when the eruptions ceased. According to the seismic report, the only visible sign of volcanic activity at present was a minimal release of gases from the cone of Crater C.

Earlier this month, Adriana had contacted Jayna Rowan, owner of Rowan Geologic Consulting and Lenaia's boss, to ask for a consult. No one doubted Arenal would erupt sometime in the future, but Adriana wanted to know if the giant was sleeping or napping. Sleeping meant a drop in volcano-related tourism, but also ensured the safety of local residents for a time. While Arenal wasn't a particularly dangerous volcano, it had the potential to become one if the pressure of rising magma continued to build. She was glad to help, but Costa Rica held many bittersweet memories of time spent with her uncle, hunting and identifying new species, before their big argument had changed things between them. A swell of sadness overwhelmed her. She hadn't talked to him in months. With a shake of her head, she pushed thoughts of him to the edges of her mind.

In the last packet of information, Lenaia found the recent seismic map showing minimal earthquake activity across the whole mountain, with the exception of one area on the southwest side. Ground elevation sensors detected a sizable bulge there. It might be a magma infusion or merely a build-up of gases. Only a field investigation could determine the truth.

She checked her GPS and set out for the coordinates of the bulge. Lava rock, in varying shades from dish gray to coal black, crunched under her feet. The muscles in her calves burned from climbing the steep incline. After a few hundred yards, her oxygen-starved lungs demanded a break. She shrugged off her pack and took several deep breaths.

Turning her head, she looked down to the tree line. Standing halfway up the immense mountain highlighted her smallness. Her one life would come and go and this mountain would still rise above the jungle. The sense of awe grew, but she had no one to share it with. Her thoughts turned to the airport shuttle driver who had asked why she came to Costa Rica alone. It was the one downside to her dream job—she was always alone.

Hitching her pack higher onto her shoulders, she resumed walking. Two-thirds of the way up the mountain, she checked the GPS coordinates for the bulge again. A little west of her current position. She moved in that direction, searching the ground for steam or seeps, which could mean escaping gases. The carbon dioxide detector strapped to her belt stayed silent.

She hiked a little further. The degree of a bulge sometimes seemed large as judged by the satellite, but on the mountain it might fit with the rolling terrain and barely be noticeable. She knelt down to judge the elevation of the land. The gentle rise and fall of the ground formed a rounded protruding mound. She'd found it.

Close to the center of the bulge, a few tendrils of steam escaped, but quickly dissipated. No obvious fissures or gas vents in the general area. She walked back and forth, testing the feel of the ground. A little friable in places, but mostly stable.

She pulled the carbon dioxide gas meter off her belt and took a few readings. Somewhat high for both carbon dioxide and sulfur dioxide gas, but nothing that would set off alarms. She pressed a button to save the readings onto the meter's hard drive, then continued to crisscross the western flank of the volcano, stopping at any places with cracked ground or venting gases. Though the areas where gas escaped were spread apart, this volcano was definitely a gassy girl.

A few hours later, she took a final gas measurement and stowed the meter in the backpack. She'd review the data at the hotel, but most of the levels were on the high side. Even so, all the measurements in the world couldn't tell her more than walking around to get a feel for the mountain itself. And this hunk of rock had told her plenty. Hopefully, Adriana would handle the news okay.

***

After an early dinner in the nearby town of La Fortuna, Lenaia returned to the Arenal Observatory Lodge. Rather than go to her empty room, she sat in a chair on the observatory deck to enjoy the cool night. A cloak of darkness hid the volcano, and yet she could feel its presence. The one other time she'd come here was five years ago, when she'd convinced her uncle, who was deep into one of his big-game hunting trips, to change up their normal vacation by leaving the rain forest. At that time, Arenal had spilled glowing red lava down its slopes all night, lighting up the mountain like a massive Chinese lantern. Now, the sole proof of Arenal's power was captured in photos of the nighttime lava flows.

She took in a deep breath of the cool, humid air. This was her third volcano in three weeks, the travel only broken up by a stop at her apartment to re-pack based on the climate at the next one. But why not spend all her time in the field? It wasn't like anyone was waiting for her at home.

Shrugging off the self-pity, she pulled her cell phone from her pocket. Might as well call her boss if she was feeling lonely.

Jayna answered in a sleepy voice. "Hello?"

"Hey there. Calling in to report. Did I wake you?"

"Not yet, just resting on the couch. Growing a baby has used up my energy completely, but it's almost bedtime. How did it go today?"

"No problems, boss."

"Good." Jayna's tone became an exaggerated whine. "I'm jealous. I wish I could be there with you."

"Yeah, I wish you could too, but having a baby takes precedence."

Before Lenaia had come to work at Rowan Geologic Consulting, they hadn't known each other, but in the last year, they'd developed a stronger relationship than just boss-employee. They had confided in each other more than Lenaia ever had with a friend, much less a boss. Usually, Lenaia found other women too full of drama. But Jayna was different, even brushing off her near-death experience right after starting Rowan Geologic when her client had tried to kill her. She had survived, and somehow didn't let it change her. When Lenaia asked about her resilience, Jayna would only say that she'd endured worse things in her past.

"How is Costa Rica?" Jayna asked.

"Humid, but definitely warmer than North Carolina."

"And I'm jealous again. All I can say about Wisconsin is polar bears would feel right at home."

Several of Lenaia's consultations in the last year had been on ice-covered volcanoes. She swatted at a mosquito. Despite the abundant insect life, this climate was definitely easier to handle.

"Since it's nice and warm down there, maybe you should take a day off later in the week and go to the beach. You're only a few hours away."

Lenaia gasped. "You're my boss. You shouldn't be telling me to go play in the sand."

Jayna chuckled. "After you've completed the

consult, of course. Besides, you've earned it with how hard you've been working for the last couple of weeks."

"Maybe, I will. I might have some extra time. But you know I'm happiest on a volcano, especially one like Arenal that's not quite as likely to explode and kill me."

"Any verdict on Arenal?"

"Yeah. I have some news for Adriana, although I don't know if she'll find it reassuring or disappointing."

"The mountain's breathing?"

"More like holding her breath. There's plenty of activity underneath the west flank. The pressure's building. I can feel it. Arenal should have a hiccup again sometime soon."

"Any thoughts on when?"

Lenaia stared out at the darkness again. "That's a tough judgment call, but if I had to say, I'd give it less than a year before sleeping beauty awakens and coughs pretty loudly."

"Okay. Write it up."

"Tomorrow morning, I'll go back to the mountain to hike a little closer to Crater C where the activity has been in previous years. Depending on what I find, I'll write the report tomorrow afternoon."

"Good, I was hoping you would wrap it up quickly. That leaves two more days until you fly home, and you need a break. Go find yourself a beach."

Lenaia leaned her head against the back of the deck chair. What a great boss. Two years ago, Lenaia had thought her career was over after she'd been forced out of her position as a volcanologist for the State of Washington. Her previous bosses didn't take it well when she started to lean away from accepted ideas of geology. It could have been the end of her days exploring on volcanoes, if not for Jayna.

She shifted the cell phone to her other ear. "Actually I might have a different plan. A guy from my church and his son have been down here for a year as missionaries to a little village, called Rojo Piedra. He's the village doctor. I told him I would come visit the next time I came to Costa Rica. Only thing is, I have to figure out where the town is located. It doesn't seem to be on any maps."

A chuckle came over the line. "Instead of lying on the beach, you want to run off into the rain forest in search of a town too small to appear on a map?"

"You know I'm not a lie-on-the-beach kind of girl. Besides, my uncle brought me to these jungles several times over the years, so I know what I'm doing."

Jayna paused a moment before speaking again. "Is this a special man you're visiting?"

Lenaia's turn to laugh. "It's not like that. He's a friend."

"Uh-huh."

"And he's too old for me."

"Okay, okay. I'll back off. But seriously, you can find your way around the rain forest?"

"I'll be fine. Hunting around in the jungle for a hidden village sounds like an adventure."

"I had a feeling you'd say that. Your sense of adventure is one of the reasons I hired you."

"Really? You never told me that."

"I like to work with daring people, especially those who are also responsible. Turn in your report tomorrow, meet with Adriana in the afternoon, and then feel free to go find that village. In fact, you should ask Adriana for directions. She would know all the villages around there."

"Good idea. It's supposed to be near the Monteverde Cloud Forest, so it should be close."

"Have fun."

"Will do. And Jayna?"

"Yeah?"

"Thanks."

"My pleasure. Be safe, my friend."

Lenaia hung up the phone and stood to go up to her room. God had blessed her with a great boss, but for as much as Jayna complained about not being able to do field work, Jayna didn't understand the meaning of the word jealous. A loving husband, a successful business, a kid on the way—most women would want her life. Of course, for Jayna, it had all started with the loving husband. Not too many of those hanging out on the slopes of active volcanoes. A sarcastic laugh escaped Lenaia's lips. *Maybe tomorrow the volcano will spit one out for me.*

***

Lenaia waited for Adriana in a wooden lounge chair on the observatory deck, gazing at the jagged flank of the mountain. The volcano sloped toward her, the more recent lava flows dripped down the mountain like tendrils drawn in gray finger paint against the black backdrop of older lava rock. Where the lava rock met the jungle, she saw evidence of a constant battle for territory. Charcoal gray boulders that had plummeted down the slope during landslides held the tree line at bay, while the vegetation struggled to gain ground plant by plant, inch by inch.

This morning, she'd spent a few hours up on Crater C monitoring the gas output, then finalized her report and had a late lunch. Afterward, she packed and told the front desk staff she might not be back for a few days, but wanted to keep the room, just in case. Her suitcase and backpack were stashed in the car.

She slipped off her sunglasses to check her watch. Only three o'clock. Even if Adriana had a ton of questions, she could still get on the road before the sun went down.

The clunky steps of hard-soled shoes sounded on

the wooden deck. Lenaia looked over as Adriana Soto lowered herself into a chair. Adriana wore a comfortable, but professional, combination of khaki pants and rust red camp shirt. Her hair was pulled back in a severe bun, but she had an open, rounded face. The noisy shoes—thick-soled patent leather sandals—were classy, although not practical.

"Sorry to keep you waiting, Dr. Talavera."

"Lenaia, please. The only people who deserve the title of doctor are the ones who can save somebody's life."

Adriana smiled. "Lenaia, I'm anxious to hear what you found." With her legs crossed in front and her hands folded, the woman looked anything but anxious.

All business. Lenaia respected that. She opened a file and pulled out several maps the front desk had printed for her. "My findings confirm the results of the tilt meters, and the work done by some of your personnel. The west flank appears to be the most seismically active area." She switched the papers around so the west view sat on top. "The southwest flank, here ..." she pointed at a circle drawn over the topographic map, "... has a sizable inflation, up to five feet at the highest point of the bulge."

Adriana nodded with pursed lips.

"A displacement of rock of that size typically means a large amount of volcanic activity under the surface. Further evidence of this underground activity can be seen in the numerous gas vents in the same area."

"Similar to what we've found. It's good to have confirmation of our results, but let's get to the main reason I asked you to come." Adriana uncrossed her legs and leaned forward in the chair. "Although we have the ability to make the same measurements, we don't have the expertise to determine the extent of the volcanic threat. What we need is your interpretation."

Lenaia nodded. "You want to know if the volcano is in a coma or just napping."

"Something like that."

"Keep in mind, interpretations are subjective, not to be relied upon exclusively."

"I understand. But you've built a reputation as someone who can make accurate predictions." Adriana had to be referring to Alaska's Redoubt Volcano. Thanks to the internet, anyone could read about how she'd fought with the local geologists, warning them Redoubt would erupt sooner than they thought. If they would have listened, she could have saved more lives. She frowned and her focus slipped as images of those lost in the eruption drifted through her mind. Mothers, fathers, children. Every fatality was a failure, but the children were the hardest to stomach.

Refocusing, Lenaia gathered her hair and pushed it over one shoulder. "I expect the Arenal Volcano to take a short nap and resume activity within the next six months to a year as an outside estimate, possibly much sooner."

Adriana leaned back in the chair and stared out at the subject of their discussion. The mountain looked close because its hulking form filled their field of vision, but it was an illusion. Even a crow would have to fly over a mile to get there. Adriana's flat expression gave no clue as to whether she welcomed the information. Lenaia folded her hands and waited.

After a few minutes, Adriana turned back to address her. "At least it's job security for me. Even so, I would have liked to think the threat of eruption had passed."

Now Lenaia needed to deliver the worst of the news. She sat up straighter in the chair. "You should also prepare for more forceful eruptions than you've seen in recent years. Many times, when a volcano is nearing extinction, the magma below becomes more viscous. If this happens, the eruptions will become more explosive.

You may need to look at a larger radius of protection on the southern side of the volcano."

Adriana blew out a breath. "Wow. You really do want job security for me, don't you?"

Lenaia gave her a sympathetic smile. "My job is to tell you the hard truth. To help you protect people and property as much as possible. But please remember, these are estimates. The mountain could give you an eruption much sooner or it might hold off for a while."

"I understand. What is your sense of sooner versus later?"

"My gut tells me, sooner."

"Thank you for your honesty." Adriana rested a hand under her chin. "In fact, I'd like to get another honest opinion from you. We have written records of these volcanoes for approximately 250 years. Not long at all. So, I want your opinion on how often the location of the magma source moves. What I mean is, when one volcano starts to become dormant, does the source shift and another one take its place right away?"

Lenaia tapped a finger on her chin. "That depends on quite a lot of things. Like how much magma is available in the system, whether the lava conduits—the plumbing inside the existing volcano—are blocked, and even the composition and available pathways through the surrounding rock. Why do you ask?"

"We're seeing an increase in earthquakes in an area close to here. To the southwest of Arenal, actually. And this morning, I received a report of smoke coming out of the rain forest in an area that shouldn't have any settlements. Is it possible that Arenal isn't going dormant? Could it be changing locations?"

"Well, this area in general has had plenty of volcanic activity in its history, which means it's possible. However, up until a few years ago, Arenal was a reliable pathway for the magma to escape and relieve the pressure underground. And I think it will continue to be. But if you're seeing an increase in earthquakes, the area needs to be checked out."

"Okay. I'm glad you think so." Adriana gave a charming and somewhat guilty smile. "Can you look into it?"

Lenaia chuckled. She had seen that coming. "Sure. Where exactly are we talking about?"

"The earthquakes are happening throughout the Monteverde Cloud Forest. The smoke was reported by students at the University of Georgia outpost on the other side of the forest from here. If you drive around the southern end of the cloud forest to the outpost, you could go in from the western side. There's not much civilization around there except a little village, called Rojo Piedra."

"Did you say Rojo Piedra?"

"Yes, do you know it?"

"Actually, I was going to ask you where it is. A missionary friend of mine lives there, and I wanted to visit him."

"Ah, then you will have a vested interest in making sure the area is safe." Adriana dug into a satchel bag and pulled out a map of the Monteverde Cloud Forest along with a pen. She drew a red dot almost directly south of Arenal, at the southeast corner of the cloud forest. "This is the village. Go to the University of Georgia outpost over here." She made a second dot on the southwest side of the forest. "They'll give you a place to stay, and you can borrow one of their four-wheelers to get to the village. The students or the villagers can tell you where to look for any smoke or other anomalies."

"Sounds good."

Adriana stood and offered her hand. "I appreciate your efforts, Lenaia." She tapped the file folder in Lenaia's hand. "You'll e-mail me a copy of this report?"

Lenaia stood as well. "Already have."

"And please let me know how this additional investigation goes." Adriana gave her a sideways look. "Have you been alone in the jungle before?"

"Yes, my dad is from Costa Rica. I've come here many times, although most often with my uncle. He's American, but loves to hunt in the jungle." She placed a hand over her heart. "Not in the nature preserve of course."

Adriana looked her up and down, as if assessing her survival chances. "You have a working cell phone? Many of the ones from the U.S. don't work here."

"I've got a handheld satellite phone, in case my regular cell phone doesn't work."

Adriana nodded. "I wish I could come with you, but I have to work on my report to justify keeping my staff since the volcano isn't erupting right now. Fortunately, your work will help with that."

"Glad I could help. And don't worry about me. I'll be fine."

They said goodbye, and Lenaia headed to the car. A few minutes later, she steered down Highway 142 going south. After a few miles, she looked over her shoulder through the back window. A smattering of clouds covered the top portion of the Arenal Volcano like the white tip of a chocolate candy corn. It looked steady and peaceful, pretending to be almost harmless, when really it was lethal—a slumbering, dangerous kind of beautiful. *See you later, gorgeous.*

CHAPTER FIVE

After they both gave their statements to the police, Travis walked Harmony back to her apartment, then he headed straight to the paleontology lab. The place he could always relax. The scent of dusty rock and the continuity of history stacked inside each drawer somehow soothed him. But tonight, he needed to find one particular specimen.

He maneuvered around a rusty rock saw, with its jaws wide open, and a box of granite samples waiting for their turn to be sliced into thin sections as small as one thousandth of a millimeter. Such wafer-thin specimens for such a big job—decoding the secrets of the planet. Too bad rocks didn't come with a time stamp.

The ceiling-high shelving held rows and rows of boxes with cryptic labels. He scanned the labels until he found LC, for Late Cretaceous, followed by OVR written on the top drawer. Of course it had to be at the top. He stretched, but even his long reach couldn't quite make it. Pulling over the rolling step ladder, he climbed up and opened the drawer. He could have hunted down a picture of the specimen in a textbook, but nothing could compare to holding the fossil in his hands.

He pried off the lid and grabbed the first bones he saw. As his fingers closed over the jaw bone, he knew it wasn't right. It was the jaw of a sheep-like *Oreodont*. No matter how well-labeled the shelves, things always ended up in the wrong places. He placed the jaw bone to the side to be re-shelved and reached in again.

This time, he lifted out a skull a little smaller than a football. *Oviraptor*, a two-legged flightless theropod dinosaur. He ran a finger along the empty eye socket and down to the nasal cavity, flicking his thumb over the knife-like teeth. A natural born killer. A late-stage dinosaur. And a perfect match to Bob's picture.

Travis had Bob's picture folded in his back pocket, but he didn't pull it out. Instead, he held up the skull and tried to imagine scaly flesh and a long snout.

"Just the person I was hoping to find." Travis started at the familiar gravelly voice from below. The one that sounded like the man had swallowed too much sand at his dig sites. It belonged to Francis Haddock, professor of paleontology and newly named dean of the department.

With a sigh, Travis returned the skull to its box and backed down the ladder. Haddock stood with his arms folded, a slight smirk on his face. Maybe the man's quiet footfall was the real reason they called him the "bone whisperer." The nickname had grown popular with the press after Haddock had discovered the world's largest *Spinosaurus*—a skeleton he named Tiny. It was a one-in-a-million find. It could have happened to anyone. It should have happened to someone else.

"Professor Haddock."

"It's *Dean* Haddock now."

Travis leaned against the nearest desk and hunched over a little to the shorter man's level. "Oh, right."

The dean puffed his stocky chest out and pointed toward the shelves. "Are you preparing for a trip?"

"Not yet, but I will when the semester's over. John Campbell asked me to come to Montana."

"Ah, you can always count on John."

Travis detected a not-so-veiled insult in the tone. As if no one else would ask him to come work in their bone yards. "More visibility for the department. Shouldn't you be happy I'm going?"

Haddock stroked a thick hand down his smooth, round cheek. "I thought you might be busy with some much needed soul searching."

Soul searching? Haddock had no idea how close to the mark he was. Or maybe he did. "Nope, I'm still in the game."

"We'll see about that." Haddock narrowed his eyes. "Not that I mind the competition."

Travis folded his arms across his chest. "And exactly how could I compete with you? How many papers did you publish last year?"

"The ones I wrote myself? Or should I include the co-authored ones?"

Travis shook his head. "Never mind."

"By the way..." Haddock leaned toward him, his body twisting like a thick coil. Travis took a breath and almost choked on the nautical scent of the man's cologne. "Did you hear I got the National Science Foundation Grant?"

Travis merely raised an eyebrow. He wouldn't give Haddock the satisfaction of making a comment. The foundation didn't give money to two professors at the same college. Since Haddock had gotten the grant, he knew Travis had been rejected.

Travis pushed off the desk and took a step toward the shelves. Odd that the dean didn't ask about Bob, but then again, maybe he hadn't heard yet. If not, it was best to end this conversation before Travis had to relive it. "You said you were looking for me?"

"Corinne came to see me about the handouts you asked her to redesign."

Travis stared, unblinking, at him. No way would he let down his poker face and show the dean the depth of his struggle.

"You told her to remove the dates and to make the cladogram a box instead of a tree."

Travis pasted on a fake smile. "I use the cladogram

as a tool to inspire students to dig into the relationships between animals. Dates might hold them back from thinking outside the box." He let his smile go lopsided. "Pun intended."

Haddock smoothed one eyebrow with his index finger. As he released the skin, a twitch took over. He pressed it again with his finger. "A box doesn't show ancestry. A tree of life does. The ancestors, as the roots, give rise to branches and branches of more complex animals. The basic plan of evolution displayed as a majestic tree."

This was the dean's idea of a lecture. Travis took a step back and leaned against a desk farther from him. "Students should think critically about science. We don't have all the answers. I'm not sure we ever will."

Science had once seemed solid like concrete. But as his list of questions grew, Travis had sunk deeper into the mud of doubt. And hiding his confusion had only gotten harder.

"You refused to give dates to a student who directly asked you."

He swallowed and his poker face slipped. How did Haddock know that? "I'm trying to get the students to do their own research instead of learning everything by rote." That excuse sounded weak even to his ears. He tried again. "I prefer to use the dates as a guide."

Haddock slapped a meaty hand on the desk next to Travis. It vibrated with a rhythmic creaking. "That's enough. I'm not as easily fooled as your students." He straightened and pressed his palms together. "We discussed this last fall as colleagues. Now we'll discuss your issue in an official manner."

"My what?" Haddock made it sound like he had some kind of disease.

"I know things were hard for you after Marie died..."

Hearing his sister's name made every muscle in Travis's stomach clench. "I'd rather not talk about her."

Haddock continued as if he hadn't heard or didn't care. "The previous dean gave you a month off. Very generous, if you ask me. That was six months ago, and you keep heading further off track. At this point, I need to know, are you able to do your job?"

Good question. Travis tapped his foot. And questions were the problem. If he could stop questioning, he might find some peace. "I'm teaching every day, most of your professors teach only three days a week. I leave in two weeks for a dig in Montana. What more can you ask?"

"You won't give out simple dates and you're changing the curriculum..."

"Which is my right as a professor."

Haddock's mouth tightened. "Yes, but you're moving away from accepted facts." He brushed a pile of dirt off the desk onto the floor, then met Travis's gaze and held it. "You should be up for tenure, but I don't see it at this point."

Travis looked away. Tenure was every professor's dream. It carried the promise of security and freedom. Haddock might not like him, but Travis hadn't realized the dean would try to block his tenure, especially since Travis had good working relationships with his colleagues. Unfortunately, Haddock's vote would carry the most weight.

"I don't know what the problem is with you," Haddock continued, "but you need to pull it together. I would have gotten rid of you already, except your colleagues and students..." the dean paused, his attention moving from Travis's hair to his polo shirt and down to his dark jeans, "particularly the female ones, seem to adore you. But their adoration will only go so far."

What was Haddock saying? Yes, he'd been told a few times he was attractive, mostly by young female students who thought all professors were old and bald, but this would be the first time anyone insinuated he kept his job because of his looks. He might have laughed, if the dean hadn't threatened to fire him.

Travis pressed his eyes closed for a minute, then stared into space. As tempting as it was to blame Haddock for his predicament, the dean was right. He needed to get it together. But how could he teach something he wasn't sure he believed in anymore?

Haddock brushed past Travis and headed for the door. "Glad we could have this talk," he said over his shoulder. "Now I need to track down a biology professor."

"Which one?"

Haddock stopped and looked back. "Dr. Tiernay. Have you seen him?"

"You don't think I'd run into him in the paleontology lab, do you?"

"Well, no."

"Then you'll have to keep looking." Travis pushed off the desk. "His name does keep coming up, though."

"How so?"

Travis moved back to the bins on the shelves, forcing Haddock to follow to continue the conversation. "I've heard a few things about Dr. Tiernay's lab. Is that why you're looking for him?"

Haddock glanced to the side, studying the handle on a drawer. "No, I need a consult on a bone specimen. What have you heard?"

Travis pulled open a random drawer and pretended to look for something. "A story about one of his lab animals."

"Okay. I'll ask him when I see him. In the meantime, I'm sure you wouldn't want to spread unfounded rumors around campus. Those kinds of things can lead to problems."

Travis straightened and angled his gaze at the dean. Haddock squinted at him, his pupils trapped beneath a wedge of dark brows. "For me or Dr. Tiernay?"

Haddock shrugged, then turned to leave. Hard to believe the man would go so easily, but he appeared to have made all the jabs he'd intended.

As the door to the lab slammed shut, Travis again climbed the ladder and pulled out the *Oviraptor* specimen to take with him. He ran his fingers along the skull. Narrow, hollow eyes, long snout, thin bones. If Tiernay had reversed the evolution of a rhea bird, would it turn out something like this?

He climbed down and leaned his shoulder against the metal shelves. Since Corinne had gone to the dean behind Travis's back, he obviously hadn't hidden the problem as cleverly as he thought. Refusing to discuss dates by itself shouldn't have raised suspicion, but he'd blown her off several times when she'd asked questions about his lesson plans. Guilt welled up in his chest. In fact, he'd blown off more students in the last month than ever before. That didn't make him much of a teacher.

He sank onto the top of a well-worn desk, suddenly tired. He couldn't be a paleontologist like this. All questions and no answers.

Maybe he should resign. He took a moment to consider the idea. A tight fist squeezed inside his chest, the muscles twisting and knotting up. If he quit, he'd have to leave his two great loves—dinosaurs and teaching. No way would he voluntarily do that.

He ran a hand down his face. The timing of this thing with Tiernay was perfect, maybe even God-ordained. If Tiernay had created an ancestral form, it would prove evolution true and end all his questions. Harmony needed his help, and he needed to find out what Tiernay had done.

***

The old limestone façade of Kepler Hall stood as a

silent gray sentinel, guarding everything inside against the shadows of the night. Travis pulled out Bob's set of keys. His roommate had gladly handed them over. Drew seemed pretty convinced Bob didn't do drugs and wouldn't have overdosed, especially in the wrong bedroom. Harmony also said Bob wasn't the druggie type. Travis had to agree, the circumstances and timing of Bob's death were suspicious, but he didn't have any answers at this point. Hopefully, some of those answers waited in Tiernay's lab.

He fumbled with the key ring, surprised at his shaking hands. It wasn't like he was breaking in. He tried a key with no success, then flipped it to the back of the ring. One of these had to open the front door. After trying a few more wrong keys, the lock finally turned, the sound echoing off the other buildings in the deserted central plaza. He pushed the tall door open, and it let out a creaking complaint.

Stuffy air drifted out from inside the building. There probably hadn't been much air flow from the furnace on a warm spring day like today. He closed the door gently, but still the glass in the center panel shook. He glanced around, expecting to have alerted someone to his presence, but no one came.

Staring down the shadowed hallway lit by emergency lights every twenty feet, he hesitated. This was a risky move. Technically, he was trespassing since he had no valid reason to be here. His office was in Burskin Hall, halfway across campus. But he needed to know if a creature was hiding in Tiernay's lab and a visit during the day would raise suspicion.

He crept down the wide hallway, half expecting to run into a lab assistant or a janitor, but no one crossed his path. Having Harmony here to show him around would have helped, but he didn't want to involve her. If he got busted, she might get in more trouble than he would.

Inside the elevator, he pushed the button for the basement. When the doors parted, he stepped into a concrete walled hallway. A few offices branched off the corridor, but not much else was down here. At the end of the hallway, a massive steel door blocked the way.

He walked softly down the hall. All of the other offices had labels, except for the one at the end of the hall. There weren't any markings on the outside, but this had to be it. He tried the door handle. Locked.

Pulling out the key ring again, he pondered which of the fifty to choose. First guess was the key for the front door. He slipped it into the lock. No luck.

One after another, the rest of the keys on the ring brought no success. Finally, he rested his head on the door. This had to be it. No nameplate. No numbers. It was a perfect location for a secret lab. But apparently, Bob didn't clean inside the lab.

"Looking for something?" A deep voice boomed down the hallway.

He jumped and spun around. A heavyset security guard glared at him, one hand on the taser gun strapped to his waist. "No." He took a quick breath. It was always best to be honest. "Well, actually yes. I'm Professor Perego. Sorry to come by so late, but this is the first chance I've had to investigate some complaints I've received."

The guard held his gaze, but took his hand off of the weapon. "I haven't heard any complaints."

"This is about a research animal kept in Dr. Tiernay's lab. Do you know anything about it?"

The guard sucked air deep into his nostrils, causing them to flare out like umbrellas caught in a wind storm. "Have you talked to Dr. Tiernay about this?"

"Not yet, but I'd like to. Have you seen him?"

"I haven't seen him since last week." The guard stared

for a moment as if considering something. "But I don't think you need to worry about any more complaints."

"Why not?"

"Last week, I helped Dr. Tiernay load a crate onto a rental truck. We took it out the back door, then when I went back to close the door, the lab was quiet. I don't think he has any more animals in there."

"What was in the crate?"

The guard shrugged. "I don't know. It had a stretchy canvas cover. Whatever was inside was heavy. It moved around a lot too."

"Do you know how many animals were in the crate?"

"I couldn't tell, but it was heavier than my Rottweiler. After I locked the door for Dr. Tiernay, he said he'd be gone for a couple of days."

"Okay. Thanks for your help."

Travis swiveled his head to stare at the lab door. Tiernay had moved something out of there. But what? The creature Bob saw?

The guard cleared his throat. "So you're done here, professor?"

"Of course. I'll get out of your way."

Travis squeezed past him and started down the hallway, but then he had another thought. He turned back. The guard had just finished checking the lock on the lab door. "One more thing, sir. Did Dr. Tiernay say where he was going? I'd still like to talk to him."

"No, but I'm sure the dean could give you his cell phone number."

Travis twisted his mouth into a frown. "I'd rather not bother the dean with this."

The guard snorted out a laugh. "I know what you mean. That guy is a constant pain in my..."

"Sure sounds like him."

"He thinks he's some kind of security expert. Threatened me, too. Wanted copies of keys to all the labs on campus. Said he'd get me fired if I didn't do what he said. But I told him to go ahead. I'm ex-Navy, I don't give in to threats."

The guard flexed both biceps, which bulged like he visited the gym every day. Travis squashed a twinge of envy. If only he had the guts to tell Haddock to go ahead and fire him.

"Hey, maybe you could check with the rental company to find Dr. Tiernay," the guard said. "The truck had the name Jiffy Rent on the side."

"I'll check on that. Thanks."

Travis gave a quick salute, earning a smile from the guard. He walked halfway down the hall, then took the door marked for the stairs. Running up to the main level two at a time, he came out of the building into the cool darkness. Something had been in that lab, but whatever it was, it was gone now. Tomorrow, he'd follow up with the rental company. Maybe he could find out where Tiernay took it.

CHAPTER SIX

Holding the spare office key in her hand, Harmony paced the short distance across her lab as she waited for Tom to decide if he would help her. He had remained silent for several minutes, and she couldn't blame him. If they got caught in Dr. Tiernay's office, it could mean expulsion for both of them. But they had a small window of opportunity. This early in the morning, no one was around to catch them.

She stopped pacing to stare at the paper Bob's roommate had given her. The image of the creature Bob had drawn stared up at her with wild eyes. It was confirmation that the professor had created something. But what? As a responsible party, even as a scientist, she had to know the truth.

"Can't we just wait to ask Dr. Tiernay about this when he gets back?" Tom asked.

He had a point. Last night, after Professor Perego had made a copy of the drawing, he'd promised to look into this more, but his investigation would take too long. She could get the information faster if Tom would just hack Dr. Tiernay's computer. "I don't know when Dr. Tiernay is coming back. Besides, he would probably just lie." She reached up and cupped Tom's cheek in her other palm. "I hate to ask you to do this. But Tom, I helped him. And I don't even know what I did. I have to find out. He owes me that."

Tom went quiet again, his dark brows deeply furrowed. She gave him space and waited out the silence, knowing he needed time to decide whether to help. He probably would, if for no other reason than to protect her. He knew her well enough to know she'd try to do this on her own if he didn't help. As the time ticked by, she tried not to pace again. Tom never did anything until he was ready, and she couldn't do this without him.

Eventually, he let out a heavy sigh. "Fine. Let's get this over with."

She clapped her hands together. "Thank you."

He stood and pulled her to him. "Harmony, tell me you won't make a habit of this."

"A habit out of what? Helping a crazy biologist defy the laws of nature or breaking into his computer?" Tom frowned at her words. She gave him a sheepish grin. "I won't. I promise."

Covering the key in her right hand with a blank piece of paper, she opened the lab door and walked with confidence down the hall. Tom followed behind. No one glanced in their direction. At Dr. Tiernay's office door, she slipped the key into the lock. It turned easily, and they silently ducked inside.

Leaving the lights off, she stopped short at the disaster area that the professor called an office. A continuous lake of papers and books flooded the whole of the industrial carpet. A small foot-wide path led from the door to the desk. She kept to the swath of empty carpet until she reached the desk where she rolled the plush office chair out and motioned for Tom to sit. He gave her a dubious look, but as he sat, he pushed the power button for the CPU. The machine came to life, throwing a blue glow around the room. Harmony turned the screen so the light wouldn't shine out the glass wall and door.

"Do you need my help?" she whispered.

Tom shook his head. She watched him enter in "james. tiernay," the typical format for a university ID. More numbers and symbols than she'd ever seen in Calculus class whipped across the screen. His fingers flew over the keys, and she stared in awe for a few seconds, then gave up trying to follow the pages flashing by.

"Look for anything to do with the rhea bird. I'll look around in here to see what I can find."

She glanced around and gave a soft moan. Where to start in this paper breeding ground? Stacks of scientific papers, reference books, and scribbled notes lay on almost every surface. She sat down at the closest pile and sifted through the sheets. After half the stack, she glanced up to check on Tom. "Any luck?"

"Getting there. Give me some time."

Someone passed by the glass wall of the office without looking in. She could explain being in the office, even bringing Tom inside, but she couldn't explain snooping around on the professor's computer when he wasn't there. "Okay. The sooner the better."

He turned and raised his eyebrows at her. "Peace and quiet would be nice."

She abandoned the stack for another one, riffling through the papers faster. Nothing, except the same scientific data she'd already read. With a huff, she blew her bangs out of her eyes. Dr. Tiernay probably wouldn't keep anything out in the open anyway. She leaned back onto her hands and looked around again. Complete chaos on the floor, but the bulletin board remained a relatively clear space, displaying one sheet like a banner—a quote from Albert Einstein, "Once we accept our limits, we go beyond them." No surprise there. Dr. Tiernay had definitely gone above and beyond.

The printer let out a whine and began feeding sheets through. She jumped to her feet and leaned over the back of the chair.

"I'm printing out e-mails from a file labeled 'Rheasaurus.' " Tom said.

" 'Rheasaurus'? Wow."

"There's also an encrypted data file with the same name, but it would take me hours to break into it."

"We don't have that kind of time." She pulled a flash drive out of the front pocket of her jeans. "Can you copy it to this?"

"Yes, but not without him knowing."

She thrust the device at him. "Do it anyway."

As the printer spit out more pages, she scooped up the ones that were done. The oldest e-mail had printed first. The date was from the previous May, almost a year ago. It had no subject line and the name on the account didn't sound familiar—fulton.pike@genesysexp.org.

Dr. Tiernay,

Below are specifications for the genes I believe are the best chance for modifying the embryo to achieve our objective. This should give you a place to start. Keep me updated weekly on your progress.

Fulton Pike
Genesys Experimental Laboratory

Below the text was a table with what at first seemed like gibberish, but as she looked closer, she recognized a few shorthand names for genes and their growth factors. Dr. Tiernay had run this experiment for Genesys Experimental Lab. She'd never heard of it.

She grabbed the last e-mail as it scrolled off the printer, dated April 15, just last week.

Dr. Tiernay,

I am waiting for delivery of the specimen. Contact me as soon as you have a date arranged.

"Most of the e-mails went unanswered, but the last one had a response." Tom placed a hand on the printer. "It's coming out now."

Harmony grabbed it as soon as the printer released it. The date at the top was also April 15. Her heart skipped a beat when she realized it was also the day Dr. Tiernay disappeared.

Mr. Fulton Pike,

Due to an unfortunate incident, the specimen has been destroyed.

Dr. James Tiernay

She stuck her thumb in her mouth and chewed on the frayed nail. This answered the question of whether the professor had succeeded. Dr. Tiernay had generated some sort of biological specimen for this Fulton Pike. But something about this e-mail bothered her. If Dr. Tiernay had destroyed the specimen, why the odd disappearing act? The campus had its own incinerator. He wouldn't have had to go anywhere else to get rid of the specimen. It didn't make sense.

"Let's print off all of his e-mails from April 15. Maybe one of them will tell us where he went."

"Sure." The printer fired up again at Tom's commands.

She stuffed the printed sheets under her arm. "Are you finished?"

Tom nodded as he pulled the flash drive out of the slot in the computer.

"Let's go then."

Tom shut down the computer, and they made their

way along the clear path to the door, careful not to disturb any of the towering piles. The door jamb partially hid her as she peered out of the glass.

"There's a few more people around, so maybe we should leave separately to attract less attention. You go first and wait for me in the lab."

Tom glanced down at his watch. "I've got a class to teach in ten minutes."

"Okay, you go to class. I'll meet you at the cafeteria later."

She opened the door and let Tom pass in front of her. She spent the next five minutes scanning the remaining e-mails. One caught her eye. A receipt from International Airlines for a plane ticket with extra surcharges for freight. The flight left on the evening of April 15 going to San Jose, Costa Rica.

If he hadn't disposed of it, had he taken this thing all the way to Costa Rica?

She checked the hallway again. No one around. She squeezed out the door, twisted the lock on the inside and shut it softly behind her. She turned toward the lab, but something hit her and threw her back a step.

"Hey."

"Sorry, Charlie," she said, suddenly out of breath. "I didn't see you there."

He frowned. "It's Charles."

Of course, how could she forget? Charlie Baker started going by Charles after joining the Biology Department's doctorate program. Said it made him sound more like a professor. "Oh, yeah. I'm sorry again, Charles."

Charles took a step closer. "I was looking for you."

She breathed deep to slow her racing heartbeat. "Why?"

"*Dr.* Tiernay called." Charles emphasized the title, probably just to sound pretentious. "He said you could take the rest of this week and part of next week off. He's extending his vacation until next Tuesday."

Vacation? The professor never took vacation, but she'd play along. "Okay. Thanks for letting me know. That's fine. He didn't leave me any work to do anyway."

As she moved to pass him, he grabbed her arm in a grip that wasn't hard, but insistent. "What were you doing in the professor's office?"

She looked him in the eye, unconsciously judging which lie he would most likely believe, deciding how best to manipulate him. It was a gift she tried not to use, but sometimes it came in handy. She blinked innocently and relaxed her arm in his grip. "Like I said, I came in to work but didn't have any work to do. I thought maybe the *doctor* had left me a note in his office."

Charlie kept the hand on her arm. "What are those?" He pointed to the papers she held.

"These..." She waved them in a circle. "Are part of a paleontology lab I'm doing with a partner. She writes up half, and I write up the other half. She gave them to me in the hall earlier, and I forgot to put them in my bag." She looped the papers behind her back with a flourish.

"How did you get a key? I thought I had the only key to the office." The jealousy of a little boy came out in his tone.

"There's a spare in the lab. You know, in case Dr. Tiernay locks himself out."

Charles nodded and released his hold. For a second, he looked like he would say more, but then, he clamped his mouth shut. She turned sideways to move past him. She'd gotten away with it for now.

A few steps from the lab door, one of the papers under her arm disappeared, ripped out from behind. She spun around. Charlie gawked at the sheet like it was a photo of a naked lady. "What are you doing with Dr. Tiernay's e-mail?"

She opened her mouth to defend herself, but didn't know what to say. Rather than fumble through an explanation and give him more ammunition against her, she ran for the lab.

***

"Who can tell me if dinosaurs were endotherms, meaning warm-blooded, or cold-blooded ectotherms?"

The students stared at Travis with blank faces as if he would answer his own question. The Saturday morning class tended to be like this, full of kids thinking the professor wouldn't be as tough on the weekend. Or maybe too many of them had gone out partying on Friday night. At least the class was almost over. Travis waved an arm at the image displayed on the screen. In a jungle setting, three dinosaurs struck dramatic poses—the fleet-footed *Velociraptor* in a running posture, a huge, long-necked *Apatosaurus* munching on a tree branch, and a *Tyrannosaurus rex* looking ravenously at both.

With no responses, he tried another angle. "What do you think? Did the *T. rex* lounge on a rock to get warm like a lizard?"

A red-headed kid in the back row yelled out an answer. "Dinosaurs were warm-blooded like birds."

"Thank you for being brave enough to answer. And you could be right, but actually, this is the big question for paleontologists. We don't know for sure. Dinosaurs could have been warm or cold-blooded or some combination we've never seen." He paced to the other side of the classroom, glancing quickly at the clock on the wall. Thank goodness, only five minutes left. The class had gone painfully slow, and the students weren't the only ones distracted. All Travis could think about was the mysterious creature James Tiernay may have kept in his lab. If Tiernay had taken it somewhere, maybe he intended to leave it there. Then, Travis would never know the truth. He shook his head and returned his focus to the students. "In two weeks, you'll be turning in a midterm paper exploring the evidence for or against the metabolism of your choosing. In other words, pick warm-blooded or cold-blooded and defend your case."

The red-headed young man raised his hand again. "Can we pick a combination of both, like you said?"

Travis smiled. "You can even pick an entirely new kind of metabolism for our scaly friends. The key is supporting your position with textual or biological evidence. We'll discuss the details more next week. Read chapter eight and have a good rest of the weekend."

Students shoved their notebooks into overstuffed backpacks and filed out the open doors. A few stopped to ask questions and one even requested a slide of a *T. rex* to use as a computer background. After they left, Travis closed the laptop and turned off the projector, then glanced up to see Harmony standing by the far wall for the second time in two days. Her dark eyes squinted with anxiety as she came toward him. "I thought you'd want to know I found some e-mails in which Dr. Tiernay talks about a biological specimen. I read through them this afternoon..."

Travis held up a hand. "Wait. How did you find these e-mails?"

She bit her upper lip. "On Dr. Tiernay's computer."

"Harmony, that's stealing."

"Not really. I'm not taking them. I'm just reading them. It's more like invasion of privacy."

Travis gave her a stern look.

"I needed to know what's going on."

"So since Dr. Tiernay might have done something unethical, it's okay for you to do the same?"

Her teeth needled her lip again. "No. I just had to know for my own peace of mind."

He frowned, but held his tongue. No sense lecturing her, she'd already done it. "What's in the e-mails?"

"First, I should tell you that I had help getting this from the computer."

Great. She had brought somebody else into this mess. "Who?"

"Can I trust you to keep his name out of this?"

He couldn't promise her anything that would cause him to lie. "Look, I don't know how this is all going to shake out with the administration. If Dr. Tiernay violated university policy, there could be a hearing. I can only promise to do my best to keep this as one professor accusing another."

"Fair enough. My fiancé, Tom, helped me with the computer stuff. Let's go meet up with him, and I'll update both of you on the e-mails."

Harmony had a fiancé? In their e-mail discussions they had never talked about their personal lives. "What field is Tom in?"

"He's a graduate student in Computer Theory. It's a relatively new field that combines computer information systems with networking theories. I don't get most of it."

He nodded, grabbed his computer, and led the way out the door. They walked down the winding campus pathways in silence until they reached the cafeteria. As they went inside, they were met by the controlled chaos of students wandering around looking for other students, getting snacks, and staring at their phones. Harmony led Travis to the same tucked away table they'd met at yesterday. A burly, dark-haired young man sat waiting. Harmony took a seat next to the young man.

Travis sat across from them and offered his hand. "You must be Tom."

Tom placed a meaty hand in Travis's, and he could tell the guy lifted weights. "Professor Perego. I'm glad you could meet with us." Tom spoke with the crisp, precise diction of someone who deals in absolutes all day. Travis guessed him at a few years older than Harmony.

She tugged on Tom's shirt sleeve. "Any progress in cracking the data file labeled 'Rheasaurus'?"

"Dr. Tiernay had a file named 'Rheasaurus'?" Travis asked. That said a lot right there. He knew Harmony had modified embryos from the rhea bird, but the title 'Rheasaurus,' which wasn't a species he'd ever heard of before, confirmed what Tiernay intended to create—a dinosaur.

"The file is encrypted," Tom answered. "I haven't been able to break it yet."

"You will." Harmony nudged his shoulder.

Tom smiled at her obvious confidence in his abilities. Harmony pushed a paper across the table to Travis. He slid it over and read through a log of height and weight arranged by date, beginning in August of last year. "I found this outside Dr. Tiernay's lab the same day he disappeared. He must have dropped it. I didn't think anything of it until I heard Bob's story, but now I see Dr. Tiernay was logging data on some specimen in his lab." She pushed the log sheet closer to him to make room for the other papers in her hand. Travis tossed it into his backpack to clear the table as she shuffled through the stack of remaining papers. "The e-mails suggest he was working with someone called Fulton Pike from Genesys Experimental Labs. Does the name mean anything to you?"

"No, but this research would be unusual and costly. Someone with money must be behind it. If this guy Pike had the funds to pay for an out of the box research project, then Dr. Tiernay might be unstable enough to try anything just to see if he could." Travis tapped a finger on the table. "Question is—did he succeed?"

"I have no doubt he created something." She took a deep breath. "And I think he took it on an airplane. I found a receipt for a plane ticket with extra surcharges for cargo."

This wasn't a surprise to Travis. "That also fits with what I discovered. Last night, I talked to a security guard who said he helped Dr. Tiernay load a large crate onto a Jiffy Rent truck. I went to Jiffy Rent this morning. Dr. Tiernay left the rented truck at the airport."

"Okay, he took something big to the airport." Harmony tapped her chin. "But in one of the e-mails, Dr. Tiernay claimed the specimen was destroyed."

Travis shook his head. "He wouldn't haul an empty crate to the airport. No, whatever this thing is, he didn't destroy it. Where were the tickets to?"

"San Jose, Costa Rica."

"Costa Rica? He left the country?"

She nodded. "I should have known he would go there. He talks about Costa Rica all the time. Before I started working for him, he used to spend time there, hunting or something. But then he said the restrictions on hunting became too hard to work around, and he stopped going for a while."

Why would Dr. Tiernay take something to Costa Rica? To get rid of it? Or to protect it? "Did you find anything else in the e-mails?"

Harmony's eyes lit up. "Yes. At first, I couldn't make sense of it, especially the short-hand grids, but then I recognized some gene markers. It all fell into place a couple of hours later when I noticed patterns in the grids. The patterns pointed to changes in the underutilized portion of the genes."

She nodded her head at Travis like he was supposed to know what that meant. "So he modified the genes, but how?"

"Using the parts of the genes traditionally thought of as junk DNA."

Travis put up a hand to stop her. "Explain, please."

"A small portion of DNA codes for, or makes, proteins which help living creatures to function. But a large percentage of DNA, over 98 percent, doesn't code for proteins. Until the last few years, these sections were thought of as junk."

"And by junk, you mean?"

"Non-functional remnants left over after evolution changed parts of the DNA structure. Basically, extinct DNA."

"And now?"

"Recently, studies have shown specific functions for much of this DNA, although most of the studies have been done on mice and fruit flies." She looked into the distance, lost in thought for a second, then shook her head. "Anyway, in some of Dr. Tiernay's responses to Pike, he made it clear he modified the junk DNA, attempting to turn on genes which might not otherwise express themselves. Those were the genes he had me working on."

Travis nodded at her. Not many smart people could break a subject down and make it understandable. If she wanted to teach, she'd make a great professor someday. "Can you tell what those genes might have affected?"

"It appears he wanted to modify areas dealing with the appendages—arms, legs, tail—and the mouth, specifically the teeth."

Travis crossed both arms across his chest. "Bottom line: Did Dr. Tiernay try to recreate an ancestral form of a rhea—an actual dinosaur?"

Harmony blew out a long breath. "I believe so."

And now they'd plunged headlong down the rabbit hole. If Tiernay had really done it, that would explain the secrecy and the e-mails. But not everything fit. If Tiernay had created proof of evolution, why hide it? Travis opened his mouth to speak, then shut it quickly. A group of students strolled past, a girl with two boys. The girl eyed them suspiciously, probably because all talk at the table ceased as they approached, but Travis didn't want anyone overhearing this conversation.

After the students had gone out the north door, Harmony broke the silence. "One thing I've always found confusing is why Dr. Tiernay would use rhea embryos. They're harder to get. I asked him once why we didn't use chickens, but he never gave me a reason."

Travis had the answer for that one. "If you're going to let the thing grow, you'd get a bigger specimen with a rhea bird."

"I guess you're right."

"What I don't get is, if Dr. Tiernay created an ancestral form, why wouldn't he share it with the world?"

"See, that's the thing." Harmony took a deep breath. "I'm not sure it is an ancestral form. I did two different types of procedures for him. I turned on and off gene markers, but I also spliced in genes, which is basically introducing foreign DNA into the embryo."

Tom jumped in. "But those are opposite modifications. Why would Dr. Tiernay switch to splicing in DNA rather than keeping to his original plan?"

"Maybe some information was missing, lost from the genome over time," Harmony answered.

"What type of DNA did you splice in?" Travis asked.

The surface of the fake wooden table vibrated with the tapping of Harmony's foot on the metal support underneath as she tried to recall. "I know there was crocodilian and feline. I'd have to look back at my lab notes to see if I'd done others."

"So Dr. Tiernay tries to change the expression of the genes to get the ancestral form." Travis traced a half-circle on the table. "But let's say it doesn't work right away." He brought his finger around to complete the circle. "So, he brings in outside DNA to fill in the gaps?"

"Maybe. But gene splicing would likely create a

hybrid. A mixture of the original genes with the spliced in genes, not the ancestral form he wanted."

Tom crossed his thick arms across his chest. "You did both procedures at the same time?"

Harmony nodded.

Tom leaned back in his chair until Travis thought it might crack under the pressure. "If you're certain he created something, and we don't know which method worked, then..."

Travis finished the thought. "Then, we don't know what he created."

CHAPTER SEVEN

The phone rang as Travis spit out the last bit of his toothpaste. Only one person called him this early on a Sunday—Trudy.

"Hey, how are you?" Her voice didn't have its characteristic high energy lilt.

"A little tired this morning, which is how *you* sound."

"Yeah, Eddie has a lot of energy today. He got up at five o'clock this morning."

He smiled at the thought of his iron-willed, early-riser nephew. The boy could put any parent through the ringer. Thankfully Trudy had the strength to match him. "I'm sure you're keeping him in his place."

Her voice perked up a bit. "No doubt. Hey, the kids have Wednesday off school and we thought about making a day of it to come down and see you. Do you have time in your schedule that day?"

Good thing Trudy couldn't see his face. He was pretty sure he looked like a deer caught in the headlights. "Sorry. I can't commit. I might be out of town this week."

"Really? Where are you going?"

He should tell her the truth, even though he didn't want to, but the satisfaction of being honest wasn't always worth the trouble. With a sigh, he squeezed out the words. "Costa Rica." He braced for her next line of questioning. Trudy wouldn't let him get away with leaving it at that.

"What's in Costa Rica?"

A dozen creative answers went through his mind, but he wouldn't lie. "I need to check something out."

"What?"

He explained what he knew, hedging a bit on the reasons for his interest in the situation. She stayed silent until he finished. When she spoke, suspicion was laced through her voice. "Why do *you* need to check this out?"

"Somebody has to."

"Isn't that a job for the dean?"

"You could argue that." Travis switched the phone to his other ear while he put on his dress socks. "Harmony needs my help, and I've been like a mentor to her for years. Plus, I'd really like to find out what this thing is."

"I see."

He cringed. Those two words encompassed not only her understanding of the situation, but also her disappointment in him. Instead of guilt or sadness, irritation rubbed at him. It wasn't wrong for him to question, to want answers.

"Travis, be careful."

"I will." At least she didn't try to talk him out of it.

"I mean it. Challenging God is not a safe practice."

He pushed a stream of air through clenched teeth. "I'm not challenging God. I have questions. I can't just ignore them."

Her voice became soft with a tone of acceptance, something he rarely heard from her. "Please pray about this."

"I have." His voice cracked as a stab of conviction pierced him. He had prayed, a little, but his prayers were more frustrated than faith-filled. He grabbed his car keys. "Trudy, what I need to do right now is to get to church." He said a hurried goodbye and hung up. She had no right to treat him like a kid. She was his sister, not his mom. He could make a decision without her permission.

As he pulled out of his driveway, his mind buzzed

with the information he'd gotten from Harmony. Unfortunately, he still had more questions than answers. He listed off in his head what they knew for sure. Tiernay had created something with Harmony's help. That something was probably put in a truck, maybe loaded onto an airplane bound for Costa Rica. That something could be either a dinosaur or a hybrid with mixed genes. No one except Tiernay could say which.

A lot of maybes and probablys, but were they worth pursuing? The self-preserving part of him insisted he drop this and concentrate on his own career issues. After all, he shouldn't care about what Tiernay had done. But deep inside his motives had shifted. He'd gone from curious to desperate, because of one thought which swam in the back of his mind like a piranha devouring other, more sensible thoughts. *If this creature is an evolutionary ancestor, then evolution is real.*

To settle the evolution issue in his mind would mean having confidence in something rational again. It could restore his peace after six long months of confusion and doubt. Not to mention, it would solve his career problems.

He ran a hand over his face, swiping away the thought of what it would mean for his fledgling faith if evolution proved true. God could have used evolution, right? Problem was, the Bible didn't tell it that way.

A long sigh escaped his lips as the deep-seated restlessness smothered him again. Life used to be easy. He'd known who he was. *Dinosaur junkie. Evolutionist. Atheist.* These labels had defined him for his whole life.

His dad had been the atheist in their house, although his mother didn't have much faith either. She believed in some nebulous helper God to be called upon solely in emergencies. As he'd grown up, he discovered Dad's view made more sense. He'd never hated God. Quite the opposite. Since he thought God didn't exist, he'd lived his life happily indifferent.

Until Marie died.

At thirty-four, the lung disease that claimed her life appeared without warning during her first pregnancy. The doctors had given her six months, although somehow, she knew she didn't have even that much time. Two months later, her baby passed away. A week later, she died, too.

The day after she died, he received a letter in the mail. His tears stained the beige paper in blotches as he read Marie's last words to him, written in her smooth confident style. The last paragraph was a question, one that brought him to his knees.

Where do you think I've gone?

His tragic answer—*nowhere*—left him empty and bereft.

For months, he sank into a deep emotional hole. Finally, he decided that God existed, if for no other reason than to have someone to scream at.

Then one day, he found himself at a church, searching for some piece of her. It wasn't her church, but she loved church more than anything, and he'd hoped to feel her presence there.

An older man had found him wandering around the sanctuary near the steps to the altar. He introduced himself as Rusty. They sat side by side to talk in a creaky wooden pew. Rusty listened while Travis explained what had brought him there.

"You know she's not here, right?" Rusty asked.

Of course, he'd known. There wasn't any logic to it. "I just thought I might feel close to her here."

Rusty put a hand on his shoulder. "I understand."

"Do you think she's really out there somewhere? I can't stand the thought of her being gone, of her being nothing except a decaying lump of flesh." He expected

Rusty to recoil at his grisly description, but the man acted like he heard this stuff every day.

"Yes. I believe your sister is in heaven with Jesus."

Travis slapped a palm on the pew in front of him. "She was thirty-four—too young to die."

Rusty's expression turned mournful. "Only God knows why one life is long and one is short."

"But she was a good person. He should have taken me instead."

Rusty shook his head and twisted his lips into a frown. "He couldn't."

The answer surprised Travis. "Why not?"

"Because you don't believe. If He took your life, you wouldn't be in heaven with Him. Or with her." They locked eyes, and Travis couldn't look away. Rusty's next words were a whisper. "He's giving you more time."

More time? "For what?"

"To figure out He loves you."

It sounded like something Marie would say. She believed God loved her, even while facing a fatal disease. He remembered her kindness, her generosity, her peacefulness. He'd always thought those qualities were simply an inborn part of her, the result of a good combination of genes, but what if it was something more?

"Your sister had a relationship with Jesus, and now she's gone to be with Him," Rusty continued. "Where would you be going if you died right now?"

Again the answer was—*nowhere*. At one point in his life, that answer had seemed freeing. Like taking off a coat on a warm day, he would shed his body and cease to exist. But after losing Marie, it merely felt hopeless.

Marie had treated Jesus like an intimate friend. Travis had called it a healthy crutch, something to rely on to get through the hard times in life. He had his work. She had Jesus. But as he looked back with open eyes, he saw the truth of it. Marie had been his crutch. And he'd leaned on her more than he wanted to admit.

After several meetings with Rusty, Travis came to understand how lost he was, not just without Marie, but without God. He'd dug himself into a deep pit, spoonful by spoonful. And then one amazing day, he allowed Jesus to drop a rope down and pull him out.

If only life had gone smoothly afterward. Six months later and the first wave of peace he felt after accepting Jesus seemed like a distant dream.

Maybe Rusty would have some advice. Travis parked the car and approached the wide-open mahogany doors of the United Church of the Messiah. In the middle of the wide hallway, church members greeted people and helped first-time visitors find their way to the chapel doors. With room for 400-plus, the chapel stretched the length of a football field. A trendy coffee bar sat in the lobby outside the chapel. Even with thousands of members, the place still felt homey.

Travis scanned the crowd, looking for Rusty's copper, slightly unkempt hair. He saw the redhead bobbing up and down in the sea of bodies and started toward him.

As usual, Rusty threaded through the people, greeting friends and stopping to chat with those who looked new to church. Travis inched through the crowd until he could grab his arm. "Rusty, do you have plans after service? I need to talk to you."

He turned around and wrapped Travis's hand in a warm handshake. "Of course. Want to sit with me during service?"

"Actually, I'll listen to the sermon on tape later. I'm going to the prayer room. Find me in the café after?"

Rusty squinted at him, and then nodded. "All right. I'll see you after service."

The next hour in the prayer room passed quickly. On his knees, Travis released his fears, concerns and questions to the Lord. Thoughts of Costa Rica grew in his mind, mostly driven by the insatiably curious part of his personality—the part that always wanted the right answer. The part that usually got him in trouble. He didn't come away with any clear answers, but felt a cleansing in his soul.

He'd left the door to the prayer room open so he could hear when the service ended. Now, a rush of voices echoed from the entryway. He left the room and weaved through the stream of people on their way out. His stomach growled at the rich scent of coffee beans. He couldn't remember if he'd eaten breakfast this morning.

Finding a seat at a high table in the café, he scanned the crowd, catching sight of Rusty. He waved him over. Rusty sat in the chair opposite him, and focused intense light blue eyes on Travis. "What's going on?"

"Some strange stuff on campus." He brought Rusty up to date on what Harmony had found and what he suspected. It struck Travis right then that he'd told two uninvolved people about this, Trudy and now Rusty, but he still hadn't told the dean, even though Trudy had suggested it. The reason why hit him like a smack to the face. If he told Haddock, the dean would likely forbid him from going to investigate, and he'd either have to defy his boss or give up the idea of chasing after the creature.

As Travis finished filling him in, Rusty sat back and folded his arms across his chest. "Interesting." Rusty stared at the open doors to the sanctuary, smooth wood with a delicate cross cut out of the top. When he looked back at Travis, the crease between his eyes seemed to have etched its way a little deeper. "Let's pray before we talk over the options here."

They folded their hands, and Rusty led them in prayer. "Dear heavenly Father, Travis and I come before you with questions. We know You have the answers and will provide them at the needed time. Give us wisdom to know what decisions to make."

Travis had prayed off and on since yesterday, but the power of two people praying together gave him a measure of hope. "What are you thinking?"

The older man jutted out his chin and rubbed a hand across his face. "This biologist has some nerve thinking he could create something the God of the universe Himself didn't create. And yet, whatever this man did, God knew he would do it."

"Do you think he created an evolutionary ancestor?"

Rusty studied him. His probing blue eyes seemed to reach down and pluck Travis's true motives right out of his soul. "That's the problem, isn't it? You're afraid."

Travis blinked. "Afraid of what?"

"Maybe a lot of stuff, but let's start with the obvious. You're afraid of never knowing for sure the Bible is true. You're afraid to have faith. As a scientist you deal with facts, things you can prove." Rusty leaned forward. "God won't fit into your nice tidy box, Travis. You think maybe this creature will prove evolution is true so you can finally put down the war inside you. Problem is, the war isn't between evolution and the Bible. It's between fear and faith."

Rusty always cut issues to the core, but this time his words sliced into the soft underbelly of all Travis had kept hidden. Travis lowered his head. "I need to have answers when people ask me about millions of years or evolutionary trees."

"I know your job won't let you stay silent on the issue." Rusty touched Travis's arm. "God made you to question. He made you logical, focused and determined. All of that is good, but without faith, there's a big hole in your logic." He cleared his throat. "And your life."

Travis looked up at the ornate carved beams in the ceiling. Was he really afraid? He only knew he couldn't avoid the questions or rest on easy answers like others did. And what about his colleagues and the dean? They wouldn't accept answers like "because the Bible says so." If he was going to give up his career, he needed to know the truth.

Travis fixed his gaze on Rusty. "I need to go to Costa Rica to track down this animal. If I can get a sample of its DNA, I'll know for sure what it is."

Rusty bowed his head. His lips moved as if uttering a short prayer. When he raised his head, his eyes were pinched by his wrinkles. "I'm not saying you shouldn't go, but I want you to think about this. Make sure you're going for the right reasons."

Travis gave a nod, but inwardly he cringed. He had reasons, but only wrong ones. Like discovering if the creature's DNA proved evolution. Or finding out why Tiernay lied to hide the creature. Or even just wanting to see what a living, breathing dinosaur looked like. All selfish reasons.

He thanked Rusty and got back in the car, not any closer to finding peace in this decision. If she were alive, he'd call Marie about this. Might as well go see her.

Taking the next turn, he drove to the cemetery, parking next to the elm tree in the far corner. He stared at the crooked rows of headstones for a few minutes before he got out and walked to the granite stone that marked Marie's life, and death. Pain knifed through his heart. All that was left of her in the world lay under the cold slab. He never knew whether to look down where her body lay or up to heaven where he believed she was now, so he let his head hang as the familiar conflicting feelings flowed over him.

Marie, I'm sure you can see I'm struggling. I wish I could talk to you. You'd know what to do.

Had she kept tabs on all he'd been through since her death? After he'd accepted Jesus, it hadn't taken long for the problems to come. He couldn't talk about Jesus at work for fear of ridicule. He would sneak into church hoping no one would recognize him as a professor. And he constantly carried the weight of betrayal. If he believed in the Bible, he betrayed paleontology, and if he believed in evolution, he betrayed God. The conflict yanked him one direction, and then another until he felt like a frayed piece of cloth ripped down the middle.

This creature, whatever it was, probably wouldn't help him meld the two together, but it might help him choose between them—that is, if the creature was a dinosaur.

He knelt down on the soft grass in front of the headstone and ran a hand along the top, savoring the feel of the curved, rough stone. The rock stood for something immovable, something eternal. The way Marie's faith had been.

If only his faith could be as strong. But it wasn't. He had to know for sure. He had to go after this creature.

CHAPTER EIGHT

On his first morning in Costa Rica, bright rays of sunshine streaked through the dirty window of the hotel room, nudging Travis awake. He might be crazy, but he didn't regret coming. Still, a persistent voice in his head reminded him that his just-do-something attitude had gotten him in trouble before.

His cell phone rang, and he rolled out of bed to grab it. He checked the caller ID before answering. "Harmony?"

"Professor Perego, I got your message. Are you in Costa Rica now?"

He dropped into a chair by the window, which was so low to the ground his knees came up to his chest. "Got here last night." He glanced out the window at the view, a dirty block wall holding up the hillside behind the hotel.

"I thought you should know. Dean Haddock found out about the e-mails I took off Dr. Tiernay's computer."

"How?"

"This guy, Charles, caught me with the e-mails coming out of the professor's office. I thought he'd only tell Dr. Tiernay, whenever he got back in town, but apparently Charles wants to score points with the new dean. When the dean asked me about it, I confessed." She paused before finishing, her last words a sad whisper. "He fired me."

"Does that mean he kicked you out of school?"

"I don't think so. He said I'd have to find a different thesis adviser and a different topic."

"I'm sorry, Harmony."

A long sigh came over the phone. "I knew the risk. I just hope I don't lose my work study scholarship too." Her voice picked up in speed. "But that's not why I called. I wanted to warn you. Dean Haddock asked me if anyone else saw the e-mails. I told him you and Tom had, but I didn't tell him what you were doing. I hope you don't get in trouble."

"Don't worry about me. I'll be fine." If only that were true, but he couldn't add to her burden.

"What's your plan to find the animal?"

"Plan A is to visit the rental shops around here. Wherever Dr. Tiernay went, he would have needed a vehicle big enough to carry a crate in the back. Maybe the rental place will know where he was headed or at least how many miles he traveled."

"And Plan B?"

He ran a hand through his disheveled hair. "Don't have one yet."

Silence blanketed the conversation for a few seconds until she spoke softly. "There might be a better way."

"I'm listening."

"Let me see what I can do. I'll call you back in a little bit if I can help."

"Okay, thanks. And, Harmony..."

"Yeah."

"When I get back, I'll see what I can do about getting your research assistant job back."

"Thanks."

He hung up and ducked into the bathroom for a quick shower. The magnitude of what he'd done hung over him. By encouraging Harmony to pursue this, he'd likely damaged her future, not to mention his career. And she might face further problems when Tiernay got back. Tiernay didn't seem like the forgiving type.

He let the water wash away his concerns. It was too late to change things now. He had to find the creature to get answers for both of them. To find out if this had been worth it.

After toweling off, Travis changed into jeans and a T-shirt. He sat in the chair and pulled his computer from his backpack. A sheet of paper slid out with it and landed on the floor. He picked it up. The log sheet from Tiernay's lab that Harmony had shown him. He glanced at the height and weight on the last line—five-foot-nine and ninety-two pounds. If that was the size of the creature, he had better be cautious. He tossed the paper back in the pack.

A quick computer search brought up a map of San Jose, Costa Rica. Where would Tiernay take the creature from here? Somewhere away from the city. Somewhere without a lot of people.

Maybe a national park? He scanned the labels on the map. Several national preserves were situated to the north of the city—La Selva Biological Reserve to the northeast and Monteverde Cloud Forest to the northwest. He pushed the computer away and leaned back in the tiny desk chair. Tiernay could have gone in either direction. Both La Selva and Monteverde would have a vibrant ecosystem and protection from human encroachment. Even the Arenal Volcano had a protected national park, although it was smaller, which typically meant more foot traffic.

The phone rang again. It was Harmony. He grabbed it and moved to sit on the bed. "Hello?"

"Professor Perego."

He hadn't expected to hear from her this soon, and her voice sounded like she'd swallowed nails. "Are you okay?"

"No. They had it on the news. The autopsy results for Bob. His arms and chest were bruised. The police think someone held him down and gave him the drugs."

"Bob *was* murdered. Who would do that?"

"The news report said the police don't have any suspects." She went quiet for a minute. "Do you think someone killed him because of what he saw?"

Travis didn't want to jump to conclusions, but the timing didn't seem like a coincidence. "It's possible," he finally said.

"It couldn't have been Dr. Tiernay because he's been gone."

Travis shook his head, even though she couldn't see him. "Not unless Dr. Tiernay had someone else do it."

"I can't believe anyone would want to hurt Bob. He was a good guy."

Travis tapped his foot on the carpet. "If Bob was killed because of what he saw, then *you* could be in danger simply because he told you. Does anyone else know what Bob told you?"

"No one, other than Tom, and Drew, Bob's roommate," she said. "Although Charles probably suspects something since he knows I stole some e-mails."

"You should be safe then."

He heard her blow out a breath. "This is all my fault."

"Bob's death?"

"If I wouldn't have helped Dr. Tiernay do whatever he did, none of this would have happened."

Travis gripped the phone tighter. "We don't know for sure Bob died because of this creature. And Dr. Tiernay would have found someone else to help him if you hadn't done it. Maybe someone without as much of a conscience."

"Do you think I should go to the police?"

"And tell them what? You have some e-mails between Dr. Tiernay and somebody we don't know, talking about a creature we haven't seen and claiming it was destroyed. They won't see how this is related to Bob's death. *I'm* not even sure it is."

"You're right."

"Even so, you and Tom need to be careful."

"Yeah, I know." She cleared her throat. "Anyway, I discovered a way for you to find the animal. I thought Dr. Tiernay might have put a tracking device on it, mostly because he's such a control freak. In his e-mails, we found the user ID for a tracking website. Tom hacked the site and changed the password, so no one else can get into it."

She gave him the website and the ID number for the animal. He wrote it on the pad of paper by the phone. "And the password?"

" 'ForBob,' " she said in a sharp tone. "Please find this thing, professor."

"I'll try." As soon as they hung up, Travis went to the table and opened his computer. He typed in the website address and waited. A huge colored map appeared of the world rotating in space. Off to the side hovered a wide login button. He clicked on it, entered the ID number and the password.

The world view rotated, froze for a second, and then zoomed in on a blinking purple dot surrounded by a sea of green. He zoomed out a notch. The green sea was a mass of jungle with no structures visible. He zoomed out some more. A river came into view, along with a large lake to the north of the dot. The terrain rose and fell, but still he couldn't decipher the area.

He clicked on the road and city buttons on the side of the screen. Near the town of Santa Elena? He jumped out of the chair and grabbed the guide map he'd bought in the airport. He held it next to the screen until he found Santa Elena. The lake could be Lake Arenal situated right next to the Arenal Volcano. And the dot was at a right angle between the two.

He zoomed back in. The dot on the screen moved rapidly then stopped for a minute. It moved again but didn't stray far from the river on the southwest side of the lake.

He glanced again at the map in his hand. If this was the creature, it was inside the Monteverde Cloud Forest.

A campus messenger notification popped up, obscuring the screen. He clicked on it. From Haddock. This wouldn't be good.

Where are you and what are you doing? Taking time off right now will not be good for your future with this university.

He considered ignoring the dean and dealing with the fallout when he got back, but it might cause more problems if he didn't respond.

I'm out of the country on personal business. Sorry about the timing of the trip. I'll explain when I get back.

He held his breath, waiting for an instant reply.

Nothing came through.

Haddock would be steaming mad by the time Travis returned to the states, but what else could he do? He wouldn't go back without finding the truth. He needed to know. Not just for the sake of dealing with his issues regarding evolutionary theory. If Tiernay reverse-engineered this creature, it was the closest he would ever come to seeing a real dinosaur. Most people couldn't understand what it was like to love something you would never see in life, to hold the bones of a creature and dream about how it looked—like having a love affair with a ghost.

When he didn't get a response from Haddock after thirty minutes, he typed one final message with shaking fingers.

I'll come to see you as soon as I return.

Hopefully, it would be enough to keep Haddock from doing anything rash. He switched back to the map. The purple dot hadn't moved much. Time to get on the road before he lost this one lead on the creature.

Travis left the city and drove for three hours on some of the highest, most pitted gravel roads he'd ever seen. Apparently, Costa Ricans didn't worry much about safety. No shoulder. No guardrails. And drivers who thought the rules of the road were more like guidelines.

As he entered Santa Elena, the largest town close to Monteverde Cloud Forest, he was surprised to find the downtown area swarming with cars, ATVs and motorcycles. He'd expected a village, not a city dedicated to ecotourism. Signs for zip lining, bungee jumping and extreme rafting decorated the landscape.

He pulled into a gas station and parked at the pump. An attendant came over to pump the gas for him. He got out of the car to stretch his legs and use the restroom. At this altitude, the temperature had dropped to the mid-70s and the humidity cooled his skin. He could understand why people would want to live here.

When he returned, he paid the attendant, got in the car, and pulled out the road map of the area. The tiny town of Monteverde sat on the outskirts of the cloud forest. After the road to Santa Elena, he wondered how bad the roads in the preserve would be. Maybe he should rent a four-wheel-drive vehicle. But most of the places around here would rent by the hour. He might need it much longer than that.

A glance at his watch showed the time was a little after noon. This close to the equator the sun would set each day at about 5:30 p.m. all year long. Definitely enough daylight left to start the search.

A knock on the window made him jump.

"Sir, do you need help?" the attendant asked.

He rolled down the window. "Yes, I'm going to Monteverde Cloud Forest. How are the roads?"

The man smiled. "About the same as everywhere else. But you won't get lost if you follow the signs. The main road here," he pointed behind them, "goes to the town of Monteverde, then dead ends at the cloud forest where you can pay to follow the trails around."

"Can you go off the trails and hike farther into the forest?"

The man shook a thick mop of black hair. "No one is allowed farther in."

"Are there other roads that go deeper into the forest?"

The man cocked his head and narrowed his eyes. "Why?"

Travis opened his mouth, but hesitated. How much did the guy need to know? "I'm a scientist with Grant Commonwealth University." No reason to tell him what kind of scientist.

"Oh, you want to study the animals."

Travis nodded.

"I thought maybe you were a poacher. Instead of taking this road, go back to the highway and try the gravel road a little past the turn for Monteverde, but before you get to El Socorro. It will take you through some buildings, owned by the University of Georgia, and then to the base of the cloud forest. The road goes farther in, but it's not a good road."

As if any of them were good roads.

The attendant gave him a wide smile. "You will see many animals in the forest."

He only needed to find one animal, but he thanked the man and left. The gravel road the attendant mentioned turned out to be the driveway for the satellite campus of the University of Georgia. He followed it past several wooden buildings painted red. No way to tell if anyone occupied the buildings, but if they did, no one bothered to worry about him. The road curved and turned into a dirt path as it headed beneath the trees. A strange half-twilight surrounded the car. The overhanging trees split the sun's rays into gleaming daggers of light that sporadically blinded him as he peered into the darkness.

The road turned northeast and the slope increased. He crossed over a wooden bridge spanning a creek barely deep enough to warrant a bridge. The road was dirt, but it didn't look too bad. Might as well go as far as he could in the car. He revved the engine to coax the car up the incline and around a curve. The trees hugged the road closer, stealing more of the light.

Another mile later, the road bucked and twisted, its surface wrinkled with muddy ruts. Even so, the tires on the car dug in, slowly trudging upslope. He kept steady pressure on the gas pedal.

A flash of movement from the right side of the road caught his attention. Something large darted out in front of the car. He hit the brakes. The car slipped, fishtailing in the mud.

He gripped the steering wheel tight, trying to regain control. The wheels kept sliding. As if in slow motion, the car veered off to the right. The right front tired dipped down off the road, then the bumper slammed into a tree. Travis smacked the steering wheel with his forehead, but the force hadn't even been enough to deploy the airbags.

Pushing open the door, he stumbled out of the car, almost falling in the mud. He bent at the waist, put his hands on his knees, and raised his head. Every muscle froze.

Yellow topaz eyes stared at him from the middle of the road. A jaguar crouched, its mottled body stretched tight, ready to pounce. It glared at him, the animal's rib cage expanding with each breath. A skinny jaguar was *not* the animal he was hoping to see.

Neither of them made a move for a long moment. If the animal thought he was bigger maybe it would decide he wasn't worth the effort. Slowly, he stood to his full height, pushing his elbows out to widen his profile. The jaguar coiled deeper into its stance until he stopped moving. Then, the animal leapt into the line of dark trees.

He stared after it. Without hardly trying, the jaguar had made a ten-foot leap. Reality crept over him, stealing into every crevice of his mind. He was alone in the jungle, full of dangerous creatures, with few supplies and not even a guidebook. Sheer stubbornness had propelled him this far. But now what?

He kicked at the moist dirt. Standing here marveling at his own stupidity wasn't going to help. He got back in the car, put it in reverse and pressed the gas pedal. It rocked a little, but made no progress.

He pressed the pedal harder. Still, no backward movement.

A faint whirring sound came from outside.

After scanning the trees for signs of danger, he opened the car door and looked down. His front left tire had sunk deeper into a puddle of mud. He got out to circle around to the other side. The front right tire hung out in space above a tree-lined drop, some fifty feet to the forest floor below.

The car wasn't going anywhere.

This misadventure was over before he'd found anything, except a jaguar. He checked his watch, only two o'clock. Still time for a quick search of the area. Sliding into the car, he pulled the computer from his backpack and turned it on. The internet browser came up with a "no service" notice. Of course, he wouldn't have internet out here.

No problem. His phone still had service. He entered in the website and user information.

The purple dot came up again at relatively the same position. It wasn't moving much. Maybe it stayed in one area to be close to the river. But what did he know about tracking live animals? He only knew how to dig up dead ones.

Squinting at the screen, he found the scale for the map. Best guess, about two miles northeast of his location.

He checked the paper guide map. Rough hiking, but no major rivers or other obvious obstacles between here and there.

Just a quick stroll through the jungle. He'd worry about the car later.

From his suitcase, he pulled two pairs of jeans and several shirts, then stuffed them in the backpack along with a raincoat and all the water he had. He'd only brought one sweatshirt, a maroon one with a University of Chicago Rock Jock logo, the school where he'd earned his doctorate. He tugged it on over his head, slipped the computer into the front pocket of the backpack, and slung it over his shoulder. As he closed the door and automatically hit the lock button on the key fob, he chuckled. No one was around to steal it out here. Then again, maybe someone from the university camp would find it and tow it back for him. He unlocked it just in case, but took the keys with him.

At the edge of the tree line, he hesitated. Hopefully, the jaguar was long gone. He stepped inside, letting the dark green wall of foliage swallow him. Until he'd stepped into the shadows, he hadn't realized how bright it was on the road.

Low hanging branches caused him to stoop over, but these thinned out as he moved away from the road, replaced by entwined limbs forming a rustling roof overhead. Wood crunched under his feet as he walked, the sound cushioned by a carpet of moist fallen leaves.

About a half-mile in, he found an old stump to sit on. He drank a bottle of water and for the first time relaxed a little. No other big cats had surprised him, but multitudes of quick-footed lizards scurried away. The deep emerald leaves made a fitting backdrop for the burnt-orange and salmon-colored flowers hanging from the trees. He touched a pointy flower peeking out from under a bush, the color of a spicy red pepper. Vines snaked their way up the sides of ferns and trees alike, greedy for the sun. He glanced down at the stump. An orchid grew out of the wood, the milky-colored petals sliding through his fingers like silk.

A guidebook could never do this place justice. But he had to stay on task. It might take a while to find the creature and get a sample. He turned on his phone to check the location. The website didn't come up automatically. Instead, a screen popped up with the words "Satellite connection not found."

He shook the phone, as if that would help. The screen stared back at him, displaying the same message. He held it over his head, hoping to get it closer to the satellite.

He stood on his tiptoes, peering up at it. The screen repeated its frustrating message.

The canopy of trees must have blocked the connection. He shoved the phone back in his backpack. Opening the outer pocket, he grabbed his compass and the map. The compass showed he was still headed pretty close to northeast. A couple of miles to go. Based on the contours, the terrain ahead looked steep. Hopefully it was an illusion created by the scale of the map.

He weaved between the largest trees, ducking below some branches at eye level and pushing thick vines aside. Surprisingly, the ground level of the forest grew mostly low ferns, probably not enough sun for anything else. He easily stepped through the foliage, his feet crushing the plants growing there and snapping the twigs dropped by the trees above. Good thing he had a while before he reached the target area, because the animal would surely hear him coming.

The farther he walked into the preserve, the more mist swirled up around him. Probably why they called this a cloud forest. The mist grew thinner when he would come over a rise, then thicken on the way down into a valley.

He checked the compass often, especially in areas where the mist was heavy. Every patch of jungle looked the same, the sole difference being whether he was headed up or down in elevation. After walking for more than a mile, he'd seen a few hummingbirds, a frog, and the backside of a wild pig.

After another half-hour of walking, strange chattering noises filtered through the trees in front of him. As he rose over a hill, the mist dissipated a bit and the noises crystallized—the sound of excited birds screeching. What was the commotion about? As he hurried downslope, the filmy mist circled around him again, stealing what little visibility he had in the thick trees.

Movement to his right caused him to spin around.

Something big slammed into him. He bent over at the waist to keep from falling. Brown skin or fur whizzed by in a blur.

He whipped around, but the animal had already disappeared back into the mist. Was it the jaguar again? Or something else?

There was only one way to find out. He huffed out a breath and ran into the trees ahead.

CHAPTER NINE

Lenaia revved the four-wheeler along the pitted dirt path. The director of the University of Georgia outpost said this road led to Rojo Piedra, but it didn't look like people came through here on a regular basis. From the outpost, the path had swung up and down with the undulating terrain, weaving through the misty cloud forest. A mile in, she spotted a stuck vehicle with no one around. Who would think a car could make it down this road?

After two long miles, she prayed to find the village soon, before her teeth fell out from all the jostling. Even so, she was glad to finally be on her way. The entire day's delay, waiting for the mechanic to fix the brakes on the ATV, had tested her patience. But she couldn't exactly complain about it since the director had loaned her the vehicle for free.

At the top of a hill, the four-wheeler broke out of the trees and into a small clearing. She hit the brakes to keep from running into a three-foot-high stone wall. In the middle of the clearing, was a settlement of about twenty houses.

She steered the vehicle through a break in the wall. The dirt path widened and smoothed. This place had to be a mud pit every time it rained. And yet, clean stucco houses huddled on either side of the street. Sunlight glinted off the metal roofs and the plaster walls were painted in bright shades of orange and red. With the shadowed jungle hovering in the background, this town was like a shiny red gumball dropped in the grass.

She parked her vehicle next to a sky-blue barn, got out and walked slowly in a circle, noticing the sideways glances from a few locals sitting on a porch. Her father was born in Costa Rica, and physically, she looked like she belonged here. Unless she spoke in her American-accented Spanish, the locals most often assumed her to be a native Tico. She looked down at her jeans and coral-colored T-shirt. Her clothing didn't stand out much, but the town was small enough they obviously knew she wasn't a local.

A young woman approached Lenaia, speaking in Spanish. Lenaia smiled and answered her quick greeting in Spanish.

"Do you speak English?" the girl asked.

"Yes. I know my Spanish isn't the greatest."

The young woman shook her head. "It's not that. I love to speak English." She hooked her thumb and pointed over her shoulder at an older man on his porch steps. "Nobody else wants to practice English with me, except for my cousin. I come to this village to visit her, but she's doing chores right now. My name is Nina."

"I'm Lenaia. Is this town called Rojo Piedra?"

Nina smoothed her hair back from her face. "Yes. Can I ask why you've come here?"

"I've got some work to do, but I'm also looking for the town's doctor. Gordon Klein."

"Of course. Dr. Gordon and his son are the only Americanos in the village."

So, even here, Gordon went by his first name. He had always said it made his patients more comfortable. "I knew him before he came here. He used to go to my church."

Nina smiled as if it would make perfect sense for Lenaia to travel all the way to Costa Rica to see an old friend. With one arm, she motioned farther down the main street. "His house, which is also the clinic, is on the right, almost at the end of the road. Let me show you."

They walked along the small pressed dirt road, and then down a dirt walkway to a light green plastered house. Nina knocked on the door, her dainty hand barely making a sound. A blond-haired young man answered. "Owen, this woman is here to see Dr. Gordon."

Owen looked at Lenaia, tilting his head for a second, before a big smile broke across his face. He reached for her hand. "Lenaia. Good to see you."

She shook hands with him. "Good to see you too, Owen. Many of the kids in youth group still talk about you." She raised a hand high above her head. "You've grown taller since I last saw you."

"Well, that was almost two years ago. I might have grown a little." He twisted at the waist and yelled into the house. "Dad, you have a visitor."

Gordon came to the door, holding two vials, one in each hand. "What, Owen?" When Gordon saw her, he stopped and handed the vials to his son. He wrapped her hand into a gentle handshake. "Lenaia, how are you? What brings you here?" Before she could speak, he drew attention to Nina. "Oh, I'm sorry, nice to see you too. Please, both of you, come in."

They entered and sat on a large, lumpy couch. Gordon sank into a chair across from them. Owen disappeared down the hallway, probably to put away whatever the doctor had been carrying.

Lenaia smiled at the doctor. "I'm doing fine. I'm in Costa Rica for work and thought I would come visit."

Gordon crinkled his nose at her casual answer. "But aren't you a volcanologist?"

Nina gasped. "As in volcanoes?"

"Yes, I investigate volcanoes themselves, but I also assess the potential of volcanic activity in other areas."

Gordon nodded while grimacing. "The earthquakes we've been having."

"There's that, and also some reports of smoke in this area. Because Arenal is so close, they want me to assess the threat level."

Gordon rubbed a hand across his thinning hair. "Smoke? Could be the poachers."

"Poachers?"

Gordon grunted in what sounded like disgust. "They steal animals and sell them to the highest bidder. We've been trying to get rid of them since we got here."

"And you haven't been able to?"

"We've sabotaged their traps, but it doesn't seem to bother them much. When we first moved here, they broke in and stole my supply of tranquilizers. Now, I keep the drugs locked up, but somehow the poachers find more." Gordon gave Nina a guarded glance, then turned his attention back at Lenaia. "Let's just say, we think they may have some local help."

"Well, unfortunately, poachers would be a better explanation than the start of a new volcano, so I hope you're right."

Owen brought in some cups and passed them out. "Mango juice," he said as he left the room. Lenaia let the sweet juice slide down her throat to wash away the dust of the long drive.

"You're going to go out in the jungle alone to look for smoke?" Gordon asked.

"Gases, actually. Anything suspicious I find, I'll take carbon dioxide measurements."

"By yourself?"

"That's the plan. Don't worry, I have experience in the jungle."

Gordon looked at Nina again, then back to her. What did all these glances mean? Did they know something that she didn't?

"Forgive me," Gordon said as if he'd read her mind. "I'm concerned for a reason we've been trying not to talk about."

"What?"

He took a deep breath before continuing. "Nina and her cousin, Mirabel, saw a strange creature in the forest a few days ago. It ripped apart a wild pig right in front of them. No fear of people. And since then, several heads of livestock have disappeared from our small pastures. We find the animals torn to shreds inside the trees."

Lenaia turned to face Nina. "What did this creature look like?"

"Kind of scaly on the head and furry on the body. It has a snout like a crocodile with sharp teeth."

Weird description. But local girls should know all the other animals around here. "Did it stand on two legs or four?"

"Two, but leaning over with short arms. If it stood up straight, it would be tall, but it leaned at an angle with its tail sticking out. It has a long, thick tail. And claws on its feet."

"How tall was it?"

"About my height leaning over. If it stood up it would probably be taller than you."

At five-foot-eight, Lenaia towered over Nina. And she said the animal at its full height would be taller. What animals were that tall? An ostrich or a giraffe? It didn't sound bulky enough to be an elephant or bear.

Lenaia inhaled sharply, a realization coming to her. The description—she'd heard it before. Swallowing down her surprise, she internally chided herself. It couldn't be. That animal wasn't supposed to exist.

She continued to question both Gordon and Nina, but neither of them seemed to know where the animal had come from. They talked for a few more minutes before Lenaia said she needed to get some field work done.

Lenaia said her goodbyes to Gordon and Owen. When she left, Nina followed. As they walked down the street, another young girl came out from the house closest to the jungle. She ran to them and threw her arms around Nina's neck. The two girls could have been twins if not for the height difference. Nina was a few inches taller. "Lenaia, this is my cousin, Mirabel."

Nina graciously explained to Mirabel why Lenaia was there, all in English. Mirabel's eyes grew bright, and Lenaia realized how eager the girls were for a break in their routine. They probably didn't get much excitement in this sleepy little town.

One finger pointing at the sky, Nina nudged Mirabel's arm. "If Lenaia can't get back to the outpost before dark, can she stay at your house?"

"Of course. I'm sure my parents would agree."

Nina turned to Lenaia with a shrug. "I'd ask you to stay at my house, but my grandmother and I live in a town that's a twenty minute walk from here."

Lenaia nodded to Mirabel. "Thank you. I'd appreciate it." If she didn't have to drive back to the university camp, she could investigate for at least an hour longer. Besides, she wouldn't stay with the doctor and his son because it would give the wrong impression.

Mirabel gazed at the line of trees beyond the stone wall. "Are you going to be okay out there?"

"Dr. Gordon and I already warned her about the creature," Nina said.

"I'll keep an eye out for it. Don't worry, I've got pepper spray." Lenaia patted her pocket. "I'll be fine."

"I wish we could go with you," Nina frowned. "But Mirabel's parents and my grandmother have asked us not to go into the forest until they decide what to do about the creature."

"That's probably best. I have to go out there for my

job. You don't." But now that she'd heard about the animal, she wasn't going to just hunt for a volcano.

She thanked her two new friends and left them standing in the middle of the road. As she stepped into the trees, the jungle swallowed her whole. After turning on her carbon dioxide detector, she spun in a large circle. Was the animal Nina described out here?

What could it hurt to look? It would be easy for her to search for volcanic activity and track a large animal at the same time. Tracking itself wasn't hard, once you knew the clues to look for—a broken twig, a disturbed pile of leaves, a scratch mark on a tree—merely an extension of the observational skills she honed as a scientist.

She easily found a path, indicated by broken branches, where a large animal had come through. Could have been a jaguar or perhaps the animal the girls had seen, the one that shouldn't exist. She followed the trail which led her deeper into the forest, fortunately not shrouded in mist right now. She followed for half a mile, confident of the way, until she came over a small rise where all the markings jumbled into a confusing mass. The area was a small clearing with a multitude of human and animal footprints, interspersed with crumpled leaves.

Her head down, she scanned the ground, trying to sort them all out. On the east end of the clearing, animal tracks disappeared into the jungle. Maybe the trail resumed there. She took one step into the trees.

Behind her, a twig snapped.

She froze, then slowly turned around.

Three men stood in the clearing. Their bodies formed a wide line in front of her.

A tremor of fear seized her muscles, paralyzing her. The middle one held a rifle, the man on the end gripped a machete.

CHAPTER TEN

Travis trudged by a group of trees that seemed familiar. Was he walking in circles? The late afternoon light made everything hazy and shadowed. After losing the trail of the animal that had slammed into him, he'd tried to pick it up again, but he was no wilderness tracker. Obviously, getting a DNA sample from a creature running around in the wild wouldn't be as easy as he'd hoped.

Lord, where am I, and what am I doing here? The prayer sped through his mind, but he wouldn't say it aloud. If he had to guess, the Lord hadn't really sanctioned this trip in the first place. No, this one was all on him. A fanatical idea to clear out all his doubts. And now he was wandering in the woods alone.

Eventually, he would have to find a place to spend the night. Not the car—too far to walk back. Maybe a thick bush could give him some shelter and hide him from predators.

The sound of a deep voice to his right stopped him in his tracks. It was a male voice, but Travis was too far away to hear clearly. He crept closer, consciously keeping his rustling of leaves to a minimum. If this was some sort of dispute between locals, it would be better for him not to get involved.

The voice said something in Spanish, then in English. "What are you doing out here?"

Funny, that was the same question Travis had just asked of himself. But Travis couldn't see who the man was talking to. He crouched down, parted the leaves of a thick bush, and peered though.

A cocoa-skinned woman, her long dark ponytail draped across one shoulder, stood across from three large men. She held her hands up as a barrier between them. Tension radiated from her taut muscles. She looked like she wanted to flee, but was smart enough not to turn her back on the men.

"Don't you want to talk to us?" said a heavyset man with a machete in his hand. From the look on the men's faces, they had more on their minds than talking. The heavyset man glanced at one of his friends, a muscular man with long stringy hair and a tattoo of a snake curving around his bicep. He carried a rifle slung over one shoulder. "We like to talk to girls. Right, Tanol?"

Oddly though, they were talking to themselves as if they didn't expect her to answer. With her ebony hair and caramel skin, she looked like a local. Maybe she only spoke Spanish.

"Of course." Tanol shoved an elbow into the machete man's ribs. "Why do you think she's out here?"

The woman didn't answer. She backed toward the edge of the small clearing. He knew what she was thinking, but the men would be on her before she could disappear into the trees.

"I want to go first," whined a short, stocky guy wearing a ripped T-shirt.

The machete guy nodded. "Go ahead, Christian."

Christian crossed the space between to the woman quickly, grabbing her by the shoulders. "We've been looking for some special meat, and then here you are." She tried to pull away, but he put both hands on top of her shoulders and shoved her straight down. She landed on her rear end with her legs bent. A fierce look turned her peaceful expression into the face of a lioness. She looked ready to spring back up, but must have thought better of it because she stayed in the awkward position on the ground.

Her right hand moved to her pocket. Did she have a weapon in there? Whatever it was, it wouldn't likely stand up to the rifle.

The machete guy waved his blade in the air and yelled something in Spanish at her. Travis had taken Spanish in high school, but didn't remember much of it. Still, the woman didn't respond. Her gaze darted from man to man. Travis eyed the rifle, but the guy didn't seem interested in using it, or maybe didn't think he needed to.

The men stared at her, seemingly confused, as was Travis. Even with three leering men standing over her, she wasn't cowering in fear, and she stayed silent. The defiant look on her face, made her dark, delicate features seem regal.

"Maybe we don't have time for this," Tanol said. "The rich Americano is paying us well to find the big animal. Plus, we still have orders to fill for Manuel back in the village."

What big animal? Could it be the same one Travis was looking for? And why were these guys now speaking English again? Maybe so the woman wouldn't understand.

Christian looked up at Tanol. "I just want to have a little fun first. We have time for both."

Tanol looked between his two companions before making a decision. "Fine."

Travis shifted on his knees to relieve the pain of crouching behind the fern bush. They had almost walked away. *Come on, Lord. Make them give this up.*

A breeze flapped leaves around his face, obscuring his view. When the bush settled, he again peered between the feathery leaves. Christian had knelt down next to the woman. A slimy grin contorted his face. Travis had to do something before they hurt her, or worse.

The best option would be to take the man with the weapon out first, then deal with the other two. He'd had his fair share of fist fights in high school, but always in self-defense. He'd never attacked first.

The leaf-carpeted floor wouldn't yield much for a weapon. Leaves, branches—nothing that would go up against a machete. And then, a few feet away, behind another bush, he noticed a dark rock about the size of a baseball. In high school, he'd been an all-star pitcher. Although, he hadn't played in quite a while, he couldn't come up with any other option.

Using his foot, he hooked the rock and slid it over. He rolled it in his hand, estimating its weight and the force needed for a throw. Next, he searched around and found a thick tree branch—Plan B in case the rock didn't hit the mark.

When he looked back, Christian had gotten in the woman's face, his thick lips moist as he inched closer to her. She leaned away, but Christian had a tight grip on her leg. The rifle lay on the ground next to him within his reach. Even though he wasn't directly threatening the woman, she had to know he could get to the gun before she could.

Tanol and the machete guy spread out on either side to get a better look. The machete guy now had his back to Travis and blocked his view of what Christian was doing with the woman. The only man he had aim on was Tanol.

Travis's fingers shook with anger and adrenaline. He took a calming breath, moved to where he'd be partially hidden by a tree, and silently stood up. No one had seen him yet.

He pulled his right arm back, rotated his shoulder and pitched the rock with all his force at Tanol's head.

It hit Tanol in the temple. Tanol whipped his head around, stunned but not disabled.

Travis grabbed the tree branch, darted out of the bush, and smashed it into the back of the machete guy's head. The man fell to the ground with a *thunk*.

Christian and Tanol looked down at their fallen friend for a second—not long enough. When they both looked up, they came at Travis together, Tanol first, Christian hopping over the woman to follow.

Travis slipped through a small space between the trees, hoping to isolate the two so he could deal with them one at a time. As expected, Tanol reached him first. This man had seemed less interested in the girl before, but now his face had come to life at this new challenge. He snarled and drew back to throw a punch.

Travis dodged the blow, but felt a sharp pain in his left side. Christian had come up from behind to deliver a sucker punch.

Rubbing the spot near his kidney, Travis angled his body to bring both men in front of him. This was another first. He'd never fought two people at once. Luckily, they had chased after him so fast they hadn't thought to grab the big guy's machete or the rifle off the ground. Christian must have had the same thought, because he turned and ran back to the small clearing.

Maybe Travis could beat Tanol and get out before Christian returned. His mind flashed to the woman on the ground. Hopefully, she'd already gotten away.

Travis took a few steps backward until he came up against a large tree. Taking a wide stance, he raised his fists. Tanol gave a crooked grin and let a punch fly.

On instinct, Travis ducked and dodged to the right side. Tanol's fist hit the tree, driving a spray of bark off the trunk. He screamed at a high pitch that a soprano would envy.

Travis punched him in the nose, silencing him. Tanol slumped to the ground.

He stood over the man, breathing heavily. Anger

and relief crashed through him. He bent over and put his hands on his knees before remembering he needed to leave fast.

A thrashing sound put him on alert again. He could run, but he didn't know what direction the noise was coming from. The last thing he needed was to run smack into the last remaining thug.

He kept his back to the tree, scanning the foliage around him. Through an opening in the trees, he saw Christian's face coming at him, contorted with anger. The man lunged, swinging the machete in a wide arc.

With both hands, Travis caught the arm holding the weapon, but Christian had pinned him against the same tree his friend had punched. They held their position for tense seconds, but Travis was destined to fail. He was stronger, but Christian had the leverage.

Christian used his free hand to punch Travis in the stomach. He bent over, his stomach cramping in pain, but he kept his hold on Christian's arm.

Another punch to the gut. Travis's insides were on fire. He still held on to the arm, but he wouldn't last much longer. He let go with one hand, holding his left arm low to protect his midsection. He blocked one punch, but the next one connected with a thud that sent streaks of pain rippling through his muscles.

Christian's dark eyes had narrowed into slits, his mouth twisted into a grimace, and his cheeks puffed with each breath.

Travis pushed, but he could only keep Christian's arm a few inches away. The machete crept closer to Travis's head. His strength was failing.

A thump sounded, like a fist hitting a hollow melon, followed by vibrations through Christian's arms. Christian's head snapped forward, smacking into Travis's forehead. When their heads moved apart, Christian's eyes had gone black with anger, his eyebrows like deep furrows in dark soil. Keeping his hands on Travis, Christian twisted his neck to look behind.

Over his shoulder, Travis saw the woman holding the end of a large tree branch.

Christian shouted a few words in Spanish. Travis only recognized a few, swear words he'd learned from other students in Spanish class. Odd what you remembered in the heat of the moment.

He tried to shove Christian away, but the man whipped around and pinned him to the tree again. Another thump to the back of the head, this one softer. The man ignored it, all the while continuing the stream of foreign obscenities.

Over Christian's shoulder, Travis saw the spray canister a second before it discharged. He closed his eyes, held his breath and tried to duck out of the way of the stream.

Christian roared.

Travis pushed on the arms holding him, and Christian let go. When he opened his eyes, the machete lay on the ground. Christian clawed at his face with tears streaming down his cheeks as his eyes trying to wash out the foreign substance. He ran off into the trees, probably looking for water.

"Did I get you?" The woman touched Travis's arm.

He blinked his eyes and rubbed them a bit. "Not much. I'm okay." As the man's screams receded, the background cries and whoops of the birds returned. Travis stared at her. She wasn't just attractive. She was gorgeous, with silky black hair, angled cheekbones, and amber-colored eyes. "Are you okay? Wait. You speak English?"

"Yes." She looked sideways at him, amusement lighting her features. "Oh, you thought I was Costa Rican."

"Natural assumption. You look like you could be."

And he had to admit, the Costa Rican people had an exotic type of beauty, but she was especially appealing.

"My dad was from Costa Rica. My mom's Caucasian. And I speak English because I'm American." She leaned back on one hip. Her eyes traveled the length of his body as if analyzing him. Although she was taller than most of the locals he'd seen, he was quite a bit taller than her. Did that concern her? Finally, she looked up to meet his gaze. "Thank you."

"I should probably thank *you*." He rubbed at his aching stomach. "I'm glad you carry pepper spray."

"Well, it was my backup."

"Your backup?"

"In case the tree branch didn't knock him out."

He looked at her thin arms. She seemed muscular for her size, but to knock a guy out with a tree branch would have been hard for her.

"What?" she protested. "It worked for you."

"True." He pointed at the strap on her shoulder. "Why didn't you use the gun?"

"They're poachers, so this is just a tranquilizer gun. Why let him sleep, when I can send him running away in pain. I would have used it, though, if the pepper spray didn't work."

On the ground, Tanol groaned and rolled over. Travis put a hand on the woman's back, turned her around, and gave a gentle push. "We should probably get out of here before someone wakes up angry."

CHAPTER ELEVEN

Travis stared at the small town situated in the clearing. The woman had led him to a village nestled into one of the few flat areas to be found in the jungle. A rock wall surrounded a dozen stone and stucco houses with metal roofs. Two wooden barns stood side by side across from the first two houses.

In front of the nearest house, the same exotic flowers he'd seen in the jungle climbed up a trellis. Small fruit trees stood near the wall, most swollen with bananas, but some dangling guava or papaya from their limbs. The whole place spoke of a simple life, an enticing stress-free existence.

He sneaked another glance at the woman walking beside him whose name he didn't even know. Long strands of chocolate hair had pulled from her clip and stuck to the back of her neck, the only evidence of their life and death struggle. The way she kept her slender shoulders pulled back as she walked gave her an air of confidence. She had glanced his way a few times, but her eyes reflected curiosity, not the coy flirtations of the college girls he was used to dealing with.

She turned toward the first house, the one with the flowered trellis. He hesitated. His only aim had been to get her back to safety, but the sun had dropped low in the sky and shadows streaked along the road. He needed to find his own place to spend the night. "Will you be safe here?"

"Yes. It's Mirabel's house. She's a friend of a friend."

She spun around and looked him over again, from his Rock Jock sweatshirt to his dirty jeans. He suddenly felt self-conscious, like he needed to prove he wasn't an ax-murderer, even though he'd just saved her. Or at least he'd tried to save her. "It'll be dark soon. Do you have a place to stay?"

"Well, there's my car." Although he didn't know how far away it was, much less in which direction.

"Where's that?"

He rubbed the back of his neck. "Crumpled around a tree and hanging off a cliff, probably a couple of miles away."

Her brows furrowed into an expression he couldn't decipher. She either wanted to chew him out or laugh at him. "You'll never make it there before nightfall. Let's see if Mirabel's family doesn't mind one more guest."

"Thanks. You know, I never got your name."

She held her hand out. "Lenaia Talavera."

"Nice to meet you, Lenaia." He took her hand in both of his. "I'm Travis Perego."

"Travis." She said the name slowly as if trying it out. "I'm glad you came along when you did, but let's save the 'Where are you from?' questions until we find you a place to sleep."

"Good idea."

They ascended the stone steps to the house where she knocked on the large wooden door. The girl who answered looked to be in her late teen years.

He heard the name Mirabel followed by a conversation in Spanish he didn't understand. So, Lenaia could speak both languages and had chosen not to respond to the poachers. Perhaps to confuse them. This was definitely a woman who could keep her head under pressure.

After a few minutes, the girl shut the door and Lenaia turned to him. "Mirabel thinks her parents will agree to let you stay, but she needs to make sure."

"Thanks for asking."

Lenaia dropped to the narrow stone steps. He sat next to her with their shoulders almost touching. She turned to look out at the jungle, and her swinging ponytail brushed softly against his arm before returning to hang in the center of her back. He pulled his eyes from her profile and also gazed out at the trees. Now that the adrenaline was fading, a wave of weariness hit him.

"So, Travis, why are you here in Costa Rica?"

He huffed out a short laugh. "Would you believe I'm just a tourist?"

"Hmm...Here's what I know. Tourists aren't allowed to wander off the trails in the Monteverde Cloud Forest. And yet, here you are, exploring in the forest alone." She kept facing forward, but the tilt of her mouth spoke of skepticism. "Somehow I don't think you wandered away from your tour group."

Should he tell the truth? She'd also been running around in the jungle alone, coincidental timing to say the least. Maybe she came here with Tiernay. Or maybe the mysterious Pike had sent her...He cut off the train of paranoid thoughts. Nothing in her demeanor seemed deceitful. Besides, he obviously wasn't prepared to handle this search on his own. Without her, he'd for sure be sleeping in the jungle. "I'm looking for a special animal."

She turned to peer at him through thick lashes, her eyes keenly searching his face. Her bold examination struck him as a challenge. One he wanted to meet head on.

"So, you're a biologist? Or just an animal lover?"

"Neither. I'm a paleontology professor from Grant Commonwealth University in North Carolina."

For a brief instant, her mouth dropped open and her eyes went wide, but he barely registered her odd reaction before she recovered. "A paleontologist is looking for a live animal?"

He hesitated to explain, but what reason did he have not to trust her? "A graduate student came to me with concerns about a biologist she works for. He was modifying the DNA in embryos."

She fidgeted on the step. "Don't scientists do that all the time?"

Tilting his head, he looked down at her. Might as well throw it all out there. "He was trying to reverse the path of evolution in the DNA of a rhea bird."

Lenaia's eyes locked onto his. He swallowed hard. Behind those luminous eyes, the color of amber stained glass, he saw her mind working. She understood the implications of what he'd said.

"Did he succeed?" she asked. Her insistent tone made him wonder, was there more than a casual curiosity behind her question?

Travis tore his gaze from hers and looked down at his feet. "I don't know. His grad student thinks he might have. She also thinks he let the embryo grow into an animal, then dropped it off here." As he finished, he cringed at how crazy it sounded, but it was his working theory.

When she didn't say anything more, he shrugged off his backpack and pulled out his cell phone, suddenly wanting to prove the creature was real. "The biologist put a GPS tracker on something in this area. Harmony, his grad student, gave me access to the tracking website." He turned on the phone. "But I think the trees kept my phone from working in the jungle."

The phone took a few seconds to start up. Lenaia leaned against him to see the screen, and her ponytail swung over to fill the empty space between them. Her soft hair tickled the back of his arm. He resisted the urge to brush it away, afraid he would give in to the greater temptation to run his hands through the silky strands.

Focusing on the phone, he punched in the commands to bring up the website, then entered the ID and password. They waited in silence for a long minute. Finally, a topographic map appeared with a purple dot blinking in the far northwest corner of the screen.

She gave a surprised gasp. "Is that it?"

He tapped the screen to zoom in on the image. "I think it's the animal. Something big bumped into me in the forest. It was headed in this direction. I went after it, but I lost it."

"You couldn't find its trail?"

"I tried, but I'm not a tracker. I don't know what to look for."

She turned her head to look up at him. Mere inches separated their faces. Frown lines circled those amazing eyes.

"Why do you want to find this animal?"

He opened his mouth to answer the question, but nothing came out. His brain had shut down. Her nearness had crippled all intelligent thought.

The door behind them creaked open. They both turned their heads at the same time and his chin hit her forehead.

"Ouch," he said.

Lenaia merely laughed.

"Are you okay?" Mirabel asked.

"Yes," Lenaia answered for them both. "We're fine."

He stood and tucked the phone in his pocket. Mirabel looked at Travis. "My parents said you could stay for a few days."

"Thank you. I'm sure that's all I'll need."

"You'll be on a cot in the living room. Lenaia, you will share my bed with me. I'm sorry, but we have only one cot."

Lenaia gave Mirabel a tender smile, reminding Travis of the way his sister Marie used to smile at him. "I don't mind sharing with you. It'll be fun."

"If you're hungry, we have some rice and beans you can have for dinner."

At the mention of food, his stomach growled. Mirabel glanced over in his direction, but not at him. She seemed uncomfortable about the next thing she wanted to say, so he waited patiently. "My parents also said, if you had mechanical abilities, you could repay us by fixing the machine in the shed."

"No problem. I'll look at it before I eat."

Mirabel pointed to an old, but well-maintained barn. "It's in the blue one."

He slung his backpack over his shoulder, taking the steps two at a time.

"Do you need help?" Lenaia asked.

He didn't really, but the idea of spending more time with this mysterious woman was tempting. "Sure, if you aren't too hungry."

She left her backpack on the steps and strode toward the barn. "I can manage."

***

The machine turned out to be an older model Cameco sugar cane harvester. Lenaia had spent plenty of time as a girl on her grandparents' farm in rural North Carolina, but she'd never seen a sugar cane harvester before. Her heart went out to Mirabel and her family, scratching out a living in the middle of the untamed jungle.

Travis stripped off his sweatshirt and dropped it on top of his backpack, revealing a close-fitting gray T-shirt. She averted her eyes, somehow feeling like she should give him privacy even though he was completely clothed. He crossed the barn, grabbed a milking stool and sat down in front of the machine. He seemed to know what to do, so she stayed out of the way and watched.

Pulling on her lower lip, she mulled over what he'd said on the porch steps. He was from North Carolina, like her. It sounded like they had heard about the same animal. And he knew, as she did, that the labs at Grant Commonwealth were the perfect place for such an experiment. Too many coincidences. The animal that wasn't supposed to exist was looking more probable by the second.

With his thumb, Travis flipped on a button, probably the power switch. Nothing happened. He flipped it back off, then ran his hands over the sides of the machine, looking for something, but she couldn't guess what. She imagined those strong hands curled around a rock, ready to throw it to defend her. He'd risked his life to save her, without even knowing her name.

She leaned against a support beam and tried to keep her voice nonchalant. "You should know. The girls I've met here, Nina and Mirabel, have seen a strange animal in the rain forest."

Travis turned around so fast he nearly fell off the milking stool. "Seriously?"

She nodded, curious to gauge his true interest in the animal, but he didn't say more. For a moment, he stared at the barn door longingly as if he was prepared to go hunt for the animal despite the fading daylight. Then, he slowly spun on the stool, returning his attention to the machine.

She opened her mouth to tell him that she too wanted to find the animal, but then changed her mind. He would likely question her motives, and she wasn't sure she wanted to explain them.

Turning his head halfway, he looked back over his shoulder. "You didn't tell me why you're here."

"Is that a question?"

He grinned, then turned back to the machine. "Yes."

She forced herself not to smile back. Despite his heroism, she barely knew him and wasn't about to be drawn in by a mischievous smile or powder-blue eyes. "I'm here because I'm curious by nature. For instance, I'm curious about where you learned to fix machines."

As she watched, he touched a small switch box and followed the maze of wires with his fingers. "You'd be surprised what breaks down on a dig site in the middle of nowhere. When the generator goes out in Montana, even in late spring, you either freeze all night or you fix it. Forces you to learn quickly."

Lenaia couldn't help staring at the muscles on his back, visible through the thin cotton shirt. His wide shoulder blades stretched the material taut. She followed the line of his back to where it tapered into a strong waist. Obviously, he stayed in shape for field work. His hair hung long enough to have a slight wave to it, but not so long as to look unprofessional. After all, he was a professor. A paleontologist. Part of the geology family, same as her.

"You didn't answer my question. Again."

She blinked and mentally rolled the conversation back. No reason to keep her job a secret. "I'm here to investigate volcanic activity in the area."

He stopped working and swiveled around on the stool again. The light from the two windows shone down into his eyes as he looked up at her. In the fading light, they radiated a crystalline blue that she'd only seen in the sky over Wyoming during her capstone field course. "Because of the volcano that's near here?"

"Yes. Arenal Volcano. They've been recording an increased level of earthquakes in this area."

"And you traveled here from the States?"

She nodded. "I live in Summer City, near the Raleigh/ Durham area."

He leaned back and stared at her, suspicion written across his face. She couldn't blame him. Summer City was only half an hour from Grant Commonwealth University. This chance meeting seemed suspicious, but it had God's fingerprints all over it. "There's a great need for volcanologists in Summer City, North Carolina?"

She crossed her arms in front of her chest. "No, which is why I'm not there right now. I travel for my job."

After giving her a quizzical look, he turned back around and finished fixing the machine in silence, which suited her fine. He kept volleying questions at her, when he hadn't answered her question earlier about why he wanted to find the animal. If he wouldn't share his reasons, then her interest in this animal was none of his business either.

When he'd finished with the machine, Lenaia turned off the overhead light, and shut the barn door. Upon returning to the house, her stomach gurgled in appreciation at the starchy smell of rice cooking in the kitchen. She hadn't eaten since breakfast at the university outpost.

At the closing of the front door, Mirabel came out from the kitchen, drying her hands on a dish cloth. She turned to Travis. "How's the machine?"

"It's working. I fixed a loose wire. I think it should run fine now."

A short man with wide shoulders came from the back hallway to drape a hand across Mirabel's shoulders. They were joined by a woman with smooth chocolate skin and dark eyes. The woman glided in from the kitchen, wiping her hands on an apron like she was performing an expressionist dance. Mirabel introduced them. "This is my father and mother. Pedro and Irene Estafani."

"Thank you for allowing us into your home," Lenaia said. Travis gave her a sideways glance, and she felt her face grow hot with embarrassment. She hadn't meant for it to sound like they were a couple.

Pedro nodded at Travis. "Thank you for fixing my machine."

"You're welcome. I appreciate your hospitality," Travis said.

Lenaia offered to help in the kitchen, and Irene put her to work stirring some beans. The two men sat in the living room. She didn't hear much conversation. Pedro's English was probably limited, and Mirabel, who was watching the coals in the stove, wasn't there to help translate.

After a simple dinner of beans, rice, and bananas, Mirabel's parents excused themselves to go check on a friend who had a new baby. Lenaia planned to help clean up, but Mirabel wouldn't hear of it. So, Lenaia ended up outside again, sitting on the top step next to Travis.

A light breeze cooled her skin, but it wasn't enough to counter the radiant heat coming from his nearness. Saving her life, fixing a machine, staring out into the dark jungle—the man just looked good doing anything. His golden brown hair glowed in the moonlight. The breeze blew a couple of locks across his forehead. When he reached up to push them away, his arm brushed against hers. The feather-light sensation caused a cascade of tingles to ripple down her arm. She scooted a few more inches away.

Travis looked over at her. The bright moon cast his eyes in shadows. Her heart beat a little faster under his scrutiny, but she didn't look away. "What made you want to be a paleontologist?"

"Dinosaurs." The corner of his mouth lifted in a half smile. "I was five when I saw my first plastic dinosaur. It was love at first sight."

She laughed. "Let me guess, a *T. rex*?"

"No, actually. A *Pachycephalosaurus*." He patted

the top of his head. "The ones with the dome on top. I used to ram it into everything I could find, even the TV. I got in big trouble for that one. When my mom told me dinosaurs were real, or at least they had been..." He gazed up at the sky with an almost pained look. "That's when I knew what I wanted to be when I grew up."

"I can understand why. There's something incredible about dinosaurs—their size, their abilities, their extinction." She averted her eyes, absently playing with a loose chunk of stone from the step. "I wanted to be a paleontologist, too, for a while."

"Really? What changed your mind?"

"As much as I loved dinosaurs, I couldn't see myself sitting in the dirt all day. Or spending all day looking at bones under a microscope. I wanted more excitement. No offense."

"I know what you mean. Too many digs, and I'd end up a crazy old hermit. That's why I teach. To break up the monotony and give me some human contact." He turned to examine her again, but she didn't look up, instead she watched him from the corner of her eye. "So you got into volcanology for the action?"

"Not exactly. I'm no adrenaline junkie. When I'm on the volcano, I know the risks, but my goal is to help save lives."

"Not an adrenaline junkie?" He nudged her with an elbow. She gave in and met his gaze. "Seems like maybe you are when you decide to go off into the jungle on your own."

She lifted an eyebrow and squashed the natural urge to protest. After today, she couldn't pretend to be invincible. "You're one to talk."

The sound of footsteps from down the road drew her attention. Pedro and Irene walked down the dirt road arm in arm in the moonlight. She watched their bodies move in sync until they came to the stone steps where she and Travis sat.

Lenaia stood to let the pair go up the steps first, then she followed them inside. Travis entered last, going immediately to the low cot in the main living area. His knees pushed up to his chest as he sat. Lenaia sat on the worn couch across from the cot, her knees only a foot from his.

Pedro and Irene patted Mirabel on the cheek and said goodnight. After they retreated to their room at the back of the house, Mirabel took a seat next to Lenaia on the sofa. The tiny living room felt cramped.

"My parents go to bed early," Mirabel said, "because the sun comes up early."

Travis scooted forward on the cot. "Mirabel, how did you meet Lenaia?"

A spike of frustration tightened Lenaia's shoulders. Why'd he ask that? She'd already told him. Was he checking her story?

Mirabel turned her eyes to her feet, probably nervous to talk to an older, attractive foreigner. Lenaia pressed a fist to her forehead. She had to stop thinking of him as attractive. It would only get her in trouble.

"My cousin, Nina, brought Lenaia to my house today."

Travis nodded and leaned in closer. "Lenaia said you saw a creature in the forest. What did it look like?"

Mirabel described the creature in almost the same way Nina had at the doctor's house, then she mentioned the reports of missing livestock found shredded inside the cloud forest. As Mirabel spoke, Travis's eyes took on a mysterious glint. Excitement? Fear? Maybe equal parts of both.

"Any idea of where the creature hangs out most of the time?" Travis asked.

Mirabel shrugged. "I don't know. Nina thinks it sleeps along a little creek to the north."

Lenaia turned to Travis. "You said the animal you're seeking has a tracker on it."

"Yes, but when I go into the trees, I lose access to the website. What I need is someone to help me track it through the rain forest."

Hope stirred inside her. This was her opportunity to find the animal without going back out there alone. But if Travis knew why she wanted to find it, he might refuse her help. A sliver of guilt poked at her conscience. She pushed it away. If he didn't ask why she wanted to help, then he didn't need to know. It wasn't like she was deceiving him. "I know how to track. And I've hunted in this area before."

"I was thinking about taking a man from the village. Besides, I couldn't take you away from your search for the next Costa Rican volcano."

"I could do both. The website put the creature about two miles northwest of here. That's a good radius to search for volcanic activity. I can wear my gas meter while we hike. It will alert me to any excess carbon dioxide. And along the way, we can check the area for smoke."

Travis leaned his elbows on his knees and rested his head in his hands. What was he doing? Praying? About the time she was ready to ask if he was okay, he swung his head up and drilled her with a stare. His sky blue eyes had clouded over. "After what happened today, you still want to pursue this?"

Mirabel looked at her with wide eyes. Lenaia gave her an I'll-tell-you-later look. "Running into those men was a fluke. And they might have let me go." She was grasping at straws. Even if those men hadn't killed her, they would have done things that were just as bad. "Next time, I won't be caught unprepared. A machete will be in my hand from now on."

Travis shook his head slowly. "I heard them say they were also looking for an animal. If it's the same one, then we'll probably run into them again."

No way would she let him play the weak-female card without a fight. If he could go, so could she. "What about you? Those men are angry at you now, and you're still going, aren't you?"

He fixed his gaze on her again. "Those men might kill me, but they wouldn't do to me what they wanted to do to you."

With a quick breath, she blew a few stray hairs out of her eyes. He was right, but so was she. Being out there was dangerous for both of them.

He thumped a hand against the metal brace of the cot. "We can talk about this in the morning."

Fine with her. He couldn't stop her from going out there.

They each said good night, took a turn in the bathroom, and headed for bed. Mirabel's room was small, but at least she had a full-sized bed for the two of them to share. As soon as Lenaia's head hit the pillow, Mirabel reached out and touched her arm. She rolled onto her side to face the girl.

"What happened in the jungle today?"

"Some men attacked me."

Mirabel let out a heavy sigh. "Three of them?"

"Yes. How did you know?"

"We've had some problems with poachers. They steal animals from the cloud forest. There's actually four of them in a camp a mile west of here, but usually only three leave at one time. They've never come into the village, and we've never confronted them in the jungle."

"You should avoid them. They aren't nice guys. Could they be the ones taking the livestock?"

Mirabel shook her head. "Not likely. Those men are looking for exotic animals to ship to wealthy people, not livestock."

At only sixteen years old, Mirabel seemed more adult then most American teenagers. Maybe because she'd grown up with danger all around. "Do you go walking in the jungle by yourself?"

"All the time. At least, before the creature came. Now, my parents won't let me."

"And you've never had problems with the poachers?"

She gave a little giggle. "I've seen them, but they haven't seen me."

"Weren't you afraid?"

"No. They crash through the jungle like wild pigs. I'm quiet. No one sees me unless I want them to."

She touched Mirabel's elbow. "Your parents were right to forbid you from going into the jungle right now."

"I don't know if I agree. The jungle is my home. The beauty there comes with risk, but it's worth it."

Lenaia smiled in understanding. An hour ago, she said something similar about volcanology to Travis.

Mirabel grew quiet for a minute. When she spoke, her voice held a touch of sadness. "If you find the animal, what will happen?"

"It depends on what the animal is."

"What do you mean?"

Lenaia let out a long sigh. No doubt Mirabel would know if she stretched the truth. "If the animal is a new species, lots of scientists will come. They'll want to see it and study it. Maybe even take it to a lab for research."

Mirabel gasped. "The Costa Rican government would never allow it. We are proud of our conservationist attitude."

Lenaia envied her naiveté. "I hope you're right, but money can make things happen. And American scientists have plenty to spend."

"Maybe we shouldn't tell anyone about it."

Lenaia glanced at Mirabel's silhouette outlined by the moonlight coming through the open window. "Travis doesn't seem like the type who would hurt the animal. We can talk about what to do once we know what we're dealing with."

"I wish I could come with you." Mirabel rolled onto her back. "I'm a good tracker."

"Who do you usually go tracking with?"

"Nina. We are safest together. Sometimes, Owen comes with me, but he makes so much noise I can't listen for danger. Plus, he doesn't blend in with the jungle."

"Owen? You mean, Dr. Gordon's son."

Mirabel's voice grew softer. "Yes. You know. He's white, and I don't just mean gringo, I mean *white*. He stands out like a snowball among the leaves."

Lenaia laughed. "I'm sure he'd appreciate the comparison. So he's your boyfriend?"

Mirabel brought her voice down to a whisper. "Don't tell my parents."

"Why not?"

"They are accepting of gringos, but they don't want me to date or marry one." She let out a huff. "I don't want to get married right now anyway, but girls in my village usually marry by seventeen. I have other plans."

"What plans?"

Mirabel lowered her voice even further to where Lenaia could barely hear the words. "I've never told this to anyone except Owen. I want to be a doctor like Dr. Gordon."

What a shame for her to be afraid to tell her parents her hopes and dreams for the future. "You should tell them."

"In our village, that's not what girls do. They marry a Tico from the village, have babies, and take care of their families." Mirabel rubbed at her eyes. "I do want a family someday, but I also want more."

"And you think your parents will be afraid to lose you?"

"No, because they wouldn't lose me. After I become a doctor, I want to come back to the village to help the people here. But it would be disrespectful and ungrateful to say I didn't want to be a wife and mother, even if I only wanted to postpone it. It is a woman's privilege and duty."

Lenaia touched her arm. "You're a good daughter, Mirabel, but don't give up on your dream. Pray, and let God make a way for you." She felt an unexpected pang of conviction. She and Mirabel were opposite sides of the same coin, both struggling to trust God with their future. Lenaia already had the career, but the family...

"What do you think of Travis?" Mirabel asked.

She stumbled over her answer. "He's...uh... interesting."

She could just make out Mirabel's smile in the moonlight. "I think he finds *you* interesting, as well. He looks at you like Owen looks at me."

Thankfully, the darkness hid the blush rising in her cheeks. "I don't know much about him."

"He's cute."

More like hard to resist. But Lenaia had practice resisting temptation. "There's more to life than being attractive."

"Like being kind. He saved you from those men."

Lenaia rolled onto her back. "Okay, enough already."

"Why don't you want to talk about him?"

She hesitated. Although she sensed she could confide in Mirabel, she didn't know if the girl would understand. "Do you believe in Jesus?"

"Of course, He's my best friend."

Maybe she would understand. "I don't think Travis does."

The bed vibrated as Mirabel nodded. "If he doesn't believe, then he would not support your devotion to Jesus."

"Exactly." Lenaia had compromised her faith for a man before and ended up far from God with a heart in tatters. No way would she go down that road again.

CHAPTER TWELVE

Harmony couldn't wait to get back to the solitude of her apartment. After the weird weekend, she'd found it extremely hard to concentrate in class. Then, Charles had cornered her after her first class. He thought she'd gotten off easy, only getting fired for what she did. He threatened to make sure the dean expelled her if she kept prying into Dr. Tiernay's business. Although she didn't care what Charles thought, she feared the little suck-up might actually get the dean to do something crazy, like expel her.

At least she was able to go home after class since she didn't have any research hours to put in. The late afternoon sun sliced through the windows in the stairway of the apartment building, creating a shifting kaleidoscope of rainbow-colored light along each stair. When she'd signed a lease here, she'd thought the lack of an elevator would be great motivation to keep in shape. And it was, but on a day like today, when all she could do was wonder what was happening in a foreign country, the third floor seemed a mile away.

At the landing, the light shone more fully, the scattered colors gone. She rounded the corner and caught sight of her apartment door. It stood wide open. She stopped and stared. Without fail, she closed and locked it every time she left.

She took slow steps to the threshold and leaned in. The door didn't appear damaged and the rest of the apartment looked fine. She stepped inside. The sun traced a line along the carpet as it forced its way through the blinds. Had she forgotten to pull them up this morning?

As she looked around, she had the eerie feeling she was in the wrong apartment. But it was hers. Same beige sofa. Same empty glass sitting on the end table. What was it then that nagged at her?

She set her backpack down on the floor by the desk and closed the door. Nothing seemed different, except...A little piece of white paper was tucked under the desk chair. With the toe of her shoe, she tugged the paper out and picked it up.

It was a receipt for a book she'd bought in the campus bookstore earlier this month. It should have been in the top drawer of the desk. The drawer where she'd put...

Oh, no. She grabbed the handle of the top drawer and yanked it open. Her heart dropped to her toes. All of the printed e-mails were gone.

A shudder tore through her body. Someone had broken into her apartment. She couldn't stay here. Leaving her backpack behind, she ran out the door and up the two floors to Tom's apartment.

By the time she reached his door, her fear had turned to anger. She walked in without knocking, knowing Tom didn't lock his door when he was home. "They're gone," she shouted to his back.

He spun his computer chair around to face her. "What's gone?"

"The e-mails. Every last one that we took from Dr. Tiernay's office." She flopped down on the couch.

He rolled the chair over to her side. "How?"

"Somebody broke in."

"Into your apartment?"

His hand pressed onto her shoulder, bringing her comfort. "The door was wide open when I came home and all the e-mails were gone."

"We should call the police."

"And tell them what? That someone broke into my apartment to steal the e-mails I stole?"

Tom crossed his arms over his thick chest and spun the chair in a slow circle, his way of thinking. Comfort time was over. "Nothing else was taken?"

"I don't think so, but I didn't take inventory."

"Okay, let's start with who knew you had the e-mails."

She slammed a fist down on the worn leather as the truth sunk in. "Charles. He found me after class today and told me to stay out of Dr. Tiernay's business. He threatened to have me expelled."

"Why would Charles want the e-mails?"

"To protect Dr. Tiernay?"

"Maybe." Tom planted his feet to stop the spinning. "Seems to me somebody is working hard to keep this creature to themselves."

"What are you getting at?"

"I've been thinking. What if Charles and us aren't the only ones who know the creature survived? What if the Genesys guy figured it out too?"

She balled her hands into fists again. "That would be worse, because we don't even know who he is."

"True, but there is some good news."

She looked up at him. "What?"

"Whoever broke into your apartment didn't know about the flash drive. We still have the Rheasaurus file. It might take a couple of days, but I'll hack into it."

Gratitude poured over her, loosening her fists. Tom had taken the same risk as she did when they'd stolen from a professor, and he'd done it for her. She jumped up and laid a passionate kiss on his lips. "You're the best."

"It's about time you realized it." Tom grinned while wagging a finger at her. "No more kisses or I'll forget all about hacking."

She pressed her palms together in a promise to be pure and wholesome. If she couldn't be in Costa Rica to help Professor Perego, then they needed to help him by getting all the information they could on this creature.

***

The jungle pressed in on him from all sides of the hunter's blind, but Dr. James Tiernay came alive in the harsh setting. With his exceptional hearing, he could sense the presence of animals outside the foliage. Nothing large enough had passed by yet.

He risked a glance beyond the concealing branches. A leaf from some species of fern he'd never seen before tickled his nose. He'd explored half a dozen jungles in the world, but Costa Rica ranked as his favorite. No two acres were the same. New species of plants and animals popped up around every turn. It made this area the perfect home for his creation.

He leaned back, pushing at his bushy hair, made more shrub-like by the humidity, and shifted his position. A cramp seized his right thigh. He lifted each leg to stretch them. In this stage of life, his body had a hard time keeping up with his mind.

The heavy footfall of a large animal on the game trail caught his attention. He sat up in the hunter's blind and peered through the leaves. As he squinted, he recognized the unique bob and weave movements of his creature running at full speed. She couldn't be done with her brunch already. No animal dangled from her mouth and no blood smeared her muzzle. Something must have gone awry.

Instead of heading back to her lair under a log fifty feet away, his Rheasaurus jumped into the dry creek bed, sprinting directly for him. The blind, really just a foliage-covered hole in the wall of the creek bed, didn't conceal him completely, but still he ducked under the branches and hid behind the leaves. Not that it would make much difference. Rheasaurus could certainly smell him.

The creature stuck a nose in between the branches and breathed deep. He inched further back though he longed to reach out and stroke Rhea's snout. This mission was to study how she survived, how she inserted herself into an already thriving ecosystem, and how she managed the threats against her. No sense interfering with her adaptation to the environment.

After a minute, Rhea moved away from the opening. He risked a glance out. The rear flank of the creature disappeared into a clump of trees on the other side of the dry creek. Apparently, hunger had again taken hold.

Tiernay settled back with his field notebook and jotted a note of concern about contaminating this experience for Rhea. This was the first time she had openly acknowledged his presence. Had he somehow kept her from fully immersing herself into her new home?

His pen froze in mid-sentence as a low growl came from directly outside the blind. It sounded like a jaguar. Maybe that was why Rhea had run.

He held every muscle still, barely daring to breathe. The jaguar sniffed the branch where Rhea had stuck its nose. A thick paw poked through in the same spot.

Using his foot, as quietly as possible, he slid his tranquilizer gun closer until he could grab the handle. In a practiced motion, he swung the gun up and shot, hitting the jaguar in the shoulder. A noise like a barking seal came from the animal, and then a thump as it dropped to the ground.

He climbed out of the blind and stared down at it. Silky, thick coat. A little skinny, but muscular. The head would look awesome on his wall. But he already had two jaguars mounted in his basement. This one could live. Still, he had to get it away from Rhea's den.

Half an hour later, he shuffled down the creek bed,

dragging the jaguar on a mat made from branches he'd strapped together. He could do this for his creature now, but he couldn't stay here to protect her forever. Even so, he knew Rhea's biggest threat wouldn't come from other animals.

The poachers, whose home base he'd seen about a mile away, didn't know about Rhea yet. Someday though, they would discover her and if they tried to take her, they'd probably get more of a fight than they expected.

***

Travis rolled over on the cot and stretched his muscles. The details of the dream had started to fade already, probably a good thing. He'd dreamed of an open door with a shadowed woman on the other side. Every time he tried to cross the threshold to get to her, he inexplicably fell on his rear end. The muscles in his lower back ached as if he'd actually fallen over and over.

He yawned and looked up at the ceiling. The plan for today was to check the location of the animal, then go find it. Same plan as yesterday.

No noises came from down the hall. The girls were probably still sleeping. If he left quietly, he could go it alone. But Lenaia would probably follow him, and then she'd be out there on her own again. He shuddered at the thought of her running into those men when he wasn't around. Plus, he'd promised to talk about it with her this morning. The idea of disappointing her sounded equally unappealing. He swung his legs over the edge of the cot. He would try to talk her out of going, but if she was dead set on it, they'd go together.

He went to the bathroom, splashed water on his face and brushed his teeth. Still no noise from the other room. He returned to the cot, where he retrieved his phone and pushed the power button. He'd made a habit of powering it down out here to save the battery. When the screen came to life, he pulled up the tracking website. It displayed a purple dot in the same location as yesterday morning. Maybe the animal had a lair there.

He watched for a few minutes, but the dot stayed put. It could be sleeping. Leaving the phone on the cot, he walked silently into the kitchen and grabbed a banana for breakfast. He returned to the front room and glanced again at the screen. No change.

"Good morning."

He jumped. Lenaia sat on the couch, long legs crossed, dressed in a navy tank top and form-fitting jeans. Her dark hair fell in sheets around her shoulders. Her skill at moving silently probably made her an excellent tracker, but it completely unnerved him. "Good morning." He sat across from her on the edge of the cot.

She uncrossed her legs and leaned forward. "The way you talked last night, I thought you'd be gone."

"It crossed my mind, but I figured you'd follow me anyway."

She gave him a sideways grin. Looked like he was right. "So what's the plan?" she asked.

"The website puts the animal about the same area as last night, two miles to the northwest, near a small creek."

"Then, let's grab some supplies and get going."

She took his backpack and headed for the kitchen. He hesitated, reluctant to take much from the family. "I'll put enough for both of us in your pack. Mine has other supplies we might need." She looked back and must have noticed his reluctance. "Don't worry, I've already given the family some *colones,* and we can give them more money later, depending on what we use."

She scrawled a note for Mirabel, telling her what direction they were going, and they headed out the door. They walked down the dirt road side by side, past the stone wall and into the shrouded jungle, but the jungle today was a different experience for him. The forest floor held a camouflage layer of dry and freshly fallen leaves interspersed with sprays of wildflowers, like gemstones growing up from the depths of the earth. The scent of moist dirt soaked into his lungs, filling him with the peace he usually found only at a dig site. Even the pervasive mist didn't seem as oppressive today.

Lenaia tapped his arm and pointed. He followed her gaze to a pair of sand-colored hummingbirds, one cuddled into a tiny nest and the other flitting near it. He wished he could hear the soft beating of their wings, but the volume of other sounds overwhelmed his ears. The chattering of other birds, the squeals of animals he couldn't identify, even one that sounded like a baby crying, all evidence of a rich, teeming ecosystem. Tiernay couldn't have picked a better place to drop off his pet project.

He took the lead, walking slowly, pushing leaves and branches back to make a path. Lenaia had hooked a machete to his backpack, but he didn't need it for the foliage, and he preferred to have his hands free. True to her word, she carried her own machete in her right hand. He'd be willing to bet she still had the pepper spray in her pocket. On her belt, the gas meter blinked its red light, the only indication it was scanning the air for toxic gases.

Thirty minutes into the hike, he began to look for evidence of the creature. She must have had the same thought because she slipped by him to move in front, her eyes scanning the ground intently.

"Do you see anything?" he asked.

She nodded and held her finger to her lips as a signal for quiet. He didn't want to spook the creature, especially since he had yet to formulate a plan for how to collect the samples he needed from the creature. Although he should be working on a plan, his focus kept drifting to her. As he trailed behind, he admired the way she moved, smooth and comfortable in her own skin. He guessed her to be an athlete, maybe a runner like him. She'd captured her hair in a loose bun, but a few stubborn strands drifted free along the nape of her graceful neck. What would it be like to cup her neck in his hand and...

Whoa. He hung back a little further. Maybe some distance would help. As a professor, he'd grown used to dealing with young, attractive women and seeing them only as students, but with Lenaia, detachment proved more difficult.

The rhythmic trickling of a small river joined the background noise. Lenaia suddenly stopped and motioned for him to come near. He moved to her side and leaned down so she could whisper, her breath tickling his ear. "I think we're close. A large animal came through here, but there's no way to know if it's the one we're looking for."

He squinted at her. "What else could it be?"

Her perfect brows arched up. "Did you read anything about this area before you came?"

Busted. "Well, it was a spur of the minute thing."

"This area has large cats, like jaguars or pumas, and then there's the tapirs and wild boars, although their tracks are usually pretty distinct." She looked up into his eyes for a second, clearly amused and pretending to be annoyed. "You didn't even bring a guidebook, did you?"

He shrugged sheepishly, but couldn't hold back his smile. Her fake annoyance was more attractive than any other flirting she could have done. But she probably wasn't meaning to flirt with him. He definitely had to work harder on detachment. "What's the difference between a jaguar and a puma?"

She rolled her eyes and ignored the question.

He let her take the lead again as they pushed through the next group of trees. The leaves parted to reveal a river spanning six feet across, but only a foot deep. After the discussion of big cats, this area seemed exposed, too out in the open. What if a jaguar was waiting on the other side? He took the lead, brushing past her and wading into the water, glad he'd brought his field boots. A glance back told him Lenaia had worn waterproof boots as well. She paused to look up at the trees, one hand resting on her hip, the other tucked by her shoulder into the strap of her backpack. How odd to push through the jungle with a woman who looked like she could pose for the cover of an adventure magazine. Her beauty would draw others to her, and yet she'd chosen a solitary career. Why?

At the deepest part of the river, a little water sloshed into his boots, but otherwise they made it across with no problems. A well-worn dirt path led into the trees on the other side. A game trail. The perfect place for the creature to hang out, where dinner might wander by.

He climbed out of the river, gave Lenaia a hand up, and then let her pass him again so she could look for signs of the animal. A short distance later, she stopped and turned to face him. She pointed to her ear. He listened, but all he heard was the constant background noises of the jungle that had surrounded them since they left the village. He shifted his head in the direction she indicated. Still just noise, but then ... He heard it almost as an undercurrent, a repeated sound he couldn't identify. Somewhat like a horn mixed with a flute.

He nodded to tell her he'd heard it.

Lenaia tapped his arm and moved forward. They moved as quietly as they could, which was mostly a problem for him. He slid his feet on the leaves, avoiding sticks and fallen branches. Ahead of him, Lenaia pushed branches back, scanning each new clump of trees.

After pulling back one long branch, her body went rigid. He looked over her shoulder. A narrow parting in the trees opened to a hovel protected by a fallen tree trunk. Underneath the crumbling wood, in the cool shadows, a peculiar animal slept. It looked like nothing he'd ever seen before, living or fossilized.

He held his breath, afraid to disturb it, afraid this was a dream.

The creature had tucked its snout under its tail. Dirty brown scales covered part of the head and tail, almost like armor, but the rest of the body had a tawny coating of what appeared to be matted feathers. The noises they'd heard continued, originating from its snout. The creature was snoring. Curled up, it looked about four feet long. So, it would probably be his height when standing.

He shot a look at Lenaia. Her mouth hung open, and her eyes were wide. Obviously, she hadn't thought they'd find it either.

He watched the creature slumber for a long moment. She tapped his arm and shrugged her shoulders. She wanted to know what he planned to do.

Good question. A DNA sample would be ideal, but how to get one? A feather maybe. Blood would be better. Or saliva. Could he slide a swab into the creature's nose while it snored? Maybe through the side of its mouth.

He silently eased the pack off his shoulders and placed it on the ground between his feet. A gentle pull on the zipper caused a faint ripping noise.

The creature stirred, twitching the end of its tail.

He stopped. That was far enough. His hand could fit into the opening. He reached in and searched by feel for the glass vial containing the sample swab. The creature probably wouldn't open up and say "ah," but maybe he could get skin cells or saliva from the outside of its body. He'd take anything he could get.

Crouching down, he inched slowly along the six feet of space separating him from the creature. He positioned his feet carefully, avoiding sticks and dead leaves, to make the least possible noise.

Two feet away, he noticed the teeth—at least an inch

and a half long and knife-sharp. Probably its first defense if it woke.

He slid the DNA swab out of the tube. It gave a tiny popping noise as it released. He froze in place, but the creature never moved. It must have had a late night tearing up the local animals.

Travis took a shallow breath and bent further to get closer to the creature's head.

Under the stress of the position, his knee joint gave a loud crack.

The creature's eyes flew open. Stark terror reflected in the shiny brown orbs. It let out a startled squeal, somewhere between a bark and a yelp.

It bolted, slamming into Travis's shoulder and knocking him backward.

The creature slid on the fallen leaves, then regained its footing and took off into the trees on a dead sprint.

Travis rolled onto his knees and stared at Lenaia. She gave him a shocked look. A second later, she took off after the creature.

Clumps of dead leaves swirled around Travis as he scrambled to find the glass vial he'd dropped. At least the swab had never left his grip. He found it, shoved the swab back in the tube, and threw it all into the pack.

Slinging the bag over his shoulder, he ran after them.

CHAPTER THIRTEEN

The kitchen floor was as clean as their dining room table, but Mirabel swept it anyway, just to have something to do. Her mother stood at the sink cleaning pans from the guava bread she'd made. "Don't fret about your friends. God will be with them."

Her mother spoke in Spanish, and often Mirabel would force her to practice English, but not today. "I know, Mom. I wish I was with them."

"You are too young to go out there with a dangerous animal."

Mirabel swept harder, as if she could wear the sheen off the floor. "But I'm not too young to get married and have babies?"

Her mother sighed. Mirabel hoped she would turn around, maybe have a real discussion about this. But instead, her mother stared at the pan in the sink. "You wouldn't get married until next year when you're seventeen. Your father and I merely asked you to think about the men in the village who have husband potential."

For once, Mirabel wanted to flip the old argument on its head. "And if I'm interested in someone you don't approve of?"

Her mother looked over her shoulder and raised her eyebrows. "I can see the interest between you and Owen. The whole village sees it. But your father and I said to look for a man with husband potential." She returned her attention to scrubbing the pan. "Owen, while a nice boy, would not make a good husband for a Tico girl."

"You barely know him."

"He has no idea how to handle livestock, how to hunt in the jungle or how to harvest the village crops."

"They've only been here for two years. And he's learned a lot. Those are things he loves to do, but rarely will anyone in the village help him learn." Mirabel wrestled with her frustration. Her mother had known of her feelings for Owen but ignored them, hoping she'd do what ... grow out of it? Part of her wanted to explode at her mother's explanations, but it wasn't in her nature. "How can you judge him for being gringo?"

"He's not like us. He doesn't understand the way we do things."

Mirabel rested the broom in the corner and brushed her hands on her jeans. "Neither do I."

Her mother kept her focus on the soapy pan. Mirabel left through the front door, happy to have gotten in the last word. Not that it would do her much good in the long run, but it was satisfying for now.

She flopped down on the front steps. The line of trees, where Travis and Lenaia had disappeared hours earlier, marked the line between her two worlds. In the jungle forest, she explored freely, wherever she wanted to go. Here in the village, limitations put a strangle hold on her. Just because every Tico in this village had married another Tico didn't mean she had to. Jesus judged people by their hearts, not their birth place.

"Hey." Owen came around the side of the old blue barn. He walked up slowly, his expression softening when he sensed her mood. His blond hair stuck out in front and bobbed when he moved, like it was waving to her. Today, even that couldn't make her smile. He stopped in front of the steps. "You want some company?"

She nodded, but turned her gaze back to the trees.

He sat one step below her and stayed quiet. That was one of the things she liked most about him. He knew when to let her think and had the patience to wait until she wanted to talk.

After a few minutes, she swiveled to look at him, letting herself sink into the deep pools of his light green eyes. He hopped up to the step beside her and put a tentative arm behind her. She leaned against him, not caring if her mother saw. She smiled at the surprise on his face. In the cover of the jungle, they had kissed a few times, but she'd made it clear they couldn't show affection in town. And even as she boldly allowed it, she knew there were others in town besides her mother who thought a Tico and a gringo didn't belong together.

"There must be something wrong with me. I want to be a good daughter. All of the other Tico girls make their parents proud."

With his fingertips, he rubbed her arm. She melted into the tingling sensation brought by his touch. "Mirabel, you're a great daughter. Your parents love you very much. Give them time, and they will open their minds."

She let out a sigh that sounded quite a bit like her mother's. "When they find out what I want to do, they might lock me inside our house. Right now, our fights are about marriage ... and you."

"You fought about me?"

"Yes, my mother can see we care for each other."

He bent his head to get close to her ear. "Do they know we're in love?"

She could feel the heat rising in her cheeks. "No, but if my mother is looking out the window, she might guess. And then I don't know what she, or my dad, would do."

"Maybe they'll surprise you."

The surprise would be finding out which would make her parents more angry--marrying a gringo or leaving home to go to the university. She tilted her head and looked at him with one eye. "Or I could wait until next year, then leave for the university without telling them."

Owen tapped her chin. "You wouldn't do that."

She shook her head. "But I wish I could."

He smiled like he knew better, but she knew her parents. They were kind and generous, and also stubborn when they had their minds set. She wanted to honor them, God said to honor them, but what would she do if they forbid her from leaving the village or, worse, from seeing Owen?

***

Good thing Travis could hear Lenaia running, because he sure didn't know how to track like she did. Branches grabbed at him, pulling like greedy hands, as he ran. He followed the crashing sounds until he almost bowled her over, stopping his forward momentum just in time to keep them both from tumbling over the edge of a ravine—a fifty-foot drop.

"What happened?" his words came in ragged gasps. Running through the jungle was much harder than jogging in the city.

"It jumped into the trees about halfway down the hill."

He sucked in another breath and gave her a playful tap on the shoulder. "And you let it get away."

She shot him an annoyed look and waved her arm at the steep hill. "Be my guest. Jump."

He put a hand on her arm. "We'll find it."

She turned to him, eyes narrowed. For a second, he thought she might push his hand away, but then her features softened into something akin to wonder. "I've never seen anything like it."

"Me either." He tugged a broken tree branch from her hair. "Good thing you know how to track. Lead the way, Pocahontas."

She glared at him again, but this time with a half-grin. "You're in a good mood, considering we just lost the animal."

"What can I say? I love field work." He continued in a more serious tone. "Actually, I'm relieved. Until five minutes ago, I still thought this might be a wild goose chase."

She rolled her eyes, then started picking her way down the slope. He followed, placing his feet as she did in the v-shaped space made by the trees as they stretched up for sunlight. By unspoken agreement, they both kept quiet, knowing any noise could spook the creature if they happened upon it again.

He placed a foot, grabbed a tree, swung the other foot, and grabbed another tree. The next one bent under his weight. Catching a nearby trunk, he regained his balance. These trees weren't as hard as the ones in North Carolina. In fact, now that he looked closer, the tree which bent under his weight wasn't a tree at all, but a group of vines growing together in a thick mass, desperately seeking the light. He chose his next foot placement more carefully.

As they descended, he found himself repeating the creature's noises over and over in his head. Not the snores, but the startled yelp before it bolted. He strained his ears to filter the constant jungle noise and listen for anything resembling those sounds.

Nothing came close. Only the raucous clamor of a monkey, or a bird, maybe even a cat.

He looked down at Lenaia, five feet below him on the slope. He probably should have gone first. If he fell now, he'd take her down with him. And if he'd have gone first, he could have caught her if she fell. Of course, she was the one who knew how to track, but tracking on the wall of a ravine couldn't be easy.

Another few feet down and his fear came to reality. Lenaia pitched forward, her body slamming into a tree trunk. He slid partway to her, anchored his left hand on a nearby trunk and grabbed her under the arms with his right. He supported her weight until she balanced again on the trunk next to her. She clung to it with both arms wrapped around the tree.

"Thanks," she said in a hushed tone. "I stepped in a hole. Look out for it."

He moved to the other side of the tree to avoid it. "Here let me go ahead."

Grabbing a thicker tree trunk just past her, he circled his legs to swing in front of her. On the way by, his leg brushed her thigh, her skin as smooth as silk. He pushed down the swell of non-platonic thoughts swamping his mind and focused on climbing down.

"How will you follow the trail?" she asked.

He glanced back. "Let's get down first. When we're on more level ground, you can try to pick it up. You can always look on the way for obvious signs the creature veered off this course."

She nodded, and he noticed a faint crimson color to her cheeks, making her skin look like cinnamon. Was it from almost falling, or had she also felt the accidental brush of their legs?

He resumed their painstaking climb down, trying not to stare at the bottom of the ravine, still twenty feet away. Although heights didn't bother him, staring straight down reminded him every second of the consequence of a misstep. Once, he heard a squeal behind and braced to catch Lenaia with his back, but she'd caught herself before she fell.

He did his best to scan for any sign of the creature, but even as he did, he marveled at the craziness of it. To come all the way to Costa Rica to meet a beautiful girl from North Carolina and take her on a hunt for a frightened, potentially dangerous, creature. For what, to satisfy his professional curiosity?

No, it was more than that. When he'd become a Christian, everything had changed. His world had fragmented into Christian Travis and Paleontologist Travis. The two couldn't coexist for much longer. He needed to find a way to make sense of the world again. And his world had always included evolution.

A few feet from the bottom, a dark brown blur ran past, knocking him into a tree trunk. He bounced off and slid the remaining distance to the bottom of the slope, landing on a pile of broken tree branches.

"Are you okay?" Lenaia asked.

Probably a bruised backside, he thought, but otherwise no harm done. "I'm fine."

"Was that the creature?"

"Not sure." If so, it had knocked into him twice now. Part of its defense mechanism or an attack? He motioned for her to crouch down and come down the hill. Might as well try to take away the creature's line of sight.

She knelt beside him on fairly level ground behind a clump of ferns. They kept their breathing quiet and listened. There, off to the left. A distinct rustling in the underbrush. He swiveled his head. No movement that he could see.

His pack had fallen to the ground after the slide down the hill. He inched it over and slowly pulled the machete out of the bungees. He held the blade end well away from his body in case the creature dive-bombed again. He didn't want to lose a leg from a wound made by his own machete. A glance behind told him she'd also retrieved the machete she'd stowed during their descent.

Before yesterday, he'd never wanted a gun, but this was the second time in two days he'd wished for a rifle, not so much to protect himself, more out of a caveman-like desire to protect Lenaia. Although, he would hate to hurt the creature. Its only crime was being created in a lab by a crazy scientist.

The rustling stopped and the excited chattering of birds filled the air again. Until the other noises returned, he hadn't realized the whole jungle had gone silent. Were the birds scared by the attack, if he could call it that, or maybe they didn't know what to do around such a foreign creature?

He leaned toward Lenaia. "I think it's gone," he whispered.

"Me too. Why don't you let me try to track where it went?" She bumped his arm with her elbow and gave him a mischievous grin. "Besides, you might be better off behind me. It apparently doesn't like you."

Her calm demeanor impressed him. But of course she would be accustomed to taking risks. The field work she did for a living outranked his in danger level.

For the next several hours, he watched her pick through the jungle, sifting a thousand bits of data, looking for one telltale sign to track. They stopped to have a simple meal of dried meat and bananas, and then continued the hunt. He knew the kinds of things she looked for, but didn't know how she interpreted them. She would check a broken tree branch or examine prints in the scattered spots of mud, and use it to point them in a new direction.

She stopped to release her hair and finger comb through it. Her slender fingers slipping through the silky strands mesmerized him. He shook his head to clear it. When he stared at her for too long, his mind wandered. All the questions he should ask seemed to float away. Like why she had volunteered to help him track this creature. Was it out of curiosity? He sensed there was something more, but couldn't fathom what.

Maybe she'd helped him because she couldn't resist his animal magnetism. He laughed at the internal joke.

"Something funny?" She threw him a suspicious glance as she clipped her hair up into a messy bun.

"No, sorry. I hang out in my head sometimes. Didn't realize that came out."

She took a step, coming close to him, rose on her tiptoes and put two fingers on his temple. "Spend a lot of time up there?"

Heat rushed through him at the soft touch. He wanted to grab her hand and pull her closer. "More than I'd like."

She nodded once, like she understood. "I think it went this way." She moved away and pointed northeast. "But we have a problem."

He swatted at a mosquito swooping near his ear. "What?"

"It'll be getting dark soon."

"Already?"

"In the jungle, the trees block much of the setting sun, and the walls of the ravine won't help either. We could make it partway up the ravine, but not back to the village before dark. And it would be nearly impossible to camp on the slope if we didn't make it all the way up. I think we're better off staying down here for the night." She patted her backpack. "We should have everything we need."

"Were you on some survival show that I missed?"

She laughed, a musical sound among the chatter of animals and the buzz of insects. An instant later, her face turned sober again. "There's just one more problem."

He ran a hand through his hair. "I wish you'd stop saying that."

"Unless you brought one, we have only one hammock and one mosquito net."

"We can't just sleep on the ground?"

"We could, but I wouldn't recommend it." She pushed the hair off her face. "Easy prey for snakes, scorpions, and spiders. Plus the mosquito net won't work unless it's away from your skin. You can't lay it over you like a blanket."

He slapped at another of the blood-sucking critters. A mosquito net sounded like a good idea. "You take the hammock. I'll sleep on the ground under it."

"I appreciate the thought, but the net won't reach to the ground. And I won't sleep if I know you're getting eaten by mosquitoes and spiders all night."

"You forgot snakes and scorpions."

"We'll just have to share, platonically, of course."

"Of course."

"Can I trust you?"

Her expression said this was less of a question and more of a warning. He got the message. Putting a hand over his heart, he held up two fingers, even though he had never been a Boy Scout. "You can trust me."

He hoped it was true. As extra insurance, he sent up a quick prayer for strength. Lying close to Lenaia would be a temptation of epic proportions.

CHAPTER FOURTEEN

"Just so you know…" Lenaia peered at Travis, but could barely make out the features of his face in the darkness. "I don't usually have so many problems when I'm doing field work. Like being attacked or falling down hills. I like to think I'm pretty competent in general."

"That's easy to believe."

She pulled at the sleeves of her sweatshirt. Was he being sarcastic? Her knee still ached from her close encounter with the tree trunk. Not her finest moment.

They lay side by side in the hammock, the mosquito net tucked under their bodies and billowing out in the light breeze. The temperature had dropped at least ten degrees. They'd gone to bed with their shoes on for warmth, and despite how unnervingly close he was, she was already glad for Travis's extra body heat. She shifted more onto her back, hoping to relieve the pressure on her knee and to keep the slope of the hammock from pulling her toward the middle, toward him.

"I'm serious," he said. "You're very independent and capable."

Maybe a little too independent. At least, that's what her mother always said about her marriage prospects. *No guy wants a girl who can outdo him in everything.* Before the criticizing thought could take root, she banished her mother's voice from her mind, but it was quickly replaced by another admonishment. *Why haven't you told him the truth? If he knew about your uncle, he wouldn't be so willing to trust you.* She pinched her eyes closed and cleared her mind. The two of them were stuck in a hammock together for the night. This was no time for confessions.

"But I've enjoyed saving you on occasion."

The teasing in his tone made her smile. She opened her eyes to focus on his silhouette. "Even when you got beat up to do it?"

"Worth every punch." His tone had changed to something more intimate, almost whispered. A rush of heat flooded her body. He was too close, but she had nowhere to go.

She reached down to rub her aching knee. As she shifted, the hammock pulled them together like a flytrap closing. She managed to get her hands out before their bodies thumped into each other. Her palms pressed against his soft sweatshirt. She felt the contours of his strong chest underneath. His heart beat was steady and strong against her right hand. "Sorry."

"Don't be."

His voice had lowered into a husky whisper. She was in big trouble.

The brush of his fingers along her cheek was so light it could have been a feather. His fingertips traveled over her lips and under her chin. The smooth anticipation of a kiss from Travis melted over her, followed by stark panic.

Whoa. Lord, I need some help here. I can't get pulled in. I barely know him, and he doesn't know everything about me.

Sharing the hammock had been a bad idea. She had to do something, say something, anything. This heat between them could burn her heart to ashes.

"Travis, why is it so important to you to find this creature?" Nobody would come all this way to check on what another professor had done. He had to have his own reasons.

His hand dropped. She squirmed away as far as she could, but the spicy scent of his cologne, or maybe his deodorant, lingered in her nose.

He stayed silent for a long time until she thought maybe he wouldn't answer. But she wanted an answer, so she pressed him. "Not many people come out to the jungle to look for something they can't prove exists."

"I need to find out how the creature was made."

An academic answer, not good enough. "But creating an ancestral form is impossible, because that would verify the theory of evolution, which I know isn't true."

She felt his body stiffen next to her. "Says you. Millions of people believe in evolution compared to what...a handful who believe God created the Earth in seven days. A better question is how can you be a geologist and not believe in evolution?"

She'd faced this attack before, and yet somehow it felt different coming from him. "I could ask you the same thing. If you really believed in evolution, why are you down here trying to find an animal that proves it?" A different possibility hit her. "Unless, you're trying to steal the discovery."

He shifted and the change in weight distribution caused the hammock to sway. She braced her good knee against his leg to keep from falling against him again. In the moonlight, she could make out his hand resting on his forehead. She'd probably pushed too hard, but before things went too far between them, she needed to understand why he'd come here.

"I don't have to justify myself."

She placed her shoulder as a wedge between them. "No, I guess you don't."

They lay in silence, in a jungle that was never silent. The soft buzz of insects and rustling of nocturnal animals seemed louder in the void. About the time she thought he'd fallen asleep, he spoke in a quiet voice. "Why are you here, Lenaia?"

"I told you."

"I know you said you're looking for volcanic activity, and I believe you, but you seem as anxious to find this creature as me. Why?"

Perceptive question. But she couldn't answer it without explaining more than she wanted him to know. Besides, if she told him the truth about her interest in the animal, he'd probably think she was working against him. "I have my reasons."

He let out a soft sigh. "Well, I'm grateful for your help. Good night, Lenaia."

She lay on her back as much as possible, trying to decide which Travis she found more frustrating—the one who had tried to kiss her or the one who was giving her space. Did she want him close or far?

It didn't escape her that he hadn't answered *her* question. Was he out here to steal the discovery for himself? She didn't believe it, but then again, she didn't really know him at all.

***

Sleep fell on Travis like a tarp. One minute he pondered what Lenaia might be keeping from him and why exactly he'd thought about kissing her, then the next minute he slipped into a frightening dream. Lost in the woods, someone screamed in words he couldn't make out. He turned to find the screamer, catching movement out of the corner of his eye, but everywhere he turned he saw only dark leaves. He woke with a racing heart to a darkness blacker than any he'd seen.

It took a full minute to remember he lay on a hammock in the jungle next to a beautiful, but secretive, woman. The rhythm of Lenaia's breathing calmed him.

At least he hadn't woken her. He breathed in and out in long stretches and began to relax. They were fine. The intense darkness was merely because the moon had gone behind the clouds.

Her hand had come to rest on his chest. The unconscious touch comforted him, but she'd probably yank it away when she woke. He cradled her small hand and gently moved it back to her side.

His eyes drifted closed, but they popped open again a short time later. He'd heard something. Or was it another dream?

The soft whine of insect wings, the croak and chirp of frogs, nothing sounded unusual. His eyes grew heavy again. They had almost closed, when he heard it. In the distance, but coming closer. A high-pitched yelp like the scream from his nightmare, although less sharp, less human.

He turned his head in the direction of the sound. The sun had barely started to lighten the sky to a milky gray. He could see, but not far.

The noise continued every thirty seconds or so for a few minutes, coming nearer each time. Then it stopped altogether.

A new sound replaced it, the crack of branches and leaves breaking. Something large was coming toward them fast. If it didn't slow down, it would slam into them in seconds. He wrapped an arm around Lenaia and braced himself.

The next few seconds dragged as he anticipated the collision. Was it the creature again?

A heavy weight plowed into his back. Lenaia woke with a scream. He held her against his chest as the hammock jerked in an awkward arc.

The crashing in the underbrush began again. He pulled Lenaia on top of him, away from the bottom of the hammock, and braced for another hit.

This blow came from the other side. Harder.

The hammock overturned, dropping them on the ground. He landed on his right shoulder with Lenaia mostly on top of him.

He kicked against the mosquito net to untangle them. Once he got her legs free, she jumped up and unzipped the net. He'd just gotten his second leg out, when he heard the same thrashing in the brush.

"Run," he shouted.

Jumping to his feet, he grabbed her hand and took off into the jungle away from the sound. He managed to dodge the larger trees, but soon the whipping branches forced him to let go of Lenaia's hand so he could keep his arms up as protection. Hopefully, she was doing the same.

After maybe a hundred yards, he slowed down. Lenaia wasn't behind him. He stopped to listen, but needed to catch his breath before he could hear anything.

He put his hands on his knees and sucked in great gulps of air as he turned around. The jungle behind him was empty. Where was Lenaia? He shouldn't have run so far ahead without knowing she was near. If something bad happened to her, it would all be his fault.

As his breathing slowed, he listened closely. No sound of an animal or anyone crying out for help.

"Lenaia?" he whispered.

No answer.

Maybe he had come from a slightly different direction. He made a quarter turn and tried a little louder. "Lenaia."

Still no response.

CHAPTER FIFTEEN

After hitting the ground hard, Lenaia smothered a scream and let her body go limp. The animal thrashed in the brush close behind. Her best option was to play dead. In front of her, crunching leaves and slapping branches told her that Travis had kept running. She was all alone with this unknown animal.

The thrashing grew louder. As it came closer, Lenaia fought the urge to get up and run. It would only trigger the animal's prey drive.

The animal broke through the bushes at full speed. It spotted her and jumped into the air, leaping over her with ease. Through squinted eyes, she stared at the yellowish underbelly as it flashed by.

It landed just beyond her head, digging its claws into the soft ground to gain traction. It swung its large snout around to pierce her with a hunter's intense gaze. She didn't dare move a muscle, not even her eyes, focusing her gaze in the distance beyond it. Her heart beat wildly, shaking her chest. Surely, it could see her rib cage vibrate.

After a steamy huffing breath, it turned away and took off in the direction Travis had gone.

As the noise from the animal faded, Lenaia let out the breath she'd been holding. The way it moved, the power in its legs, the fire in its eyes. The animal was amazing, exquisite, and more dangerous than any she'd ever seen. It was exactly as her uncle had imagined.

After lying there for about twenty minutes, the noises from the jungle returned. She hadn't realized they had quieted. She sat up, brushing her hair back. The animal was gone, but so was Travis. Since he hadn't come back searching for her as she'd hoped, she faced a decision. Try to track him or return to camp.

Finding the animal wouldn't do Travis any good without getting a DNA sample. For that, he'd have to eventually make his way back to camp. She got up and retraced her steps.

Their backpacks and the hammock were right where they'd left them. She let out a heavy sigh. His pack still sat on the ground untouched. He wasn't here.

So, she waited.

And waited. For several hours.

What happened to him?

She warily scanned the surrounding trees. The animal had attacked them here and every minute she stayed raised her blood pressure a notch. Even if Travis didn't come back, it would eventually.

She pulled on her sweatshirt and touched the pepper spray tucked into the pocket. Her machete lay on the ground beside her.

Squinting at the sliver of sun she could see through the canopy, she guessed it was a little after noon, possibly one o'clock. After this amount of time, she had to assume Travis wasn't coming back. Maybe he had lost his bearings. Or maybe the animal had attacked him, and he needed help. She hadn't known him long, but her heart ached at the thought of him injured and alone. She had to go look for him before it got dark.

She inspected the hammock and mosquito net. The hammock had made it through okay, but the mosquito net had a small tear. She tied a knot to cover the hole in case she had to use it again and shoved them both into her pack.

She couldn't carry two packs. His would have to stay here after she removed the food. She fingered the zipper on the outside of it, feeling somehow like leaving it here was giving up on him. But that was silly. She knew her way around the jungle. It was her duty to go look for him. To try to help him if she could.

She unzipped the main compartment and transferred the dried food, crackers, and an energy bar to her backpack. The only things left were his phone, laptop and wallet.

After slipping his phone into a side pocket of her pack, she picked up the wallet, running her hands over the worn leather. His fingers had rubbed the surface to a shine. The memory of his fingers trailing along her cheek made her pulse quicken. She might have let him kiss her last night. But what did she even know about him, except he had a gene for stubbornness as strong as hers?

She'd done plenty of field work with men—in fact, most volcanologists were men—and never had a reaction like this. The two of them had chemistry for sure, but he could be a serial killer for all she knew. After only a second more of hesitation, she flipped the wallet open. Yes, it was snooping, but "Thou shalt not snoop" wasn't in the Bible.

Sixty dollars, one credit card, one debit card, university identification, a library card, and a driver's license showing a terrible picture of him with his eyes half-closed. Nothing else.

What had she expected? A membership card from serial killers anonymous? She was about to close it up when she noticed something. A ragged corner of paper poked out from behind the credit card. She tugged it free. A picture of Travis with a woman and three kids. Her stomach lurched. Was he married? She hadn't seen a wedding ring, but then again, she'd been so distracted by the rest of his body that she might have missed that detail.

Another picture fell to the ground. It had been stuck

to the back of the first one. She picked it up. Travis with another woman, this time without kids. Another wife? That would make him a bigamist. She didn't think so, but she couldn't exactly trust her instincts when it came to men.

Well, if she was going to snoop, she might as well do it right. She placed the pictures on a bed of leaves and opened the rest of the wallet wide. A waterproof flap tucked behind the cash caught her attention.

She flipped the pouch out and pulled the edges apart. Inside was a folded piece of paper. Carefully, she inched out the white square with two fingers. It had been folded at least ten times to make it fit. The sweet smell of perfume drifted up from the paper as she unfolded it.

A letter from a woman named Marie. Maybe she was one of the women in the pictures.

The even lines took up the whole page, the script precise and pretty, like an elementary teacher had written it. The paper filled with fading ink trembled in Lenaia's hand as she read it.

Dear Travis,

I wish things could be different, but I'm filled with a certainty that my body will not last much longer. The pregnancy started a chain reaction in my lungs and now, since my precious child has gone before me, I long to join her. Don't take this as giving up. I will fight to stay here with you and Tony, but somehow I know I will go home soon. At that point, these words will be the only thing you have left of me.

We've talked many times about heaven and Jesus. I know how you feel, but this is my last chance to tell you how I feel on the downhill side of this life—when my faith may soon become visible.

Jesus is real. Heaven is real. Hell is real. In our talks, you have brought up many objections to these statements, all of them focused on this world. But what happens when you leave this world, Travis? All you have worked to build in this life won't matter then.

You have to make a choice. A choice more important than your reputation, more vital than scientific knowledge and greater than your fear.

At the end of your life, what God thinks of you will matter more than all the accolades given here on Earth. Do you remember the speech I gave in Vail when my article won the McCrea award? Remember how they told me the audience, full of hard-nosed reporters, would frown on any mention of God? And yet, I got up there and praised Him for ten minutes before they practically yanked me off the stage. And they were right, the audience didn't appreciate it, but God did. Don't give up eternity in heaven, because you're afraid of what it means for your life here.

You can't buy your way into heaven with money or prestige or intellect. Faith is the only currency God uses. When I do leave, please think about this very important question: Where do you think I've gone?

If you believe I'm in heaven, please ask Jesus to show you the way.

Love,

Marie

Lenaia's hand trembled. She'd gone too far. This was too personal. How would she explain it to Travis if he found out she'd read this note? And yet she didn't regret it. She sat on the stump of a fallen tree and read the carefully penned words again.

After refolding the letter, she placed it back in the waterproof pouch in the wallet. Travis carried this wherever he went, so this woman must have been important to him, but who was she? Lenaia couldn't ask him or he'd know she snooped. For that matter, she needed to find him before she could ask him anything.

She grabbed the laptop and put it in the front pouch

of her pack, along with his wallet. The sun would set in another couple of hours. She would search for Travis along the way, but she needed to at least get up the ravine slope in the daylight.

As she walked through the carpet of fallen leaves, she listened for sounds of larger creatures. A few times, the low growl of a jaguar rumbled in the distance, but not close enough to worry about. At the base of the ravine, she picked up a fresh trail. The unmistakable pattern of an animal using trees to make a path up the hill. Probably not Travis, but if he'd made it out, maybe she could pick up his trail at the top.

She pushed up on a tree trunk, braced her shoulder on the next one, and then slid her feet up the slope. Sort of like mountain climbing, except with big trees. She repeated the motion over and over, content with making slow progress. Working against gravity felt easier than working to squash down the one question that kept pushing its way to the front of her mind. The question that suddenly mattered most.

Had Travis made his choice?

CHAPTER SIXTEEN

Travis swallowed the fear rising in his throat. If the animal had gotten to her, he was sure he would have heard a scream. But, then again, maybe he'd missed it in the noise of their escape. Or maybe she fell and knocked herself out cold.

He'd continued to call her name for hours while he backtracked their run through the trees. He pushed aside another set of branches, again expecting to see the camp just ahead, but he only saw more trees. So much for his stellar sense of direction. In the past, he'd prided himself on being able to get around in the wilderness on his own, but then he'd had a compass as a backup. Now, his compass sat useless in the backpack at camp. A camp he still hadn't found even after hours of wandering around.

A howler monkey swung past, tendrils of mist swirling as it swooped by. It made another pass and screamed in his face, probably not used to a person being this far into the rain forest. He ignored the monkey, more concerned about the animal he'd heard scream last night. It was big and the noise had sounded like *the* creature after they'd awoken it by the river. And it had attacked them.

Maybe he should reconsider this whole endeavor. Pack up and go home before anyone got hurt, if Lenaia wasn't hurt already. But he still needed answers. The war raging in his head demanded answers, it demanded the truth. And what better place to work out his inner demons than in the middle of nowhere?

The saving grace in the whole situation was the steep wall of the ravine, on his left, like a lighthouse in a storm. But if he decided to climb out, he'd essentially give up on reuniting with Lenaia or finding the creature. Then again, maybe it was better if they separated. That way he wouldn't bring her down with him.

It had to be close to midday, but the mist persisted, leaving his sweatshirt damp. The way he normally checked the time was on his phone, but he'd left that back with their supplies. He stopped to gaze up at the high sloping walls. If he went up, he might be leaving her behind. But maybe she had already gone back to the village.

Without supplies or even a hammock, he didn't have much choice. He needed to get out. Powerlessness gnawed at his gut, but he couldn't do anything for Lenaia now. Hopefully, she had gone back to the village instead of waiting for him.

Hitching his foot up onto a tree, he started upslope. Half an hour later, sweaty and exhausted from the climb, he knelt over a small fern. After catching his breath, he stood and looked around. Although somewhat brighter outside the ravine, the sun already cast long shadows along the forest floor. It was later than he'd thought. He needed to find the village or some sort of shelter soon. Putting the setting sun to his back, he headed east.

He followed the slope of the land up steep ridges and down into low valleys, all the while wondering if he'd make it back to the village or pass right by without knowing it. As the light faded, the shadows shifted and danced through the trees, throwing confused shapes at his strained eyes. The mass of leaves blended together until they turned into variegated gemstones—deep emerald, light peridot, even blue-green malachite.

The rise and fall of his legs became monotonous, like the background noise of shrill animal calls, until he tripped over a large square stone. What was it doing out here? He'd seen a few rock outcrops sticking out of the wall of the ravine, but nothing since then. He searched the jungle floor with his feet and found another stone a few feet away. Couldn't be a coincidence.

He continued shuffling along the ground. Sure enough, the stones were part of a crumbling wall which sliced through the trees in both directions. Odd to find a stone wall out here with no clearing, but if he couldn't find anything else, it would afford him some protection for the night. He followed the remnants of the wall for fifty feet to where a decrepit stone building suddenly appeared, as if it had grown up from the rain forest floor.

Two walls of the homestead had survived, the other two were half crumbled, causing the wooden roof to buckle. He sighed in relief. Though sagging and splintered, it had a roof. He gently pushed open the crooked door, careful not to break the rusty iron hinges. A strong scent invaded his nose. A heavy mixture of mildew and mold, strengthened by a dash of urine. Lovely accommodations, but better than nothing.

The shack-sized structure didn't have windows, but gray shafts of weak sunlight made their way through the missing portions of the walls and the gaping hole in the roof. At least he would have some protection from predators and mosquitoes.

After clearing out a few lizards, he leaned back into the corner made by the two surviving walls. He sat there for a few hours praying and listening to the jungle sounds as night fell. Eventually, he drifted off to sleep with thoughts of Lenaia. Her adventurous nature, the gentle way she talked to Mirabel, even the annoyed looks she gave him.

He woke with a start. Something had awoken him, but what? The cool air clung to him like a moist blanket.

He couldn't have been asleep long because a sliver of moonlight still shone through the broken part of the roof.

He held his breath and listened.

A faint rustling. Had he really heard it or had he crossed over into paranoia?

He kept his body rigid and strained his ears.

There, no doubt about it. Something large moved outside the door.

He jumped to his feet as the door to the shack opened a crack, then stopped. He froze every muscle, waiting to see what lay beyond the sliver of darkness. Was a jaguar forcing the door open?

Another rustling sound, and then the door swung open in a wide arc. Silhouetted by the moonlight was a long, slender shadow, holding a flashlight. Definitely not a jaguar.

"Travis?" Hearing that sweet voice shocked him like a baptism in frigid water. She swept the flashlight to the side, so he could see her. Her hair was tangled and dirt smudged her cheek, but she had never looked more like an angel to him.

"Lenaia." He closed the distance between them and gave her a bear hug. When he pulled away, he tugged her inside and ran his hands down her arms. "Are you okay? You're not hurt?"

"No. You?"

He gave an exaggerated scoff. "Of course not. Just call me Tarzan."

"Uh, huh, swinging with the monkeys, I'm sure."

"Hey, at least I found shelter."

"Leave it to you to find the only rock house in the center of a rain forest." She playfully punched him in the arm, but he captured her hand. He wanted to touch her, to make sure she was really here. "How did you find me?"

She closed the door with her free hand and moved farther into the room before clicking off the flashlight.

In the weak light coming through the exposed part of the roof, he could just make out the features of her face, the outline of her thin nose, the high cheekbones. Her eyes, though, remained in shadow.

Her lips turned up into a smile. "Your trail isn't exactly hard to follow, although a bit harder in the dark."

"Ah, yes. I forgot. I'm glad you're with me again, Pocahontas."

She laughed, and the sound bounced along the rough stones like marbles on a floor. "I followed your trail this way until it got too dark to track. I was about to set up the hammock when I stumbled upon this place."

"Come sit." He pointed at the corner. "I've chased all the rats out of this area."

She sat with her knees up, her back resting on the pitted wall. He lowered himself beside her. After a minute, he took her hand again, tracing along each finger with his thumb. "I didn't mean to leave you. I walked around for hours looking for camp—"

She stopped him by putting her other hand on his arm. "You didn't leave me. I know that. We got separated."

"I'm glad you're here." He'd already said that. Now he sounded like an idiot. "Did you see the creature again?"

"No, but I'm pretty sure it was what tipped our hammock."

"How do you know?"

"I've never seen any other jungle animal act that way."

He leaned back against the wall, keeping her hand in his. "How do you know so much about the jungle?"

"My uncle has a fascination with jungles, especially Costa Rican ones. He started taking me with him when I was a teenager."

"It's a beautiful place."

"Sounds like you're finally gaining an appreciation for the rain forest."

He reached up to wipe away a smudge of dirt from her cheek with his thumb. Her skin felt as soft and smooth as exotic silk. "It helps to have good company."

She didn't respond. Maybe he'd embarrassed her. He rested his head against the coarse rocks, his thoughts turning to the problems at hand. Things hadn't gone as he'd hoped. He hadn't thought the creature would be aggressive, hadn't thought he might endanger someone else, hadn't thought getting a sample would be this difficult. But here he was. He needed to stop kicking himself for impulsively getting into this mess and start figuring out what to do. "Getting DNA from Rheasaurus is turning out to be difficult.

"Rheasaurus?"

"The name of the project file in the professor's computer."

"Hmm." She tapped a finger on her chin. "I like it. Sounds feminine."

"Yeah, I guess it kind of does."

"Do you think it's a female?"

"I don't know. Maybe." He squeezed her hand as an idea formed. "In your jungle travels, did you learn anything about traps?"

She pulled her hand away to lay them both on her knees and then let her head fall back until she stared through the hole into the night sky. "Some. The problem with a trap is that after you capture the animal, it flails around trying to get free. Since we don't want to kill this one, we need a way to immobilize so it won't thrash around. Maybe Dr. Gordon has some tranquilizers. If we mixed it with some food, we could drug the creature."

"Good idea. What kind of trap could you rig up?"

She turned to look at him. He didn't think she could see his face any better than he could see hers, but she stared for a long moment. "Are you planning on taking this creature back home?"

"I don't know." He wanted to reach out to her, to revisit the closeness of last night in the hammock. But they had also fought last night, and his instincts warned him of a fight coming now. "At first, I just wanted a DNA sample, but now I'm not sure what to do. I'm afraid the locals might kill it for attacking their livestock, or worse, what if someone else finds it and sells it to the highest bidder?" She raised her eyebrows at him. "What?"

"You still think it's an evolutionary ancestor?"

"Maybe." The word fell flat even to his own ears. "You don't?"

"No, absolutely not."

If only he could see her eyes, maybe some of her conviction would flow into him. "How can you be so sure?"

"I'm sure because of my faith."

He raked a hand through his hair. "I don't get it. You decided to believe in God and then your scientific mind flew out the window?" As soon as the words left his mouth, he knew he'd crossed the line.

Lenaia took a slow breath before answering, but thankfully she didn't turn away again. "It's not like that. Evidence exists which can be interpreted as for evolution or against it, depending on your starting point. Everyone has to choose where to start." She paused a moment as if deciding whether to say more. Then, her words came out with enviable peace. "My choice will always be with God."

"Despite scientific evidence?"

She tilted her head. "Have you looked into the evidence for creation?"

"Some."

"Then you probably know the problems with evolutionary theory." Her words were challenging, but her voice was soft, even, patient. "Tell me, how can natural, supposedly random, processes add information to make animals more complex? Because evolution says we went from simple to complex organisms. That sounds pretty intelligent for random processes."

"I don't know," he conceded.

"Or how did a complicated structure like the eye evolve when there isn't any evolutionary advantage to it until it's complete? Or why does the evolutionary tree have gaps where transitional forms should be? Darwin said the gaps would fill in as we found more fossils, but they haven't. If anything, the gaps have gotten larger."

"Well, you've certainly done your research." A stupid comment in the face of legitimate questions, but he couldn't think of anything else to say.

She put a hand on his arm. "Believing in evolution is just as much a leap of faith."

The muscles along his back and shoulders tightened. He fought to control the defensive tone in his voice. To treat this discussion as she had, as a debate among equals. "And if this creature is an ancestral form? Would that be enough evidence to convince you evolution is true?"

"No matter what this creature is, I wouldn't doubt God." Her tone was sad, almost apologetic. She bowed her head. He didn't know if she was staring at the dirt, praying or sleeping until she raised her face and tilted it up, allowing the dim light to hit her eyes. Her dark orbs radiated smoky fire. "Faith comes from love, especially in the absence of proof."

He had to think about that a moment. "So because you love God, you have faith He didn't use evolution?"

"God could have used evolution if he wanted to, but the way they understand evolution today contradicts the Bible. The Bible says some animals were created before evolution says they evolved. And God wouldn't give us wrong information in the Bible."

The note of confidence in her voice gave him pause. "I wish I had your faith." The hollow words echoed off the surrounding rock walls and into his soul, shaking it hard. If he really wanted that kind of faith, would he be trying this hard to disprove it?

Her answer came so soft he almost missed it. "Me too."

CHAPTER SEVENTEEN

A lone cricket chirped in the front room as Mirabel softly opened and closed the door. From the porch, she stared at the trees, wishing for Travis and Lenaia to appear. The unbroken line of trees stared right back, like emerald statues.

She glanced in the other direction. A dusty brown rabbit darted down the deserted main street through town. Her father had already left to visit one of the pastures, but her mother still slept. Mirabel had a precious hour before her mother would stir.

She crossed the road, sneaked around the side of the old blue barn and sat on a pile of hay where she had a view of the trees. Lenaia seemed like she could handle herself in the jungle, but they hadn't come back last night. If they didn't get back by the time her mom got up, she'd beg for permission to go look for them.

Heavy footsteps sounded from the side of the barn. Owen came around the corner, carrying a book under his arm. He sat beside her, close enough for her to smell the clean scent of soap. He must have just showered.

He balanced the book on his lap. Mirabel reached for it, but he put a hand on top of hers. "Have you told your parents yet?"

"I can't."

He lowered his head. "It seems wrong to be sneaking around like this."

"I haven't lied to them."

"Maybe not, but this feels too much like lying."

"I can't tell them. They would refuse to let me learn. I'll tell them this summer, before I start applying to universities in the fall."

"And if they find out before you tell them? Like they suspected about us."

It was a risk she had to take.

He released his hold on her hand and let her grab the book. She bent her knees, rested the book against them, and began to read where she'd left off. He pulled a small loaf of bread from the pocket of his sweatshirt and offered her a piece, but she waved him off, intent on studying.

The anatomy book covered the nervous system and disorders associated with the nerves. The descriptions pulled her in, especially the accounts of extreme disorders. Each nerve, each cell had a part to play, a necessary function. The pieces all fit together to make a whole, sensory human being. After an hour, Owen nudged her as a reminder to get back before her mother missed her.

She reluctantly gave the book to him and grabbed his other hand. "Thank you, as always."

He scanned the area in a circle, then brushed a kiss across her lips. "For what it's worth, I think you'll make a great doctor."

She watched him leave, then got up to return home. She came around the edge of the barn, touching her lips with her fingers. Every stolen kiss was a treasure to hide away in her heart.

As she stepped into the dirt road, someone grabbed her arm, whirling her around. "Mirabel. What are you doing out so early this morning?" Manuel, the village treasurer, held her elbow in a firm grip.

She looked at his dark eyes and saw the accusation there. Had he spied on her and Owen? "I'm getting some air. It's stuffy in the house."

"Ah, but the place for a good Tico girl is in the house, where she's safe. Not sneaking off with unpredictable young men."

So he had been spying. She pulled on her arm, and he let her go. "Owen is not unpredictable." She had to tread carefully here, otherwise Manuel might tell her parents. "He's a good man."

Manuel ran a finger along her arm from her elbow to her wrist. She forced herself not to cringe. "That boy is hardly a man. You need an experienced Tico to show you the good life."

"Tico or not, a man is a man. And Owen's actions speak louder than his skin color."

Manuel lifted his pointed chin. "Like the light-skinned Americano who is staying at your house? Are you interested in him as well?"

"Of course not."

"You've had many foreign visitors lately. The Americano, the girl who looks Tico, but isn't. What are they all doing here?"

As a town official, Manuel had the right to demand an answer, but she didn't want to inform on her friends. "They're looking for something in the jungle."

"So, I've heard. Tell them to be careful. Sometimes people who don't belong in the jungle get hurt." His brows scrunched over his eyes. He closed a hand around her wrist again, more gentle this time. "I know you're worried about your friends. Convince them to leave, Mirabel. They don't belong here."

She backed away. He let her wrist slide out of his grip. She turned and walked to her front steps, looking back once. Manuel was gone. Hopefully he wouldn't go to her parents with what he'd seen.

***

Lenaia blinked her eyes open. Her head rested on Travis's chest, his heartbeat thumping strong in her ears. Had she sought him out during the night or did he pull her over? She listened to the reassuring beat for a few more minutes, marveling at her sudden desire to stay snuggled close to his warmth.

When a crick in her neck complained, she sat up and leaned against the wall, cool as an icepack compared with his chest. Thin rays of sunlight filtered through the ramshackle roof. She looked over at his sleeping form, quickly deciding she had to stop doing that. Every time she looked at him, the confusion and concern of last night melted away, replaced by a desire to lean into him.

Her heart had already gotten entangled, but she knew from experience not to trust it. Her heart picked out distant men. The ones who would stay at arm's length. *To preserve your independence*, her mom have told her. Usually, she broke up with them whenever they wanted to get serious. Even the last one, Zayden—the one she'd come the closest to settling down with—she'd left to follow her career, although she probably should have left him earlier. They had fought constantly, mostly about God. Zayden wanted to sleep in on Sundays instead of going to church with her. He resented the time she spent helping with youth group. And he didn't like her "churchy" friends. He'd called them stuck up. But their disagreements weren't really about her friends. He'd never understood the biggest part of her life: Jesus.

After their breakup a year ago, Uncle Jim had brought her to the northern part of this same cloud forest. In her uncle's misguided attempt to help her work things out, he tried to get her to work out her anger the same way he would—by shooting something. And not just anything, Uncle Jim wanted to bag a jaguar to put another head on his wall.

She remembered trekking through the dense tangles

of leaves and vines, keeping an eye out for snakes, with a pistol at her side because Uncle Jim had insisted she carry a gun. She had hunted with him on previous trips, but this time she had no interest, not even in tracking.

"Pull your gun up. You'll feel better if you shoot something." Uncle Jim lifted his leg and nudged the weapon with his foot.

"No matter how many times you say that, it doesn't make it true. And be careful, I might shoot your foot off." She gave him an evil grin. "By accident, of course."

Despite his overbearing, pushy nature, she always enjoyed seeing her uncle. He doted on her in his own way, which usually meant nature walks. In her teen years, her mother had tried to limit the time Lenaia spent with her uncle, probably afraid Uncle Jim would convince her God didn't exist. And he definitely tried. But mom needn't have worried. Uncle Jim's challenges only made her examine her faith harder, drawing her closer to Jesus.

"You don't have to go for a jaguar. Look for a sheep or something." His idea of sarcasm. Sheep didn't exactly wander around in the rain forest.

"I'll get right on that." She'd given him her most serious look. "Uncle Jim, I just need to process. Emotions are not just a chemical release to be replaced by some other chemical. Sometimes you have to sit with them and figure out why you're feeling them."

"So have you figured out why you're mad at Zayden?" He stopped to look at her. "You are mad, aren't you?"

"Yes." She pushed past him and brushed aside another clump of vines. "I think because he didn't fight for our relationship." In truth, she aimed more of her anger at herself. Their beliefs hadn't been in line from day one. She shouldn't have dated Zayden in the first place. But her uncle wouldn't understand that.

"You didn't fight for it either. You chose your career first, a move that made me so proud, my dear."

She didn't respond.

A great tangle of vegetation rose up before her. She stopped and moved back so Uncle Jim could swipe at the thick curtain of vines with his machete. "And if he was hurt by your decision, you probably told him he shouldn't have gotten too emotionally involved."

She squinted at him. "You think this is helping?"

He shrugged and continued his assault on the plant curtain. "Just pointing out the obvious."

The machete ripped through the last of it, leaving once vibrant vines hanging in tatters. She walked through the opening, then glanced back. "I don't miss him much. And I didn't even think he was *the one*."

"Are you looking for the one?"

The question caught her off guard. "Of course. I mean, isn't everybody?"

"Not everybody."

And then she was mad again, this time at Uncle Jim for being astute, when he was normally clueless about people.

She wanted a family, and while every passing year increased the desire, her uncle had been right. The idea of finding *the one* brought waves of fear. Fear of losing herself in someone, fear of being left, and even the fear she would leave the right person because she couldn't handle it.

She glanced over at Travis as he slept. His mouth slightly open, his brow relaxed, all of him was at peace. At least Travis didn't act like the distant men she usually fell for. In fact, when she looked into his eyes, she saw a fire she didn't yet understand. No, he certainly wasn't frigid, but his pursuit of this animal bordered on obsessed. Would he be rational if she told him about her uncle and the secrets he kept? Travis probably wouldn't trust her again, and even though they hadn't known each other for long, his trust mattered to her.

His azure eyes popped open, searching. For her?

She sucked a breath in through her nose. *Clear out the guilt. Tell him now.* She opened her mouth, held it open, then let the breath escape without a word. Maybe later. After she knew what he intended to do with the animal.

"I'd ask how you slept, but it's not exactly a deluxe hotel," he said.

She folded her legs under and pressed her lips into a smile. "At least we got more sleep than we did in the hammock."

He stretched, twisting his torso until she could see his solid chest through the sweatshirt. She averted her eyes and feigned interest in examining the soles of her shoes.

"Are you okay?" He placed a hand on the crown of her head and smoothed her hair, his hand stopping in the small of her back.

Warm tingles followed the path his hand took down her spine, followed quickly by a twinge of warning. Sleeping next to him for two nights was making this seem all too natural. "Fine. Just tired."

She toyed with the laces on her tennis shoes. How did he overwhelm her senses so quickly? *Come on, focus on something else.* A troubling question bubbled up from the well of her mind. This might not be the right time, but it was definitely a distraction. "Travis, who's Marie?"

He pulled his hand away and placed both of them on top of his knees. "Where did you hear that name?"

"I know I shouldn't have snooped." She reached into the front pouch of her pack and retrieved the wallet. He held out a hand. She sheepishly placed it in his palm.

A dark cloud rolled over his face, turning his eyes rainy day blue. He flipped the wallet in his hand twice while still holding her gaze. "My sister. She was my best friend." He cleared his throat, but his voice still sounded strained. "She died six months ago from a lung disease. In here, I keep the letter she wrote to me before she passed. I suppose you read it."

She hung her head, but kept one eye on his face. "I'm sorry. I shouldn't have been nosy. I...I wanted to know more about you."

He stared down at the dusty dirt floor. She wanted to ask why he kept the letter in his wallet, but couldn't. She'd invaded his privacy enough.

When he spoke, his voice sounded raspy, like he'd swallowed gravel. "It took her dying for me to see the world through her eyes. I didn't—no, I wouldn't—listen while she was alive." He pounded his fist into the dirt, but without any force behind it. "I came to know Jesus because of that letter."

She bit her lip to keep from smiling, not an appropriate response right now, but a small part of her heart soared at this new information. Travis knew Jesus. Even so, the rational part of her kept a tight rein on her emotions. He obviously had issues to work out. "It must have been hard to lose her."

"You would have liked her. Everyone did." He ran a hand through his sandy hair, which looked a shade darker under the shadow of the roof. "The first month or so after she died, I threw things and yelled—at God mostly, even though I didn't really believe He was there. Of course, I had heard all I needed to know about God, and Jesus, from Marie before she died, but at the time it sounded like a pointless story. I didn't need Jesus to be a good person." He sighed and turned his head toward her, his vivid eyes revealing the pain of a not-yet-scabbed-over wound. "After the first wave of anger passed, the sadness came. I asked God why she couldn't stay. She deserved to stay, at least more than I did. I didn't feel like a good person anymore. And I had this awful thought

I couldn't shake. I thought Marie died because of me." Tears misted his eyes as he held her gaze.

She couldn't look away. He wasn't just opening up, he was opening up to *her* and wanted her to know it.

"It doesn't make sense, I know, but before she passed, she said that if it took her dying for me to come to know Jesus, then it would be worth it. After she was gone, I read that note until I thought it would fall apart. It was all I had left of her. Then one day, I read it and something hit me, literally." He gave a humorless laugh. "I threw a turkey baster at the wall. It hit on the bulb side and came straight back at me. The pointed end smacked me in the forehead. This sounds crazy to say out loud, but I thought God threw it back at me. His way of saying, 'You idiot. Marie died, but she didn't die for you. I did.' A week later I found a church. Within a month I got baptized. The weight of Marie's death lifted off me, which I'm grateful for, but other things have gotten harder since then."

Lenaia put a hand on his cheek. "Life's never easy. Knowing Jesus just means you have somebody to fall back on when things get hard."

He placed a hand over hers, holding it while he shook his head. "You handle problems with faith. Not questioning like me."

She winced at his overinflated opinion of her. "I have my own issues."

"I feel like God's asking me to give up my career." The pain reflected in those words ran deep.

She knew how he felt. "And if He is?"

He dropped his hand. "I don't want to let it go."

"Travis, you can't mold God into your chosen career path. God wants us to accept Him—what He has done, His plans, all of it. That means we have to trust."

He ran a hand through his hair until the front stuck straight up in a sexy, rumpled way. "I wish I didn't struggle. Like you."

Although she enjoyed the praise, she knew from experience that seasons of questioning usually led to the most spiritual growth. "Oh, I've struggled." She still did, but they didn't need to go there. "Two years ago, I lost my job at the Washington Geological Survey. You don't know how hard it was to work my way up in a male-dominated field. It took me years to get there, and I had the same fear of God asking me to give up my job, my life."

"And did He want you to?"

She gave him a sad smile. "Yes."

"That's comforting. Thanks."

She softened her voice. "Actually, that's the point. God knows sometimes we need to confront our greatest fear. He wants you to love Him above everything else, including your job. I wouldn't be a volcanologist right now if it weren't for my boss, Jayna. She hired me when no one else would."

Travis bristled. "God wants blind faith, then? I don't know if I can do that."

"Not blind, but definitely faith. He's not asking us to abandon our logical minds or pretend we don't see things in the natural world. When I started looking into the evidence, I saw proof of design everywhere. In fact, my pastor gave an example once, about a wristwatch."

"A wristwatch?"

"Hear me out. Our pastor made it the focus of a sermon. He said, if you were on a nature hike and came across a wristwatch sitting on a stump, you wouldn't think natural processes created it over millions of years. Why?"

Travis shrugged. "Because I would know what it's used for."

"That's the point. If even a wristwatch looks designed to us, why would we think our bodies, which are a thousand times more complex, formed by chance?"

He stared ahead as if considering her words.

When he stayed silent, she continued. "The problem is, what you already believe determines how you interpret it. If you don't know that the metal on the watch dial had to be processed and formed into a dial, then you could suppose it formed randomly on the stump with bits of metal coming together slowly. In the same way, if you assume natural processes formed our bodies, then you'll search for natural ways to explain how it could happen. Like maybe a fish's fin turned into an amphibian's leg bit by bit, even though we've never seen this kind of change happen in nature." A bird alighted on a patch of roof, distracting her for a second. She kept her eyes pinned to its brilliant blue feathers. "But if you start with God, you'll see the evidence of design everywhere."

A sigh leaked out of the side of his mouth. "Maybe that's my problem. I can't decide where to start."

The bird flew off so she turned her gaze back to him. "I understand. I'm a questioner too. God made us this way. But He wants us to turn our questions to Him."

Travis nodded as if deciding, but deciding what exactly? He grabbed her hand, curled his fingers inside hers and tugged her hand to his lips. He brushed a soft kiss over each knuckle. "Pray for me."

Her stomach dipped as tingles raced up her arm. The vulnerable moment had passed, the confident man had returned, and he seemed intent on testing her reactions. She nodded slowly, not trusting herself to speak.

CHAPTER EIGHTEEN

Travis let Lenaia take the lead on the hike back to the village. She obviously had a better sense of direction than he did. They need to go back to get more supplies, ask the doctor about animal tranquilizers, and check in with Mirabel, who was probably worried about them.

As far as he could tell, Lenaia led them along a game trail. Easier walking since it had a wider path for their feet, although sometimes they still had to push through tree branches growing above waist-high. As Lenaia pushed through one, she let it swing back. Instinctively, he whipped his hand up and caught it before it smacked him in the face.

She looked back. "Sorry."

He released the branch. "That could have been a serious injury. You can make it up to me later."

A blush rose on her cocoa cheeks, before she turned away.

"What? I meant you could get me some dried mango when we get back to the village."

She twisted her head around again to give him a scalding look. "Be careful or you might find a few more branches flying your way."

A smug grin earned him a huff from her. It was too easy, making her blush, and a little bit addicting.

Facing front, obviously ignoring him, she continued to lead the way down the trail. The sound of animals filled his ears, but the noises didn't seem intrusive any longer. He'd grown used to the volume. A butterfly rode by on a breeze, zig-zagging, then landing for a fraction of a second on Lenaia's shoulder. He was starting to understand why the villagers continued to live deep in the forest.

"I'm still confused. What do you think this creature will prove to you anyway?" she asked. The butterfly took flight again.

Hadn't they already gone over this? Was she picking a fight? "Look, I'm not trying to prove the Bible wrong."

"Actually, you are, but let's put that aside for a minute, what I want to know is why?"

"Why?"

"You might lose your job. I get that. But you could always get another job." She glanced back at him before turning away again. "Seriously, there has to be more to it. What would happen if you declare you believe in creation?"

Only the death of all the respect he'd garnered over the last five years. "Everyone I know would think I'd gone crazy. They'd laugh at me, accuse me of bias, of having an agenda, and no one would believe any of my research in paleontology."

She nodded her head. "Now I get it. This is about prestige. Your reputation as a scientist. You need the respect of your peers."

Anger churned his stomach at how well she'd pegged him without hardly trying. "Everybody wants the respect of their peers."

"Hmm. Maybe you're right."

He knew her point. Not everybody would put the respect of their peers above God. Problem was, she was speaking from personal experience, and he couldn't refute that, so he said nothing. They passed the next few minutes in a not-so-comfortable silence.

As they came around a bend in the path, Lenaia halted in front of him. He looked over her head to see a dozen fallen trees, like an over-sized beaver dam, blocking the path. The dam stood about five feet high with creeping vines and thick shrubs on either side. No good way to get around.

He moved past her and pushed on the dam to test its strength. "Rock solid. Or maybe wood solid. Are you sure we're going the right way? We didn't see this before."

She shrugged. "My compass says we are, but we're coming into the village from a different direction, because of how we left the ravine."

"Let's take a break. We've been walking nonstop for hours."

He lay down on the leaves in the middle of the path, while she sat on a small log. "Be careful," she said. "Fire ants sometimes like to hide under leaf cover."

Of course, they did. Where else would fire ants hang out? He sat up and brushed the leaves out of his hair. Crossing his legs, he bent at the waist to touch his toes and stretch out his hamstrings. A tickle started at the crown of his head and worked its way to his neck—ants. He raised a hand to swipe at them, but Lenaia put both palms up, motioning for him to stay still.

The tickle continued to travel to his shoulder, and then he felt a pinch. Like a claw.

"A quetzal," she whispered. He raised his eyebrows. She answered his unspoken question. "A bird."

He slowly lifted his head. The tickle moved to the top again. A rush of wings and a tiny turquoise bundle of feathers landed on his right knee. Its long fancy tail hung down over his leg, the feathers touching the ground. The animal cocked its head and stared at him, all the while hopping like a lunatic on his kneecap.

"They're usually quite shy, but apparently he likes you."

"You know birds, too."

She gave a sideways smile.

"Why am I not surprised? You're sure he doesn't think I'm too close to his nest or something?"

"No, he'd peck at you or buzz by your head."

She tried to hide a mischievous smile behind her hand. "Maybe he mistook your hair for a nest."

He peered at the shimmering bird. "Well, little guy, if you want some beautiful hair for your nest, I suggest hers." He pointed at Lenaia and watched with satisfaction as a crimson flush spread over her cheeks.

The bird continued its hopping undeterred. "Isn't he an amazing testament to God's creation? So perfect. So designed."

As if on cue, the bird shot up and hovered a foot above his head. It flitted back and forth in a frenetic dance. A second later, a milky stream of liquid dropped onto his shoulder. Then, the quetzal swooped away into the canopy, another gemstone taking its place in the jeweled forest.

"Oh, great. God's wonderful design just pooped on me."

Lenaia giggled, a belly laugh that almost made the mess worth it. She dug into the backpack and handed him a tissue. As he took it from her, his eyes fell on something beyond her. A small parting in the trees, too low for anyone to see while walking upright. He cleaned his shoulder, wadded up the dirty tissue, shoved it in the front of the pack, then crawled over to investigate. "Maybe this is a way around."

She swiveled her head back and forth between him and the opening. "I'll fit better. Let me see where it goes first."

He watched with a smile as she squatted and did a duck walk into the foliage. As the leaves filled in behind her, he had a moment of panic. What if they got separated again? Tension rose like a balloon in his chest until he rubbed at his sternum to release the pressure. "Lenaia?"

No answer at first, but then a shuffling noise. "I'm coming out now."

The glossy crown of her head came through, followed by her knees. She crawled over to him. "Well?"

She held up a closed hand until he looked at it. When she uncurled her fingers, a spent shell casing from a rifle lay in her palm. "It's a blind." She swept her arm toward the tree dam. "And this is a trap. Probably set up by the poachers. They could sit in the blind and wait for the trap to capture the animal they wanted, then shoot it with a tranquilizer dart. The ones they don't want, they kill."

"So the passageway doesn't lead to the other side?"

"Nope."

He got to his feet and put a hand down to help her up. "Then I guess the only way through is over. I'll spot you from the back."

She gave him a suspicious look, but then approached the dam and put a foot into the crook of a branch. She stood and the branch held. He kept his arms poised near her back. She tried a branch further up. It creaked, then snapped.

He caught her by the armpits. "You okay?"

"Fine." She pushed off him.

"Maybe try lying on the branches and almost sliding over them. Less pressure on any one point."

Her eyebrows dipped into a scowl. "I can do it." Using his suggestion, she shimmied up the dam and over.

He grinned as he climbed onto the branches. Like a toddler determined to climb a jungle gym on her own, she didn't want his help. Come to think of it, she didn't seem to like his help with anything. Independent and stubborn, not usually the qualities he looked for in a woman, but her strength made the rare moments of tenderness somehow sweeter.

***

Harmony stared at the spread out pile of papers on her coffee table. After two days, Tom had finally cracked the password for the Rheasaurus file. Inside, they'd found copies of all the e-mails between Tiernay and Pike. Tom had printed them out for her again, and she'd brought them down to her apartment while Tom searched through the rest of the electronic documents. She could have stayed at his place, but Tom liked to talk to the computer as he worked. More than a little distracting.

She ran a hand over the fanned-out sheets. If there was a clue in here as to who had killed Bob, she hadn't found it yet, but she couldn't give up. She wouldn't let someone get away with killing her friend.

All she knew for sure was Dr. Tiernay himself hadn't killed Bob. Maybe he hired someone else to do it. She thought again about going to the police with what she knew, but she had no proof of anything. Just a stack of stolen e-mails involving someone named Fulton Pike at a company that didn't seem to exist.

She dug back into the paper pile. There had to be a clue here somewhere or at least she had to try to find one.

Her phone chimed the sound of a trilling bird. A text message. She glanced at the screen. From Tom.

Get up here right now.

They'd talked only fifteen minutes ago. He must have found something. She grabbed her keys and locked the dead bolt on her way out, a new lock since the break in.

She ran up to the fifth floor where she found Tom hunched over the computer, his large frame bent almost in half. She made a mental note to get him a better computer chair for Christmas. He liked practical gifts like that.

"What's up?" she asked.

Tom turned to face her with a wide smile. "I know who Mr. Pike is, and so did Dr. Tiernay."

"Huh?"

"Was Dr. Tiernay computer savvy?"

"Not at all."

Tom turned back to the screen. "Whoever found this was. Dr. Tiernay must have had help from somebody."

She didn't have to think long to come up with a name. "Charles."

"Whoever it was, hacked into the e-mail account for Fulton Pike and discovered the e-mails were being forwarded to a dummy account on the university's server."

"Did they find out who had created the account?"

"All of the reply e-mails came from Pike's account, so they actually had to wait until someone initiated an action on the dummy account. Finally, on April 15, the creator of the dummy account deleted all the e-mails from that account. Dr. Tiernay, or maybe Charles, saw it happen before that person could clear out the action history."

They were getting close. She could feel it. "Who deleted the e-mails?"

"Administrator 541."

She put both hands on her hips. "Who's that?"

Tom pointed to the screen. On it was a table containing hundreds of entries. He used the cursor to highlight a single row.

Administrator 541.

She followed the row to the column marked User Name. Her breath caught in her throat. *Francis Haddock.* The dean had known about the creature all along. She grabbed her phone to text Professor Perego.

***

Tiernay pushed through a tangle of vines and scowled. He'd caught a glimpse of the animal an hour ago and had been following the trail ever since with no sightings. He squashed the urge to curse, knowing the animal might hear him if it was close. Instead, he focused on placing his boots silently with every step.

He lifted a branch, ignoring the sharp *whoop whoop* warning of a bird who thought him too close to its nest. And then he stopped mid-stride.

Rhea, as he'd taken to calling her, was bending over in front of a fallen tree.

The animal's feathery spine bobbed up and down as she sniffed and scratched at the ground with stubby forearms. She shifted position to the right, and Tiernay saw her preoccupation—breakfast. A coral snake lay immobile on a clump of leaves; its red color like a bloody gash on the jungle floor. Rhea placed her back foot on the head end of the snake and lowered her mouth to the body. He heard a slicing noise as teeth ripped through muscle. Easy as cutting up a steak.

Rhea dipped down for another bite. While she ate, he stared at the blade-like teeth, the pebbled leathery skin and the short, stubby arms, so like a theropod dinosaur.

He settled into a crouch to watch a while longer, but then flipped forward to his knees again. Movement along the trees on the left caught his attention, behind a rotting tree stump.

Sliding a few feet left, he peered through the foliage. A young girl leaned against the stump, her profile just visible. She seemed transfixed by Rhea. Her dark skin and simple clothes meant she was a local. But why was she here? Curiosity? Maybe he had made a mistake thinking Rhea could exist here without interference.

As he stared at the girl, a hand reached out from the bushes behind her and clamped over her mouth. An arm circled her waist. Quickly, the arms dragged her into the trees out of his view. His heartbeat picked up. Another person was out here, likely looking for Rhea as well.

He froze in indecision, torn between checking on the young girl and protecting his creation. Another glance at Rhea showed her still munching on breakfast. If he or these other people disturbed her, it could take him hours to find her again, causing him to lose valuable monitoring data.

Easing the tranquilizer gun off his back, he held it by his side as he approached the area where the girl had disappeared. Muffled whispers came from behind the leaves.

"I'm looking for a friend of mine." The small mouse of a voice had to be the girl.

"What friend?"

The gravelly timbre of the male voice sent a shiver of recognition down Tiernay's spine. It couldn't be him, could it?

Tiernay took a step forward, gently parting branches to peer through. A man with a broad back and close-cropped dark hair towered over the terrified girl. Tiernay couldn't see the face, but the body type lined up with the voice. Haddock had come to Costa Rica.

It had to be because of Rhea, but no one else except Pike knew of her existence. How had Haddock known?

Pieces of conversation floated through Tiernay's mind. Haddock saying he wanted to recreate the fame he'd savored during his *Spinosaurus* discovery. Haddock admitting to hiring a publicist to create the moniker "The Bone Whisperer." Haddock talking about leaving a legacy worthy of the history books.

What better legacy than to bring dinosaurs back to life?

Logic pointed to the conclusion that Pike was Haddock. But if so, he still shouldn't have known *where* to find the creature, unless...

The bitter sting of betrayal turned Tiernay's stomach. Charles was the only other person who knew of the tracking website. Trusting in that idiot's ambition was a mistake. Obviously, Haddock had made Charles a better offer.

"What friend?" Haddock hovered over the young girl as he repeated his question.

The girl was so terrified she could barely squeak out an answer. "I won't give you her name."

"A local?"

"No, an American."

Haddock growled at her. "Why are you following the animal?"

"Because she and the professor were looking for it."

What? More people were looking for the creature? Tiernay pushed stray curls off his forehead along with a layer of sweat. Could it be someone from the university? Charles had sent a message about Harmony pilfering some of the e-mails from the project. Maybe it was a professor she knew. The only one she'd ever mentioned was Dr. Travis Perego, the paleontology professor. A knot of tension formed over Tiernay's breastbone, and he rubbed at it. That was all he needed, another paleontologist in the mix.

He took a silent step back, releasing the leaves to cover all traces of his presence. He wouldn't let Haddock or Perego take his creation. He had to get Rhea out of here.

Walking backward, he retraced his steps until he reached the area where he'd last seen the creature. As he turned around, a sound like a collapsing thump came from behind him, like a thick branch crashing into something soft, followed by a loud crack.

At the noise, Rhea looked up from the bloodstained leaves, the snake skin hanging from her mouth. Still peering in the direction of the sound, she darted off to the southwest, dragging her meal along. Without hesitation, Tiernay shadowed her, pushing his tired legs fast through the underbrush, while simultaneously pushing out of his mind the sickening sound of the branch breaking.

CHAPTER NINETEEN

The trail on the other side of the tree dam, if you could call it a trail, wound through patches of thick trees, roughly following a meandering creek. They had left the wider game trail an hour ago when it had continued north. Travis kept his eyes on the path, not wanting to explore the feelings which arose every time he glanced forward at Lenaia. He had let his mind wander in a romantic direction for too long. This was an unusual situation in which the two of them depended on each other. Who knew where those emotions would go in a different time and place. And yet, whenever their eyes met, his sobering reminders drifted away like smoke.

The path in front of them twisted to the left, but Lenaia stopped before the curve. He caught himself before he ran into her back. She turned her head, listening. He listened for a moment as well, but didn't hear anything unusual. "What's wrong?" he whispered.

"Shhh." She pointed at her ear, telling him to listen.

Gradually, among the background screech and cry of animals, he heard something different. A loud rustling like the wings of a large bird. He would have never heard it. Proof positive he spent too much time in his head.

He nodded to tell her he'd heard it, then he moved in front. Pushing through vines and branches and high stepping on ferns to make a path, he led them toward the sound. Ten feet in, he pushed aside a thick green branch and his body froze, even before his conscious mind could make sense of it.

Face down on the ground, with her limbs folded underneath, lay the body of a young girl. Two large birds, some type of scavengers, beat their wings and took off into the canopy. As he moved closer, he saw the side of the girl's face. Her skin pale. Her jaw slack. Dead. Crusted blood on the back of her head shouted the cause of death.

Lenaia pushed his arm aside. "Nina!" she screamed and ran to kneel beside the girl.

He knelt beside Lenaia and placed his hands on her arms. "Did you know her?"

"I met her when I first came to the village. She was a sweet girl. Oh, Nina."

He remembered the name now, Mirabel's cousin.

Lenaia picked up the girl's wrist, checking for a pulse. He reached over and stilled her hands. "She's gone."

Tears began to spill from her eyes, darkening in spots on the knees of her jeans.

"I'm sorry," he said.

He stayed on the ground for a long time, rubbing a hand along Lenaia's back as she cried, knowing he couldn't do anything else. After a while, she took in a halting breath and looked up at him. With his thumbs, he wiped away the wet trails on her cheeks, then planted a kiss on the top of her head.

"We need to get back to the village," she said. "They have to come get her."

"Do you want me to carry her back?"

She shook her head. "I don't know what they do here with..." she choked on the words. "I mean, they might have some rituals they need to do. I just don't know."

"Okay. Let's go back to the village."

Lenaia leaned forward and reached behind Nina's neck. She sat back with a small oval locket in her hand. "Nina lived with her grandmother. She would probably want this." Lenaia stood and placed it in the front pocket of her backpack.

They turned to go, but he turned back. "Wait." He reached over and pulled open the back portion of Lenaia's pack. Retrieving the hammock, he laid it gently over Nina's still form and secured it with a few rocks. Not much coverage, but better than leaving her exposed to the birds.

"Thank you." Lenaia grabbed his arm. "Oh Travis, how am I going to tell Mirabel?"

Another, even more pressing, problem occurred to him. Nina's death couldn't have been an accident. Who did this to her?

He didn't think it was the poachers who attacked Lenaia because, other than the injury that killed her, Nina didn't have any other signs of an assault. But if not them, then somebody else out here had a reason to kill.

****

After Travis and Lenaia had finally made it back to the village, Lenaia had left again with Pedro and two other men to retrieve the remains. Travis had tried to get her to stay, to allow him to guide the men, but she insisted, saying she wanted to do it for Mirabel and Nina's grandmother.

Travis sat alone on the steps leading to Mirabel's house, watching the women of the village rush around inside the blue barn as they prepared a place to lay Nina's body. He didn't know her last name, had never met her, but he couldn't stomach the death of an innocent girl.

He glanced down at his cell phone. Before she'd left, Lenaia had pulled it from her pack and returned it to him. Yesterday, he'd shut it off to save the battery since he couldn't get a cell signal in the jungle anyway. Did he even want to turn it back on? The real world in North

Carolina seemed distant, somehow empty, and yet being here also felt like a dream.

No matter what, he had responsibilities. As the phone powered up, a couple of text messages came in. The first one was from Corinne, sent yesterday.

Dean Haddock is looking for you. He left a message saying you need to come back to school now or you're fired.

Great. So much for working out his issues in time to save his job. He pounded a fist into the step, then winced at the pain.

"Everything okay?"

He glanced up to see Mirabel leaning over him, her small eyebrows wrinkled in concern. He marveled that she would worry about him when any minute they might bring back the body of her cousin. He couldn't add to her troubles. "Yeah, I'm fine."

She stared at the ground in front of her feet. "Yesterday, my worst fear was what my parents would think of me becoming a doctor. It seemed like such a big thing." She wrapped her arms around her midsection. "I want to go back to yesterday."

He didn't know what to say. Going back in time would solve some problems for him, too, like saving his career. But if he erased the last couple of days, then he wouldn't have met Lenaia.

"Do you think it's really Nina?"

He couldn't lie. "Lenaia seemed to think so."

Mirabel's face sagged. Instead of nodding, she shook her head like she couldn't, or wouldn't, believe it. She sank to the steps. "I saw her yesterday. She wanted to go look for you, but I told her to wait."

"Did Nina go into the woods by herself often?"

"All the time. She was helping Dr. Gordon frustrate the poachers. They were trying to drive them away, but Dr. Gordon told us not to go out there anymore. Not until they could do something about the creature." Mirabel twisted the sole of her boot in the dirt. "Did the creature kill her?"

"I don't think so."

Even though he'd never met Nina, her death pricked at his conscience. He had the nagging feeling it was somehow his fault. It seemed like too much of a coincidence for her to be killed in the jungle while looking for them. And he didn't think the poachers had done it. But who else out here would have reason to kill a young girl?

He changed the subject. "You want to be a doctor?"

She blinked a few times, then nodded. A sad smile pulled on her lips. "But my parents want me to stay here."

"Why would they want to hold you back?"

"They want what's best for me. We just disagree on what that is."

"What did they say when you told them?"

"I haven't exactly told them, but I know what they'd say. That my purpose is here, getting married, having babies, no need for university." She looked up at the sky for a minute. "That I shouldn't question the way things are."

"Maybe God has a different purpose for you." Her eyes shot to his and surprise flickered across her face. Had Lenaia told Mirabel about his own struggles with God? And then Trudy's words from last week came back to him. *Can you honor God in this profession?* A mirror image of what he'd just said.

"I know God has a place for me here in this village." Mirabel's eyes were a dark, sea of longing. "I believe it's as a doctor. I love medicine, but I also love my parents."

Mirabel's passion struck a chord deep in his soul. More of Trudy's words pushed their way forward. *God gave you a passion for paleontology for a reason.* What reason? Could he honor God in paleontology? Could

Mirabel honor God by disobeying her parents? The questions seemed endless. For him, it probably didn't matter. He wouldn't have a job when he returned anyway.

"When I'm an adult, I will leave to become a doctor, even if my parents forbid it." The quiet certainty in her words surprised him. "I have to obey God above all else." She shook her head, and her dark ponytail bobbed along her back. "He's the one thing I won't question."

"Why?"

"Because He's the one with the best plan for my life."

Travis picked at the grass between his feet. "How do you know He won't take away the very thing you love to do?"

"He might. But He loves me like a child, more than even my mother. If He takes something away, it must be necessary to work out His plan."

He thought of Lenaia. If she would have compromised her beliefs, she could have stayed at the Washington Geological Survey. And then they never would have met. Was it God's plan for them to meet? Then, what about Nina? God's plan didn't work out too well for her. Mirabel's mouth twisted into a frown. He wondered if the same thought occurred to her.

Without another word, she stood and walked toward the barn. He watched her disappear inside, amazed at the strong faith of such a young girl. He, on the other hand, questioned everything. Lenaia said he was made to question, but for the first time, he wished he could stop.

He turned to look down the street. A blond-haired young man wandered along, searching in all directions. He disappeared into the barn where Mirabel had gone. That was probably Owen.

Travis turned his attention back to the variegated tree line. Movement in the foliage caught his eye. He pushed off the steps as Lenaia emerged from the jungle ahead of the men. When her eyes found his, she veered in his direction.

"Did you find her?"

She nodded sadly.

"The women said to put her in the second barn."

She nodded again, then pointed the men toward the barn. He watched them pass by before putting his hands on both of Lenaia's arms and tugging her toward the steps. "Come, sit." Her lack of response concerned him. She was shutting down.

She sat cross-legged, looking innocent and vulnerable, like a porcelain doll he could break with the wrong touch. He sat next to her and placed a hand on her back. When she spoke, he leaned close to hear. "Who did this to her?"

"I don't know."

"The guys who jumped me?"

"Could be, but I think ..." How could he put this delicately? "If it was them, I think she would have been found with less clothes on."

"So somebody else?"

"Probably."

She bowed her head and spoke to the ground. "As if the jungle wasn't dangerous enough already."

Another text message chimed on his phone. He set the phone on the step behind him.

Lenaia lifted her head. "Who's that from?"

"Probably Harmony, but it can wait."

She held a hand up. "No, it can't. Maybe Harmony has more information on the creature. We need to find it and figure out what's going on."

She had a point, and he admired her ability to focus during this terrible situation, but at times she seemed more determined to find the creature than he. What was that about? He picked up the phone and checked the new text message. Sent today from Harmony. As he read it, his fingers shook.

We discovered the identity of Fulton Pike. It's Dean Haddock.

Travis's stomach clenched into a rock hard knot of anger. So many things made sense now. Haddock hunting for Tiernay right after Tiernay had left. Haddock's need to get back into the spotlight. How the dean had hounded Harmony to find out who had read the e-mails from Tiernay's computer.

Could that be why Haddock threatened to fire me? Not that it mattered at this point. Travis would find out the truth about this creature, and Haddock couldn't do anything about it.

CHAPTER TWENTY

Mirabel sat on an overturned bucket, waiting with her mother and two other women from the village. She kept her head low, praying scattered prayers. She prayed they were wrong about the dead body being Nina. She prayed for comfort in case they weren't wrong. And she prayed for strength and compassion to handle this person's body in either case.

The wooden door of the barn creaked open, letting in cool humidity. The air was like a heavy blanket. It would rain soon, but that seemed fitting.

She focused on the men who entered and the canvas stretcher they carried by the handles between them. Whoever was on the stretcher was covered with a sheet, the outline of small features indented in the cloth. Mirabel's heartbeat pounded in a great rush in her ears. Her muscles tensed to flee.

The men brought the stretcher to a wide wooden bench and placed it on top, letting the wooden handles fall to the side. They moved back to the corner to let the women take over. Her mother approached the body and grabbed a corner of the sheet. Mirabel stood over her shoulder, refusing to look at the person underneath. Her mother's reaction would tell her all she needed to know. As her mother pulled back the sheet, her mouth dropped open and her skin paled. Her eyes were full of pain when they met Mirabel's gaze.

No, it couldn't be her. Mirabel forced herself to look. Instantly, she recognized the dark, wavy hair, the upturned nose. She covered her mouth to drown out a strangled cry. *Nina, what happened?*

Her mother put her hands on Mirabel's shoulders. "You can go if you want. We'll take good care of Nina."

Mirabel turned and ran. The barn door clattered as it slammed shut behind her.

Lenaia shouted something as she passed by, but she didn't stop. She sprinted beyond the houses to the tree line, and then ran parallel to it for a hundred yards. A familiar place called to her. The place where the trees bowed out to surround the village.

She swung up into the tree with an ease that came from having done so a hundred times. Their tree. The perfect size for two girls to nestle inside the crooked branches and get a view of both the town and the forested jungle. She and Nina had sat in it for hours, their rear ends aching, as they explored other nations and exotic lands in their imagination, always until sunset—dinner time. Although they hadn't visited the tree in a few years, preferring to explore the jungle together as they got older, it would forever be theirs.

She braced her feet against the trunk, laid her head back, and fought the tears. Nina wouldn't want her to cry. She hated when anyone was sad. As girls, they'd tickled each other out of their tears. She'd even fallen out of the tree once because Nina had tickled her silly.

From here, they had spied on the adults and dreamed of their grown up lives. Nina had simple dreams, to fall in love with a man who would show kindness to her grandmother. *Oh, Lord, why did you take her?*

A large hand pressed on Mirabel's shoulder, and she jumped, almost falling out of the tree.

"It's me."

She relaxed into Owen's arm. Even standing on the ground next to her, he was tall enough to put an arm around her. At the comforting touch, she almost let the tears go, but she held them in, as Nina would want.

They stayed in silence for a long time. She was grateful Owen didn't speak. She drew on his quiet strength while she dammed up the tears and drowned in memories.

One time, she glanced toward the village and saw her mother searching for her. When their eyes met, her mother saw Owen and turned away.

Rather than watch her go, Mirabel leaned back on the rough branch and stared up into the heart of the tree. She'd meant her words to Travis about trusting God, but her heart floundered in confusion as she tried to make sense of this. "Why did God do this?"

Owen brushed stray hairs from her face. He took a long time to answer. "I don't know why she had to die, and she didn't deserve to die this way, but I'm pretty sure God didn't do this."

"I know you're right, but..." A hailstorm of anger pelted her fragile soul. She'd never before wanted to blame God for anything. "He could have saved her."

"Yes, He could have."

She kicked a foot against the thick trunk. "But He didn't."

"No, He didn't."

It was what she loved most about him. Even now, in the midst of comforting her, he didn't cover over things. He didn't tell her it was okay. He didn't try to make the ugly things pretty. Her arms started to shake, and Owen held tighter.

"Mirabel, we all have to leave this earth someday."

"He took her too soon." The whining tone in her voice made her want to throw up.

Owen took a long breath, like dealing patiently with a stubborn child. "Who are we to claim that power? How our life and death fits into God's plan is His business, not ours. You're angry, and I don't blame you, but God didn't kill Nina—another angry person did."

He was right. She was mad at God for Nina's death, but she would die someday too, and only God knew how. He didn't promise a long life here on earth, but an eternal one with Him in heaven. And knowing Nina, she was having a party now in heaven.

Still, anger seeped out of the gaping wound in her heart. She leaned into Owen's embrace, allowing him to kiss her forehead. For once, she didn't care what her mother or the other villagers might say.

***

The four-wheel-drive vehicle bounced down the rough pitted road, bottoming out several times. Lenaia gripped the stability bars with white knuckles. Travis slowed for a corner, and she winced at the nearly hundred-foot drop to the valley below. The road to Polvo was steeper than the one to Rojo Piedra. Nina's grandmother had left the little town where they lived, and come to the larger town to be with friends and prepare a place for the funeral.

As they came over a ridge, the town of Polvo appeared with its stucco houses and slanted metal roofs, much like Rojo Piedra, except with more residents. Lenaia's gaze shifted to the back of Pedro's vehicle, to Nina's body wrapped in two blankets, strapped with rope to a metal grate on the back. Bringing her to her grandmother would be the hardest thing Lenaia would ever do.

"Why didn't Mirabel want to come see Nina's grandmother?" Travis asked.

"She said she couldn't face her. I think the pain is too raw right now." Lenaia held herself stiff, letting the tension of the task pulse through her like an electric current. Only God could get her through this. She closed her eyes and whispered a prayer for strength and peace.

Pedro stopped the four-wheeler at a small yellow house. Travis pulled to a stop behind him. They all got out and climbed the stone steps to the door. Pedro knocked and immediately an elderly woman threw the door open.

"Marina, we are so sorry." Pedro spoke to her in Spanish.

The old woman motioned for them to bring Nina's body into the house. Travis and Pedro returned to the vehicles, while Marina tugged Lenaia inside. She hovered just inside the doorway, watching with Marina as Pedro untied the ropes. A shudder caused Marina to tremble. Lenaia placed a hand on her arm. Both men solemnly carried Nina through the front door.

Marina directed them to place her on a board laid in the center of the main living space. Wooden chairs were arranged in a semi-circle around the board, but Marina ignored them, instead she dropped to the floor next to Nina.

Lenaia took a seat in one of the chairs directly behind Marina, somehow hoping to comfort her by being close. Travis and Pedro sat in chairs at the other end.

Slowly, gently, Marina unwrapped the blanket covering Nina's face. She gently touched Nina's cheek, holding her palm there in a moment that stretched on. Lenaia's eyes moistened at the tender goodbye filled with longing.

Several minutes later, Marina pulled over a cardboard box. Reaching in, she took out bright yellow and orange flowers and laid them one by one as a covering over her granddaughter's body.

The beauty and finality of the flower burial tore at Lenaia's heart. She dabbed at her eyes to keep the moisture from falling. Marina stayed strong, never crying, her deep frown the only evidence of her pain.

After Marina had placed the last fragrant stem, she disappeared into the kitchen. When she returned, she held a tray of hot tea and sliced kiwi. She served each of them, then took one of the chairs and turned it to face them before she sat.

She sipped tea for a few moments, calming her nerves and trying to compose what she wanted to say to Marina. Finally, Lenaia turned to Pedro. "Can you translate for me? My Spanish is passable, but not efficient."

"Of course."

She looked at Marina as she spoke. "Nina was a sweet girl. I'm glad I got to meet her, but I'm sad to lose my new friend."

As Pedro translated, a solitary tear rolled down Marina's face. Lenaia swallowed past the lump in her throat. She couldn't break down now. Not when Marina was so bravely holding herself together. Even so, they all felt the tragic reality: Grandchildren weren't supposed to die first.

Lenaia cast a glance at the men, and her gaze stuck on Travis. The sorrowful expression on his face reached all the way down to her soul, melting her to the core. His heart broke for Marina too. He felt the pain with her. He was a good man. Better than any man she'd met before. A sharp pang of guilt derailed her thoughts. She hadn't been completely honest with him. No matter what she said about his issues, her secret was a locked door, keeping them from opening up to each other. No, keeping *her* from opening up to him. Eventually, she would have to tell him all that she'd been hiding.

Marina spoke again, bringing Lenaia back from her tangled reflections. "Nina was also happy about her new friend from America. She begged me to let her go into

the forest to find you. She thought you needed help..."
Her words were choked off by a sob.

"I didn't see her." Lenaia stared down at her hiking boots. "I mean, until we found her." She felt her face pinch as she battled strong emotions. She needed to cry, but she held the tears captive. Sliding off the chair, she knelt in front of Marina. "Can I pray with you?"

Marina nodded, then clasped her hands around Lenaia's. They bowed their heads.

"Dear heavenly Father, our hearts are heavy because we have lost Nina. As a child of Yours, we know she's in heaven with You, but we miss her." Lenaia cleared her throat and gave Pedro time to catch up in the translation. "Calm our hearts, give us peace, and take care of Nina, until we meet with her again in heaven. Amen."

Marina whispered, "Amen." She leaned over and kissed Lenaia on the forehead. "*Dios te acompane.*"

Lenaia wiped more moisture from under her eyes, as she whispered, "God be with you, as well."

CHAPTER TWENTY-ONE

On the trip back to the village, Travis improved at avoiding the usual road hazards of pot holes and fallen limbs. He touched Lenaia's arm once, but couldn't keep a hand on her because he needed both to steer. Up ahead, the road curved into the jungle where the tree branches, desperate to reclaim the space taken by the tiny road, had created an arched canopy. It meant they were close to Rojo Piedra.

On a straight stretch, he glanced over and noted the dark circles, barely visible, under Lenaia's caramel skin. This had been a hard day for her. She had completely opened herself to Mirabel, Nina, and Marina. Her ability to love people she had just met showed the purity and goodness in her heart. And yet, with him, she was guarded. Something held her back. Most often when she looked at him, the metal bars of a jail door slammed shut over her eyes. Now more than ever, he wished for that to change.

They came out of the shelter of the forest and pulled into the village clearing where full access to the sun warmed his skin. This time he was in the lead, so he parked the four-wheeler next to the steps of Mirabel's house. He glanced over at Lenaia, but she didn't look his way. She shifted in the seat, refusing to meet his eyes.

Before she could get out, he grabbed her hand. "Lenaia, what you did for that woman ... well, it was beautiful."

She continued to stare in the opposite direction and

wouldn't look at him. Something was definitely wrong. "Can we go inside now?"

"Sure." He released her hand. She darted from the vehicle and up the steps. Lenaia knocked, and Mirabel opened the door, motioning for them to come inside quickly. Once they were inside, Mirabel stuck her head out, searching down the street in both directions before closing the door.

"What's going on?" Travis asked.

Mirabel locked her gaze onto him. "Someone came asking about you. He seemed unhappy."

Travis squinted at her. Who would be looking for him down here. "What did this man look like?"

Mirabel moved the palm of her hand a foot above her head. "Tall, but shorter than you. Older. Bushy hair, gray as the mist in the cloud forest."

Tiernay. But how did he find out I was here? "Was this man armed?"

Mirabel moved her hands apart a distance of about two feet. "He carried a long rifle."

"A real gun or a tranquilizer gun?"

"It looked real, but I'm not sure I could tell."

"Did he ask about the animal?"

Mirabel shook her head. "No, just about you."

Strange for Tiernay not to be looking for the creature. Maybe because he knew exactly where it was. "What did you tell him?"

Mirabel folded her arms. "The truth. That you had been to the village, but you weren't here now."

"Do you know where he went?"

"No."

"Okay. Thanks." Travis grabbed Lenaia's backpack from the corner of the room. Tiernay must be desperate to stop him if he came here. Travis needed to find the creature and find out why. He pulled out his phone, then glanced over at Lenaia. She lay on the couch, looking up at the ceiling. Her skin matched the olive color of a kiwi, and she bit into her lip like she wanted to draw blood. He put the phone down on the cot and moved to sit next to her. "What's wrong?"

Mirabel crouched down in front of her for only a second. "I'll get you some tea. It will make you feel better." She ran into the kitchen. He watched her go, wondering why people thought tea solved everything.

"I haven't told you the whole truth." Lenaia's voice came as a hoarse whisper.

He turned back to focus on her, resting a hand on her arm. "What do you mean?"

She brought guilt-shadowed eyes up to meet his. "I *am* here to look for volcanic activity. That is true. But when I heard you describe the animal, I knew exactly what it was and where it had come from."

He pulled his hand away. She knew about Tiernay's work? "How?"

"A year ago, while up here hunting with my uncle, we argued about God." She gave a rueful laugh. "Again. But this time the subject of evolution came up. He claimed it was possible to create an evolutionary ancestor, to retrace evolution in bird DNA." She pressed a palm to her forehead. "I told him it wouldn't happen. He insisted that he would prove me wrong."

Travis's lungs felt like twin lead balloons, weighing down his chest cavity. "Um..."

"I should have told you what I knew right away, but I didn't know how you'd react." She swallowed, turning her gaze to the wooden floor. "Dr. James Tiernay is my Uncle Jim."

Whoa. He hadn't seen this coming. *Her Uncle Jim.* God had a twisted sense of humor to throw him together with the niece of the man who started all of this. He drew back to sit on the cot across from her, trying to engage the rational part of his brain. Yes, she should have told him earlier. But she had a point. He probably would have thought she was working with her uncle. He probably would have left her behind. Still, her deception cut to the core of the matter—could he trust her? "That's why you're helping me find the creature."

She nodded, and her ponytail slipped off the couch, dangling over the edge. Before, he would have been tempted to run a hand through the silky strands. His fingers still itched with the desire, but now part of him wanted to pull away.

"Did you know he was here?"

"No. Until yesterday, I wasn't even sure the animal existed or if it was connected to my uncle. But now that I've seen it, I feel responsible, like I need to help protect it somehow. If we can get proof that it exists, maybe we can force Uncle Jim to find a safer place for it." She slowly sat up. "This animal might have been created by my uncle, but God allowed it to happen. It deserves protection."

She was talking about the threat from the poachers. Though he had doubts about her, he didn't question her allegiance to the creature. She would do what was right for it. And right now, she was the only one thinking about the creature's best interests. So far, he'd been self-focused, not worrying about anything beyond getting the samples he needed to find the truth. But if they left the creature here, Tiernay would control what happened to it, and who knew what plans he had?

Despite Travis's efforts to consider the creature's future, his thoughts kept circling back to his confused emotions about Lenaia. Did her allegiance lie with him, too? Or would she deceive him again just to find the creature and protect it?

***

Mirabel lay on the sofa in the living room, staring out the front window at the dusty street. When they'd taken Nina's body away on the back of a four-wheeler, she'd curled up in a ball and sobbed. Having Nina close made it somehow better, but she wouldn't be selfish. Nina's grandmother needed her most.

She couldn't imagine how hard it would be to outlive your son, daughter-in-law, and your grandchild. *I'd probably be wishing for death to be reunited with them.*

The front door opened, letting in cool, but still humid air. The promised rain of yesterday hadn't happened, although she'd cried enough tears for a monsoon. Her mother entered the room and sat in a chair beside the sofa. She must have finally finished coordinating meals to take to Marina, as if Marina would ever feel like eating again.

A fresh wave of guilt washed over her. She should be helping, doing something like her mother, but she couldn't seem to get up.

Her mother took her hand and gently pressed both sides with her palms. "Don't go near the forest, Mirabel. Please."

"I wasn't planning on it. I know whoever killed her might still be out there." She didn't dare say Nina's name out loud or she might spiral down into sobbing again. Blessed numbness had, at least temporarily, relieved her from the agonizing sorrow.

Her mother pumped her hand up and down to get her full attention. "Not even like yesterday."

She focused on her mother's pleading eyes, the same color as the coffee her mother drank every morning. "Yesterday, I wasn't in the forest. I was in our tree." She couldn't promise not to go back to the tree, the only place she felt close to Nina. Her mother waited silently for an answer until the moment became painful. She sighed, too tired to argue. "Okay, I won't go anywhere near the trees."

"Thank you. I want to keep you safe." Her mother went to the kitchen. "I know how your curiosity sometimes gets the better of you." Her voice drifted into the living room in between the rush of the faucet and the clang of a pot placed on the stove. "Look where curiosity led Nina."

Mirabel drew in a shaky breath to steel herself against the hurt that came with hearing her cousin's name. "What do you mean?"

Her mother poked her head back in the room. "Nina should have been at home taking care of her grandmother instead of running around the jungle chasing things which weren't her concern." Her mother's words were harsh, but her face was compassionate as she returned to the stove.

High voltage sparks of anger shot through Mirabel, but she couldn't direct the emotion toward her mother. She forced the fiery feeling away, and it left as quickly a lightning strike. Even so, when she answered, the hard edge in her voice sounded like someone else. "Nina didn't die because she was chasing the creature. She probably thought Travis and Lenaia needed help."

"She should have left that to the adults in the village."

"Even if she was curious about the creature, so what? The creature didn't kill her." Mirabel took a breath, mostly to keep a rein on her tongue. She never talked to her mother this way, but she couldn't seem to stop. "Haven't you ever been curious? Did you ever question anything?"

Her mother turned around to face her through the wide kitchen door. She leaned against the counter and placed both hands flat on top of her long skirt. Mirabel felt suddenly ashamed for attacking this meek and gentle woman. "Questioning leads to discontent."

Mirabel had heard the statement before, but this time she had a new answer. "Not questioning leads us to accept less than what we're capable of."

Her mother released a sad sigh. "You think my life is less."

"That's not what I meant."

"I don't regret my life here in the village, with you and your father."

"I know. But this is your life. Your choice. Not mine."

"Mirabel, your life is not your own. You must consider what Jesus wants of you."

She sat upright on the sofa. "And Jesus only wants me if I become a wife and mother like you?"

Her mother closed her eyes and took a long breath. When she opened them, Mirabel saw resignation written there. "All I know is you must bend your will to His. If you try to follow your plans, you will be the one who is unhappy."

***

"Thanks for meeting with us, Charles." Harmony crossed her legs and settled back into the chair. If she wanted him relaxed, she needed to seem relaxed, as well. She shot a glance at Tom who leaned against the far wall, giving them space, but staying alert in case Charles did something unexpected. Staring at his phone, Tom appeared uninterested, but really he was videotaping the conversation.

Charles crossed his legs the opposite way as her. "Exactly why did you ask to meet me? I can't get your job back, if that's what you want."

"No. I don't think I'm suited for genetic research anyway." Not completely a lie. Her life had flipped upside down, and she didn't know where she would go from here. She glanced around the office, grateful for the empty desks. She didn't need anyone overhearing this conversation, at least not until the police had viewed the videotape first. "This meeting is so that I can help you."

"Help *me*?"

"Yes, you. Before it's too late."

Charles folded his arms across his chest and tapped his fingers against his biceps. "I don't need any help."

"You do. You just don't know it yet." She pulled the front part of her hair back and trapped it behind her ear. *Here's where it gets tricky.* "My friend, Jenny Monroe. She's a biology student. Do you know her?"

A subtle hesitation. "I wouldn't say I know her. But I know who she is."

"She knows you, as does her roommate, Shannon Porter." His white face turned a shade paler. A vision popped into her head of a miniature Charles trapped under a glass slide, squirming under the bright lights of a microscope. Now, she needed to slide in a pointer and jab him with it.

"I know Shannon."

"When was the last time you talked to her?"

"Probably in class last week. We take Vertebrate Biology together. Well, at least whenever she goes."

"Do you know why she doesn't go half of the time?"

Charles rubbed his hands on his thighs.

"Is something making you nervous?" When he didn't answer, she pressed on. "Shannon has a bit of a drug problem, helped along because her parents are loaded. They give her as much money as she wants, as long as she stays in school. Which means, she only goes to class enough times to keep from flunking out. The rest of the time, she's out partying." Harmony touched his tennis shoe with the toe of her flats. "But you already knew that, didn't you?"

He scooted back in the chair. "Maybe I did."

Harmony narrowed her eyes. Time to smack him

hard. "Dr. Tiernay had already left town when you got the drugs from Shannon. So who hired you to kill Bob?"

Charles shot to his feet. "What? No? I..." His eyes scanned the room. Maybe afraid someone would hear. Or searching for some way out of this. "I didn't do anything."

"Please, Charles, have a seat. I told you I'm here to help." As he lowered himself back into the chair, she even managed to smile at him. "I understand how it works. The dean of the department asks for a favor. You don't know what he's going to do with the drugs. He might have even told you it was for research."

Charles stared at his feet for a moment, then she got what she needed—a slow nod.

She held back a scoff. Charles wasn't a victim here. He had found out Haddock was Fulton Pike and decided to help him tie up loose ends so he could share in the fame when the dean went public with the research.

Charles's head suddenly flipped up. He slapped a hand on the table. "It was you. You changed Dr. Tiernay's password on the tracking website."

Harmony gave an indulgent smile. "What we need to do now is go to the police. They'll probably let you off the hook if you testify."

"Probably?" He scratched at a spot on his arm.

"Unless you'd rather ask the dean how to handle this, because I'm sure he'd love to talk to the police first."

Charles threw his hands up in the air. "We can't ask him anyway. He's gone."

"Gone? Where?"

"We were supposed to have an appointment today to discuss my future at the university, but he didn't show. When I went to his office, his secretary said he was out of the office for a week."

"A week? Where did he go?"

"I have no idea."

Understanding shot through her, and she jumped up. "I do."

She ran toward the stairs. Tom followed after her as Charles called out, "I thought you were going to help me!"

At the bottom of the stairs, she rushed through the side door and into the central plaza. She dug her phone out of her pocket and dialed Travis's cell phone number. After five rings, the voice mail picked up. "Professor Perego, I hope you get this message. I found proof that Dean Haddock was involved in Bob's death, but you need to be careful. I think he might be in Costa Rica."

CHAPTER TWENTY-TWO

Travis spent most of the night tossing on the cot. It wasn't the thin material that kept him awake, he'd slept on worse. It was fear. Fear that he couldn't trust Lenaia to be completely honest, fear of what Tiernay's presence meant, fear of what might happen when he returned to the university. The smothering fear was his constant companion lately. He remembered a time when he wasn't afraid of anything, not even death, but that was ignorant arrogance.

Last night, he'd told Lenaia he understood why she hadn't told him about her Uncle Jim. And he did understand. But it didn't answer the question of whether he could trust her. If it served her purposes, would she keep something else from him?

He wouldn't be as concerned about trust issues if he preferred to go their separate ways after finding the creature, but the thought of not seeing her again caused his heart to pound so hard it threatened to rip free from his chest. Much as he didn't want to admit it, Lenaia had found the back door to his heart and slipped in when he wasn't looking. Emotionally strong, probably smarter than him, certainly with a better sense of direction, she had the drive to prove herself, a requirement for a woman in a male-dominated field. But what drew him to her was her sense of adventure. She didn't shy away from outrageous and unproven ideas. He could see himself exploring the world with her, the two of them doing and finding things they would only share with each other. Leaving her behind now wasn't an option. But...

Muffled noises came from the other room. The girls were up.

He swung his legs off the couch and ran a hand through his tangled hair. Lenaia came out of the bedroom, then stopped and stared. "Morning," he said.

"Morning." Her gaze shifted to his bare chest. She dipped her head as if embarrassed, then ducked into the bathroom.

He smirked and pulled on a mostly clean T-shirt from their shared backpack. Somehow, her embarrassment at his undress meant more than their casual flirting had.

Grabbing his phone, he powered it up and found the website. After Lenaia's confession yesterday, he'd forgotten to check on the creature. Swiftly, he entered the user ID and password. A window came up immediately.

Incorrect ID or password.

He tried again, typing slowly, but got the same error message. Why wasn't the website working? He glanced at the home screen. A missed call and a voice mail message. He checked the recent call list. The missed call was from Harmony. Maybe she'd already discovered the website wasn't working. He tried to play the voice mail, but the phone blinked at him. Low battery. He'd done all he could to conserve the battery by keeping it off, but he'd forgotten to charge it last night during the few hours the family used their generator. He tossed the phone down on the cot.

Lenaia came out of the bathroom. With her face washed clean and her chestnut hair loose and shiny, she glowed with a vibrancy that melted the lump of fear in his chest. He had the sudden urge to discover if she tasted like toothpaste.

She swept her hair up into a clip and met his gaze

with eyes that sparked fire. "Still want to chase your creature?"

Did he? And risk their lives again? Lenaia insisted her uncle couldn't have killed Nina, but he didn't share her confidence in the man. In fact, he didn't have confidence in much of anything right now. And yet, he'd come this far. He couldn't leave without knowing.

She answered for him. "I thought so. Let's go get some supplies."

He grabbed the phone, turned it off, and shoved it back into Lenaia's backpack. "The website isn't working. Harmony left me a message last night, but I don't have enough battery left to check it."

"Do you want to call her with my satellite phone?"

He picked his watch up off the ground and checked the time. "It's still early in the States, if we can't find the creature on our own, then I'll use it to call her later."

"We know it likes to hang out by the river and the game trails. Let's go see if I can track it from there."

He took his turn in the bathroom, washing his face and brushing his teeth. After getting some food from the kitchen, they went out to the cornflower-blue barn. The door creaked as it opened and the hay-filled air tickled his nose.

Before she got too far ahead of him, he touched Lenaia's arm. "Are you sure you want to do this?"

"I need to know what my uncle did."

He pushed a loose strand of ebony hair behind her ear. "It could be dangerous."

She scowled, backing up a step. "He didn't kill Nina."

"Somebody did."

She turned her back on him, moving to a shelf stocked full of supplies. She opened her pack and stuffed it with dried fruit and water bottles. "Pedro gave me a pistol for our protection."

"Do you know how to use it?"

Over her shoulder, she sent him an amused look. "I'm used to hunting rifles, but yes, I can shoot a pistol. Can you?"

"Well enough. Most of our dig sites are remote. We need a gun to protect ourselves, more from wild animals than anything else." He grabbed a coiled rope off the wall, catching a pitchfork before it clattered to the ground. He set the pitchfork back on its hook, then tested the strength of the rope by pulling hard to stretch the fibers. It would do. "Do you know how to set a snare?"

"Doesn't everybody?" The flat timbre of her voice gave her emotions away. She acted like strong Lenaia, but he heard the sad undertones. She walked over to him and picked up the end of the rope. "I don't have anything to weight it." She tugged on the end. "Somebody strong— that would be you—would need to hoist the animal up and hold it until we can tie the rope off or until the drugs take effect."

"Can do."

She gave him a skeptical look. "You seem pretty confident considering we don't know how much the animal weighs."

He twirled his end of the rope in a circle. "It's all about leverage. No problem."

Travis dug out the tranquilizer pills and secured the vial in the side pocket of his pack so they would be more accessible. How Lenaia had talked the doctor into letting her have them, he couldn't guess. From the way Mirabel made it sound, tranquilizer was more valuable than gold out here.

Once the backpack was loaded down, they left the barn and walked toward the jungle. Lenaia stepped into the foliage in front of him. "I'll lead. Maybe I can pick up a trail quickly."

The leaves closed in around them creating the illusion of isolation, as if he and Lenaia were the last two people on earth. If only it were true. He could sense the danger lurking behind every darkened tree. Jaguars. Poachers. Tiernay. They could run into anything around the next bend. Or maybe something in here was tracking them. "Can Tiernay track as well as you?"

"Better." She scanned the ground briefly. Her brow furrowed, she examined the leaves at shoulder height. "This way."

"The creature?"

"Not sure. Something big. The animal is tall enough that it's hard to differentiate between it and a man."

"I've noticed that every time I refer to it as a creature, you call it an animal. Why?"

She shrugged. "Animal seems more appropriate since it's a living, breathing thing. God might not have created this animal, but He knew it would happen."

Travis couldn't argue with that.

A frosty, yet somehow flirtatious, glance came his way next. "Can't you be quiet? You sound like a boar running through the woods."

"You try dragging around size fourteens."

They walked for a mile or so, sometimes stopping to check the surrounding area, sometimes back-tracking when she lost the trail. To pass the time, he focused on controlling the force of each foot as it landed on the leaf carpet. He'd probably never be as quiet as her, but maybe he could sneak up on a deaf sloth.

"I'm seeing a couple of jaguar footprints, but they're intermittent so I don't think that's what we're tracking."

They continued on for another half-mile. At a small clearing, she abruptly stopped. Turning in a wide circle, she inspected each branch first, then stared at the trampled leaves on the ground.

She suddenly looked up and grinned at him. "This is the place."

"For what?"

"The trap. We've got several overlapping trails." She cupped a hand by her ear. "A water source is nearby. And some large creature, taller than a jaguar, has come through here often."

"You're sure it wasn't us?"

"I don't recognize this area. I've seen a few shoe prints, but not many. And the ones I've seen aren't ours." She bumped his elbow with her shoulder. "No size fourteens."

"Could they be Tiernay's?" Despite his efforts to keep his voice even, an accusatory note came out with the man's name.

The switch flipped instantly to her sarcastic side. "Oh, yes, that's right. In my spare time I memorized all of my uncle's shoe prints."

He deserved that. "Okay then, let's do this."

While he prepped the food, a mixture of smoked goat meat and rabbit, she tied the knot for the snare. Using a rock, he crushed the small pink pills, then coated the meat in the tranquilizer dust.

"Rope is ready," she said.

He tested the knot. It should hold. She'd done well. He laid the mass of meat on the ground and circled the rope around it. The straight end, he threw over a thick branch about fifteen feet up. It got stuck in the tree twice before coming out the other side. He grabbed the end and pulled it to another tree ten feet away, wrapping it around the trunk before tying it off. "We're good to go."

They picked a spot to hide behind some ground cover, sparse enough to allow them a view through the bushes. He untied the rope, and they lay down on their bellies. The leaves from the ferns tickled his nose. He scooted back, resting the rough cord slack between his palms.

As the time passed, he did his best to focus on the snare, but his attention kept wandering to the woman beside him. If he didn't talk to her, he was going to touch her. "Lenaia, are you and your uncle close?" he whispered.

"You know, even for a scientist, you ask a lot of questions."

He didn't deny it.

She scowled, but with no anger behind it. "We were. My dad died when I was young. He used to fly airplanes until he crashed one." She brushed a crawling bug off her arm. "Uncle Jim filled in where my dad would have been. We needed each other. I think I gave him some sort of sense of family since he never had a wife and kids. But then, when I was in high school, I found Jesus. I told Uncle Jim about it, and he laughed at me. He could have punched me, and it would've hurt less. Ever since then, I've been Uncle Jim's personal mission field."

"Mission field? You mean, he's trying to turn you away from Jesus?"

"Yep. The last time I spoke to him was almost a year ago, shortly after our hunting trip here. He isn't the type to keep in touch because he's always working. Whenever he feels like it, he just calls or shows up." She rolled onto her back. "The hunting trip down here was the last time I saw him. I had a bad break up so he took me here on a jaguar hunt." She put up a hand. "I know, it's crazy, but he thought shooting something would be cathartic."

Travis wasn't prepared for the wrench in his gut at the thought of her with someone else, even if it was a year ago. "Was it a serious relationship?"

She looked sideways at him as if she saw straight into his reasons for asking. As she answered, she flipped over and went back to staring at the snare. "We talked about marriage, but had one obstacle. He believed in God, but didn't believe in Jesus. His God was low-maintenance. Do what you want, try to be a good person, everyone goes to heaven. So, in his mind, we would both go to heaven. I didn't see it that way. We argued, but as you can imagine, arguing never brings anyone closer to Jesus. Then, I moved because of my job. He didn't follow. I should have ended it before I left anyway. I couldn't have lived a lifetime with someone knowing I wouldn't see them in eternity."

Travis gripped the twined rope in his hands, the fibers rough and spindly apart, but when twisted together forming a strong cord—so much like his path through life, the rough patches seemed so pointless, but then Jesus came and twisted them into something stronger, something with meaning. "That was me before Marie died. Before I started to read the Bible."

She went quiet for a second. When she spoke, she pronounced each word slowly. "You've read it, but do you believe what it says?"

Her tone had held no judgment, but still the words cut deep. He wanted to believe without reservation, but he didn't know how to stop the wrestling match in his head. Every time he took a step of faith, the evidence for evolution would tumble through his mind. Lenaia's question from a couple of days ago came back to him. *What about the evidence for creation?* He'd studied. He knew the same evidence could support both positions. He just didn't know how to quiet the doubts.

Silence separated them until it became a thick stone wall too high to climb. He rolled over onto his back, staring at the slivers of sky visible through the canopy. The vivid blue was broken up by dark patches as if leaf shaped cookie cutters had cut out part of the heavens. He did his best not to think about anything, but even as he tried, the drag of time pulled questions through his mind. Eventually, this jungle excursion would end, and then what? He had definite feelings for Lenaia, but he had bigger issues to take care of first—like what would happen with his job.

The rope made an uncomfortable furrow between his

shoulder blades. He had stopped looking at his watch, but the sun appeared to be halfway down the sky already. Maybe they'd chosen the wrong area.

A hummingbird flitted over to a nest, rammed its beak in a few times and settled into the cocoon of twigs. Everything in this place had a home, except for him and Lenaia. And maybe the creature. Would the creature think of this place as home or would it rather be back in Tiernay's lab?

Of course! The lab. He grabbed the backpack, digging through it feverishly. Harmony had given him one piece of paper from Tiernay's lab—the log sheet for the creature. Hopefully, Lenaia had transferred it from his pack to hers when they'd gotten separated in the jungle.

He pulled out several more things before finally finding the paper in a back pocket. He was betting the creature had a well-developed sense of smell. Creeping forward, he placed it on the ground near the meat, then he crawled back to wait. Lenaia watched him, but said nothing.

Half an hour went by. He rolled onto his back again. Another half-hour passed.

The constant cry of the birds had started to lull him to sleep when Lenaia touched his arm and pointed to her ear. He held his breath and listened.

Off to the south, a snap of twigs breaking. A few second later, a snuffling sound.

He rolled onto his stomach as silently as he could. With both hands, he grabbed the rope, not putting any pressure on it to ensure the loop lay flat.

The snuffling sound came closer, zigzagging through the trees. He half expected a bloodhound to come into view any minute. Instead, the scaly snout hovered horizontally over the ground, one wide nostril huffing through the leaves while the rest of the animal stayed in the covering of the trees.

It snorted, taking deep breaths for a long time. Travis held his own breath, waiting, praying their scent wouldn't scare it away.

With a crash, the animal broke through the branches. Its rear legs propelled it quickly forward while the shorter front legs kept it balanced in a bent over position.

The creature went straight for the lab paper, bending over to sniff every inch. It pushed the paper forward with its snout, trapped it between its front legs and started to eat—the paper. Was this behavior a reflection of how it felt about Tiernay?

Lenaia grabbed Travis's arm, but he shook his head. He couldn't pull the snare yet. Only the creature's front legs rested inside the circle. If he pulled it now, the weight of the creature might throw it out of the trap. It wasn't worth the risk.

He waited, knowing he could be missing their only chance. The creature finished with the paper, hesitated briefly, then moved on to the tasty food in the center of the snare. Still, the hind legs remained outside the rope circle.

Agonizing minutes ticked by. The creature was almost done with the food, only a few bites remained.

It pushed the food forward with its nose as it ate, moving after it only when necessary.

The last bite ended up on the edge of the loop. The creature went after it and one hind leg fell within the snare.

Travis wouldn't get a better chance. Jumping to his feet, he took a wide stance, planting one foot in front and one in back. He pulled the rope with all his strength.

The rope went taut around the creature's leg. Its body swung up off the forest floor, howling and thrashing. It scratched at the trapped leg, but its small front legs couldn't reach the rope. Bending in half, it tried to reach the rope with its teeth, but couldn't quite get there. As it struggled, the rope swung it back and forth. Travis thought he'd lose his grip a dozen times, but he rode out the thrashing with a give and take on the rope, like riding the waves on a surfboard.

At last, the animal gave up and dangled there, snarling in frustration. He tied the rope to a nearby tree with a slip knot, the one knot he remembered from Cub Scouts, then he wrapped the rope around another tree and secured it with another slip knot. If the animal started flailing again, he didn't want to lose it.

From a safe distance, he approached the creature, circling to take in every inch. Scaled head with a rust colored fringe standing up like a Mohawk, feathers streaking down the ridge of the spine, short front legs or more like arms with three fingers on each. It looked exactly like an intermediate evolutionary form previously only captured by artist's imaginations in textbooks. If only he had any battery left on his phone for a picture.

He sucked in a gulp of air to calm his racing heart. *Breathe.* He had to breathe. This creature was terrifying and exquisite. So much like a therapod, the fast bipedal dinosaurs, like *Velociraptor*. A dinosaur, right in front of him! He'd longed to see this his entire life.

But was it really a dinosaur? Its genetic code would give him the answer. He crept closer. The animal had almost stopped struggling, probably due to the drugs. He waited a few more minutes. Its eyes blinked closed and stayed that way.

After a few more minutes, he picked up a stick and poked the creature in the ribs. It didn't respond.

Lenaia stood off to the side, eyes wide, mouth open. She didn't look afraid, but made no move to approach it.

Rummaging through the pack, he found the sample vials and nail clippers. When he turned back, the creature's jaw had gone slack and shallow rhythmic breathing came through its teeth.

He uncapped the vial with the six-inch-long Q-tip, careful not to touch the end. Using a stick to pull the skin away from its teeth, he exposed the inside of the cheek. He rubbed the swab around until saliva dripped off the end. With a satisfied smile, he shoved it back into the vial.

Now, for sample number two. The nail clippers scraped along the scales, which turned out to be as hard as steel. He changed his strategy. Using the clippers as a vice, he managed to pull a few loose and get them into the vial. He plucked a feather from the animal's spine and dropped it in, as well. Finally, he clipped one of the front toe nails and let it drop in.

He rolled the two glass vials up in a T-shirt to cushion them, then he tucked them into the zipper pocket on the inside of the pack. Lenaia still hadn't made a sound. He turned to where she was standing, but he didn't see her anywhere. Alarm bells went off in his head. She wouldn't disappear without saying something. Maybe she was feeling sick?

Movement to the left made him turn on his heel. The animal swung on the rope like a pendulum. It wasn't awake yet, but had stirred enough in its daze to set itself in motion. According to the doctor, they'd given it enough sedative to knock a cow out for an hour at least. This thing must have a higher metabolism.

He grabbed Lenaia's pack to see if they had more tranquilizer. The animal probably wouldn't eat any more now, but maybe he could dribble the powder into its mouth. He had to try something. He wasn't ready to let it go.

A shrill noise broke through the background of jungle sounds. At first, he thought it came from the creature, but its eyes were still closed.

The piercing noise came again, louder. A scream.
Lenaia!

CHAPTER TWENTY-THREE

Primal protective instinct drove Travis into the jungle. He slammed into several trees and vaulted a dozen bushes as he raced toward the area where he'd heard the scream. His outstretched hands kept most of the flying branches from breaking across his face. He pushed as fast as he could. No time to stop and think about what he'd do when he got there.

Pushing through a tall, dense fern, he almost tripped over Lenaia. At the last second, he jumped over her still form. Quickly spinning around, he dropped to the ground beside her. She lay perfectly still.

As he brushed the dirt, leaves, and hair away from her face, he saw it. A quarter-sized lump on her forehead, growing by the second.

She groaned and rolled, pushing her face into the dirt. He rolled her back and brushed her face off again.

"Lenaia, wake up. Talk to me."

She made a retching noise, like she wanted to throw up, but nothing came out. Her eyelids fluttered for a minute. When they finally stayed open, her eyes struggled to focus. She probably had a concussion. He lifted his eyes to heaven in relief. At least she was alive.

"What happened?" she whispered.

He tapped her temple on the other side of the lump. "I was going to ask you."

"Oh, yeah." She squinted. "I heard a noise close to where we were. I went to check. Someone grabbed me.

Then, pain." She touched the lump with tentative fingers and winced.

"Who did this?"

She thought for a moment like she only had temporary access to the memories. A groan escaped her lips. "The poachers. I saw one of them just before..."

His blood boiled with rage. They had come after her again, and this time he hadn't protected her. "They didn't hurt you anywhere else?"

"I don't think so. One of them said something like, 'Just business.' "

"Business?" Travis sucked in a breath, then let it out in a rush. "The creature."

She covered her face with her hands. "I was a distraction."

He gently pulled one of her hands away. "I'm glad they didn't do anything else."

She lifted onto her elbow. He supported her behind the back as she pushed to a sitting position. "Let's go see what they did."

"I'm not sure you can walk."

"Of course, I can."

He put an arm under her shoulder to help her to her feet. "Okay, then I'm not sure you *should* walk."

She took a few shaky steps. "I'm fine."

She actually seemed fine while walking, but he kept an arm on her because a few times she'd stop and sway like she was fighting through waves of dizziness. It took way too long to make it back. Finally, they broke through the trees to the area where they'd left the creature.

The snare lay on the ground, empty.

He left Lenaia sitting at the base of a nearby tree, while he went to investigate. "They cut the rope."

She pointed to the dirt beyond him. "I can see the tracks from here. They had some sort of wheelbarrow to take the animal with them."

"And probably more tranquilizer than we had." He threw the backpack down next to her and began to search through it. "They also took our machetes, the food, and the gun."

"What about your samples?"

He fumbled to unzip the front pocket. His fingers dug into the T-shirt to touch the glass vials. "They're here."

She pinched her eyes closed. Lines of pain stretched across her face.

"We need to get you back to the village," he said.

"No time. We have to go after the animal."

"Not with you hurt, we don't."

She grabbed his hand and locked eyes with him. "This animal is one of a kind. We can't let them take it."

At the intense look in her eyes, he hesitated. They had the samples. He could answer his questions about the origin of this creature, but what would happen to it? The poachers would probably sell it to a private collector who would cage it or butcher it as exotic meat. It didn't deserve to suffer at the hands of humans. Not to mention the science that would be lost if it disappeared.

Still, he knew where his priorities lay. He looked down at Lenaia. "I won't lose you just to save the creature."

"You won't. I'm okay."

He gave her a skeptical look.

"Yeah, my head hurts, but I can walk." She rose to her feet and stood more steadily than before. "I won't abandon this animal to those smugglers." Her voice held a determination he knew was pointless to argue with. She tapped a foot on the ground as if to give her words more weight.

He stood and moved in front of her until mere inches separated them. She was willing to risk herself to save what her uncle created because it was the right thing to do. Her strength constantly amazed him, or maybe courage was a better word. She thrust a hip out in a stance that said, "Don't argue with me." He didn't plan to. He had something else in mind.

Wrapping an arm around her waist, he pulled her flush with his body. Her eyes widened in surprise, but she didn't pull away. He ran a finger along her jawline. "Are you this brave in the real world or does the jungle bring it out in you?"

She gave a flustered smile. The first hint of weakness in her iron-clad shield. "In the real world I wander around volcanoes, which probably makes me crazy instead of brave."

"I'm starting to gain an appreciation for crazy."

He slipped a hand behind her neck. Her luminous amber eyes stared up at him, as radiant as a garnet crystal. His gaze traveled to her lips, parted just a bit. He drew in a slow breath. She smelled of citrus and fresh air, an innocent combination that somehow heated his pulse. They had danced around this attraction for too long. He wanted nothing more than to bring his lips to hers. But did she want the same or would he be taking advantage of a woman with a head injury?

As he debated, she responded, closing the distance between them. Her lips tentatively brushed against his, at once both soft and firm, stoking a fire within him. He captured her lips, deepening the kiss. With both hands, he caressed her face, savoring the moment of unguarded abandon. No questions. No fear. Just the two of them exploring this rush of feelings.

Her fingers ran through his hair, and he let out a low moan. His restraint was turning to ash as the fire inside kept building. But he couldn't bring himself to pull away. All he wanted was to extend this feeling for as long as possible.

Lenaia leaned back first, her dark eyes staring at him in shock, her fingers still entwined in his hair.

His heart pounded, still adrift in the rush that came from being this close to her. But she pulled away, so he relaxed his arms and let her go. They stared at each other, his gaze traveling between her lips and her eyes.

"I'm sorry," she said.

Sorry for pulling away or for kissing him? "I'm not."

"We probably shouldn't..." Her voice trailed off.

She meant sorry for the kiss. He took a step backward. How could she regret it? He'd felt the connection, a deeper fusing of the spark he'd felt since they first met. Surely, she felt it too. "You didn't want that?"

"Yes. I mean, no. It's not that simple." She hung her head. "I can't split my loyalty. Whoever I get close to has to love Jesus with their whole heart."

He closed the small distance between them again. Using two fingers, he tipped her head back up. "I love Jesus."

"I know you do. But you've got some things to figure out, things that affect your heart."

His hand fell to his side. How did his academic issue keep getting in between them? "I know I'm still not sure about the evolution thing. But you have to understand. I could lose my career."

"I understand more than you think. I lost *my* job, remember?"

"Lenaia, I've tried, but I can't seem to fight these doubts. Maybe if this creature turns out to be a hybrid of some sort..."

Lenaia stared at him, compassion pouring from her eyes and soaking into her voice. "But you're not even hoping for that. You're hoping it will prove evolution true, so nothing in your life has to change."

"I don't know what I'm hoping for anymore." He took a step back and lowered his voice. "But, yes, proving evolution true would solve a lot of problems for me."

"And it would create another one. How could you

trust the Bible if you don't have faith in it from the beginning?"

Her gentle objections triggered a memory. Like some sort of cosmic voice mail, Rusty's words from over a week ago came back. *It's a war between fear and faith.*

If this was a war within him, Travis would have to admit fear was winning.

Lenaia lowered her gaze. "You have to choose, Travis. Not for me. For you."

***

Mirabel sat on the warm concrete steps to her house, flipping a small envelope between her palms. An envelope full of money. Her mother said it was for "village improvements" and she needed to take it to Manuel this afternoon. She dropped the envelope in her lap and gripped the rough step with both hands, feeling the stone scratch at her palms. She'd delivered three envelopes in the last six months and had yet to see any village improvements. Not one.

She glanced up as Owen came out of the blue barn. He took a seat next to her. "What's up?"

His American greeting almost pulled a smile from her. He was much different from the young men in the village. He was free from the bonds of tradition and the need to please others. As an outsider, she knew he struggled with loneliness, even as she suffocated under the blanket of expectations draped over her. "I'm stuck at home because I promised my mom I wouldn't go near the jungle. Not even to Nina's tree."

He put his hands on the step and brushed his little finger against hers. "Well, I for one am glad you promised."

"But Travis and Lenaia went out there again today. They might need my help."

"And you could get hurt."

She sighed. He was right, but she didn't have to like it. "They shelter me too much."

He covered her hand with his. "Your parents are afraid to lose you, and not just through death. They're afraid you'll leave and never come back."

"But I haven't even told them I want to go to the university yet."

"You didn't have to."

She pulled her hand away and folded her arms, unable to keep herself from pouting. She scowled at his barely concealed smile. "She said I need to pray and find out what Jesus wants me to do."

"She's right about that."

"I know, but I feel like she wants me to be somebody I'm not."

He tugged her arms free and turned her toward him. "I understand. But having you around makes your mom happy." He ran a thumb down her cheek. "And me, too."

"Are you sure you're only seventeen? You're much smarter than the seventeen-year-old boys around here."

Smiling, he pointed to her other hand. "What's with the envelope?"

"I'm supposed to deliver it to Manuel." She remembered Manuel's warning to tell her friends to be careful in the jungle. Something wasn't right. "I have an idea. Maybe you could help me with it."

"What?"

"You'll have to indulge my curiosity."

"I'm in." He smiled, showing perfect white teeth and the dimple that made her stomach feel like she'd fallen from a tree.

Quickly, she explained the plan, and they walked down the street. As they neared Manuel's house, Owen ducked around the side to hide in the bushes. Mirabel approached the front door, a deep green wood that looked like it had been carved right out of the forest. Women decorated the doors in the village, and Manuel had never taken a wife, so his door was plain. Most of the village assumed he'd never found a woman good enough.

Mirabel knocked as loudly as she could, trying not to think of where Owen had concealed himself. Manuel's open windows would make it easy for Owen to watch and listen.

The door swung wide to reveal Manuel dressed in a bathrobe. He stared at her, running his eyes from her hair down to her toes.

She swallowed hard. "I, uh, I'm dropping off some money for village improvements."

He adjusted the tie around the waist of his bathrobe. "Ah, yes. Please, come in."

She hesitated. The other times she had dropped off money he hadn't asked her to come in. And she hadn't expected him to be in a robe, but at least she could see a T-shirt underneath. Instinct told her to flee from his hungry stare, but this might be her only chance to get him to talk. She stepped through the threshold into a wide living room. He circled around to shut the door behind.

The house had a nautical theme, and every wall held a reminder of the sea. A ship's wheel, a rudder, a painting of a whale, even a thick fishing net covered a wall, so much clutter she couldn't tell the color of the walls underneath. If Manuel wanted to feel like he was on a boat, he'd succeeded, although it certainly didn't feel homey.

"What improvements are you going to make for the village?" she asked.

He pointed at a navy blue sofa. She took a seat.

He sat down next to her. Too close. She shifted away.

"Oh, many. The whole village will enjoy them. Maybe even you."

"Like what?"

"I'm going to restore this village to its former ways."

What was he talking about? "Are you going to fix the roads or some of the buildings?"

"Not exactly."

"What are you doing then?"

"You'll find out, but not until it's done. It's a surprise. Do you like surprises?"

"Not really." She scooted a few inches farther from him, but she'd come to the end of the sofa.

He grinned at her, all teeth, like a jaguar. Instead of pursuing her, he reclined on the sofa. "How are your parents, Mirabel?"

"Fine."

"They're hoping you will find a nice Tico man, aren't they?" He reached over to run a hand along her arm. "Maybe you could talk me into telling you about the surprise."

This had gone places she hadn't expected. She stood, trying not to look at Manuel, and backed toward the door. "I have to go."

Letting out a long sigh, he swept his arm toward the door as if sweeping her away. "You know the way out."

She bolted from the house, walked down the street a hundred yards, then circled back to join Owen. The overgrown *heliconia* bush poked at her as she moved into position next to him. Thankfully, Manuel didn't concern himself with landscaping. From here, they could see in the open window and hear everything.

Rustling told her someone had entered the room above them. She saw wooden filing cabinets and the corner of a large desk. A minute went by before Manuel's voice rang out—loud, but staccato. "Yes, I've got the money."

A pause.

"Thank you for the discount on your services. This will work out well for both of us. And you are helping to preserve our Tico heritage."

A longer pause.

"Tonight if you can."

Manuel scribbled on a notepad.

"Sounds good. After that, the doctor will have to leave. He won't interfere with our business anymore."

A *thunk* as something was placed on the desk. Mirabel ducked her head in case he looked toward the window. She heard movement for a few more minutes, then nothing. She peered up into the window again. Manuel had left the room.

She looked over at Owen, her heart racing with the implications of what Manuel had said. So that was his plan for village improvements—to get rid of the white doctor.

But what exactly did Manuel have planned? Whatever it was, it would happen tonight, and she had to stop him.

CHAPTER TWENTY-FOUR

Mirabel paced back and forth in front of her porch steps. Owen had remained stubbornly mute since they had sneaked out of the bushes, but he had to be as angry as she was. She stopped to kick at a clump of dirt. One of their leaders was planning to get rid of someone in the village. She had suspected Manuel of stealing the money, but this was worse. Much worse. This could involve hurting people.

"My mom knew."

Owen put a hand up, palm facing her. "You don't know that."

"She's hated you from the beginning."

"She doesn't hate *me*. She hates that I'm interested in you." He moved to stand between her and the steps to the house. Why did he always have to be so reasonable? "Wanting a different life for your daughter and conspiring to drive someone out of town are two different things."

She weaved around him toward the house. "Well, I'm going to find out."

As she took the steps two at a time, a heavy sigh chased her from behind. "Fine. I'll wait here."

She threw open the door, startling her mother who jumped up from the rocking chair. A needle trailed thread down to a patterned skirt that rested on her lap. The sight of her mother mending dissipated some of her anger.

"Mom, I delivered the money to Manuel. Do you know what it's for?"

"I told you, village improvements, dear. Why do you ask?"

"What improvements?"

Her mother put a finger to her lips. "Well, I guess I don't know specifically. I assumed for the roads. We're getting a lot of holes."

"You didn't ask him?"

Her mother pursed her lips in the odd way she had of looking both disapproving and patient. "Señor Orosi is our treasurer. The people of the town have given him a position of trust. When he says the village needs money, then we know it will go to benefit the village."

Mirabel folded her arms and grabbed her elbows. At least her mother wasn't involved, but now she had to admit what she'd done. "Mom, I wanted to know what the money was for. After I dropped it off, Owen and I listened outside Manuel's window."

An uncharacteristic flash of anger raced across her mother's face, and then it was gone. Mirabel wished she could rein in her own emotions as easily.

"You spied on a village leader?"

Mirabel nodded, surprised at her own lack of shame. "Don't you want to know what we found out?"

"No." Her mother fumbled with the needle. A moment of silence went by. "I mean, yes. You must have a reason for coming to tell me."

Mirabel straightened her spine and stood to her full height. "Manuel is paying someone to force Dr. Gordon and Owen out of town."

"Are you sure?"

"We heard him talking on the phone. He said their plan would make the doctor leave. Manuel wanted it done tonight." The astonishment on her mother's face confirmed her mother's innocence, but still Mirabel had to ask. "Did you or dad have anything to do with this?"

The spark of anger returned, only to flee as quickly

as the first time. "Of course not. We might not approve of your fondness for Owen, but we wouldn't do that to anyone." She put the mending aside. "We need to talk to your father about this. He's down in the south pasture. Find him and tell him to come home right away. Don't tell him why. I don't want this discussed outside the house."

"Owen is the only other one who knows."

"Tell Owen we will talk with him after we have a family discussion."

"Shouldn't he go home and tell his father?"

Her mother twisted her hands together. "Yes, but no one else right now."

Mirabel went outside and told Owen to go home for now. After he left, she went in search of her father. Forty minutes later, she managed to pull him away from the sheep and get him back to the house. He didn't seem happy about the secrecy.

Once he shut the door, her mother filled him in on the situation. As she finished, she glanced at Mirabel. "I guess this is one time when asking questions turned out to be a good thing."

Mirabel smiled. In her own way, her mother had paid her a compliment.

"We don't know *what* they're planning?" her father asked.

Mirabel shook her head. "Manuel only said it would force them to leave the village."

Her mother put a hand on her father's arm. "We should go to the village council."

Mirabel shook her head again, and this time her father joined in. "The council will want proof before confronting Manuel," her father said. "They won't act before this evening."

"Then, we should go to Manuel and tell him we know what he's trying to do. Maybe he would call it off."

Her mother had never referred to a man by his first name before, which showed her disdain for Manuel and his actions. Mirabel couldn't help being proud of the breach of decorum.

Her father thought for a long moment. "If he calls it off, he'll probably reschedule it for a different time. Dr. Gordon and Owen will spend their lives wondering when something might happen." Her father shook his head again. A muscle twitched in his jaw. "No, this needs to be dealt with tonight."

***

The setting sun threaded light through the trees, making the tracking difficult, and even more so with her throbbing head. Lenaia stopped to catch her breath, placing her hands on her knees.

"Are you okay?" Travis asked.

As if he hadn't asked her every five minutes for the last hour. "I just need a minute."

Soon, darkness would close them into a black cocoon. Spending the night out here again wouldn't be her first choice, especially with the tension running thick between them, but they might not have any other option. Maybe she'd been too hard on Travis. She hadn't meant to push him. Nobody could be pushed into belief, but after that kiss, she couldn't deny that her heart had tumbled head over heels for Travis Perego. Was it wrong to hope he'd come to understand how seriously she took her faith?

Looking up from her bent over position, she caught a glimpse of something razor thin spanning the ground, six inches below eye level.

A trip wire.

She held her palms out flat to tell Travis to stay put. Crouching down, she followed the wire a few feet to an electronic sensor. This meant they were close to the poachers' camp. If they would have kept walking, the whole place would have known of their presence. Silently, she thanked God for protecting them.

Turning back to Travis, she pointed at the sensor, then high-stepped over it. If these guys had sensors, they probably had someone stationed as a perimeter guard. Mirabel had said this was a small operation of about four or five people, so if they made it inside the perimeter they could probably move about freely. She motioned for Travis to bend his head down, and she put her lips next to his ear. "We're close. They might have guards. No talking now, only whispering." She couldn't help breathing in the scent of him, an earthy smell that had replaced his long-faded cologne. As he straightened, she fought the urge to pull him back and continue their kiss from earlier. The stubble on his chin, the rumpled hair, the outline of his arm muscles through the sweatshirt, all tempted her to give in.

She turned away, glad for the coming darkness. At least she wouldn't have to look at him as much. They walked another hundred yards until the sound of voices in the distance made her stop. She motioned for Travis to go ahead. If they accidentally came upon the poachers, the men would be more intimidated if he came through the trees first.

As the last of the light faded, she watched the silhouette of his tall, lean form and wide shoulders push through the brush. Here and there, he turned to hold the large branches so they didn't fly back to smack her in the face.

She measured the time by each step forward they took, impressed by how Travis tried to move through the carpet of leaves quietly. Strange how the voices had seemed closer than this.

Travis stopped suddenly, and she threw her hands against his shoulder blades to keep from slamming into his back. Her fingers lingered longer than they should, slipping down to the small of his back before she pushed away fast. What was she thinking? Her hands reached up again as if they had their own agenda. She shoved them in her pockets. Hopefully, he hadn't noticed. The head injury was messing with her senses. Yes, it had to be the head injury.

In front, Travis crouched down and moved a low branch aside. She bent over at the waist behind him and looked above his right shoulder. They had come to the edge of a man-made clearing. A small shack made of spindly trees sat in the center. Smoke poured from a low chimney. Stumps from larger trees circled the shack like sentries. No noise came from the structure.

"Nice place. Looks like they put all their money into security around the perimeter," he whispered.

"What are we going to do?"

"Good question. I don't see the animal."

"If it's not here, then we won't be able to do anything until morning. I can't track in the dark, especially since they've got trip wires."

"Let's circle around and see what's in there."

She nodded. Circling the shack was a good plan, as long as the poachers didn't have any sensors or cameras around the building.

The two glassless windows on the front side looked as dark as the jungle. If people were inside, they were sleeping, and if the animal was inside, it was drugged. They moved along the front of the shack, keeping to the cover of the trees. No movement, no sound. The voices they'd heard hadn't come from here.

They rounded the other side with slow steps. No windows or doors here, just an uneven makeshift wall. Complete darkness finally lowered itself on the camp though it was hardly past six o'clock. Barely illuminated by moonlight, she followed the outline of Travis in front of her, feeling her way along the trees. He moved around a large tree, then lurched away from her. She crept forward, hands out until she found him. He'd stumbled onto a four-foot-wide path through the jungle, the entrance nearly invisible in the dark.

Loud voices, almost shouting, came from down the path.

And then, a deep, husky screech. *The creature.*

Travis grabbed her hand, tugging her along. At the end of the path, they found another clearing. She crouched behind him as they tried to stay out of sight. Miniature battery operated lights formed a glowing circle around several sets of animal pens. Not exactly cages. More like dog runs, the kind used by breeders. At least the pens didn't have any padlocks on them. These guys had probably never had anyone steal from them.

A few of the pens held small howler monkeys, one a sloth, another a tapir. But the activity was centered on the pen with the dinosaur-like animal in it.

Three of the poachers surrounded the pen, trying to get close enough to an exposed flank to stab the animal with a needle. The animal thrashed and screeched in a frenzy. The men cursed at it as if it could understand. A shiver forced its way down her spine when she recognized Christian, one of the men who had attacked her. He thrust the needle into the cage while the others tried to distract the animal. It turned around at the last second and snapped the tip of the needle off with its teeth.

"What do we do?" she whispered.

"Hope they can't inject it. If they get it sedated again, it won't do any good to let the creature out because we can't carry it."

"What if we used their wheelbarrow?"

"I could get it a little ways into the jungle, but we'd have to keep it out of sight until the creature woke up or they'd just take it back."

She tapped her teeth with her thumb. "We need a distraction so one of us can let the animal out."

"A beautiful woman would make a great distraction." A flush crept up her neck, and she was grateful for the covering of darkness. He reached up to squeeze her hand. "But I'm not willing to sacrifice you like that."

"Okay, so we need a different distraction..." Travis clamped a hand over her mouth, pulling her off the path, into the dense bushes. When he released her, she glanced back to see Tanol standing at the mouth of the path where they had just been.

Travis moved his body in front of hers, pushing them deeper into the tree cover. She fumbled for the pepper spray in her pocket.

But Tanol didn't show any sign of having seen them. Too lazy to walk over to the others, Tanol stopped at the edge of the clearing and shouted in Spanish. She easily translated the words, whispering them to Travis. "The rich Americano is coming to see the animal in the morning, then he'll probably take it out by boat. Hurry up and get it settled, because three of us still have to finish the job for Manuel tonight."

"We don't have much tranquilizer left to give it," Christian answered.

Tanol shook his head and rolled his eyes. "We'll get some tonight."

Lenaia leaned against a tree and peered out at the distressed animal in the clearing. These men probably didn't even know what they had, but the rich Americano would. They were going to take the animal on a boat in the morning. Problem was, in Costa Rica, morning could mean anywhere from the crack of dawn to lunchtime, which meant they had to get the animal out of here by sunrise. But how?

Maybe they could wait until the other three men left

on their errand, and then overpower the one left behind. Or maybe...

A yell came from Tanol. The three men in the clearing ran to the path, heading for the shack. Relief loosened her chest before she questioned what had made them leave.

Travis crept out first, looking in the direction the men had run. She joined him at the edge of the path. An orange glow formed a halo along the top of the tallest trees.

She ran down the path a few yards over a small rise. From this vantage point, she could see flames dancing up toward the heavens.

She ran back to find Travis gone. Walking slowly into the open, she found him at the pen that held the animal. He spoke to it in a soothing voice. It barely moved, staring at him warily. As she approached, it took one look at her and crouched into the corner, letting out a sharp hiss.

"I think the shack's on fire," she said.

Travis didn't look at her. "How?"

She grabbed the pin holding the lock in place and twisted it to the open position. "Your guess is as good as mine, but if you want this animal out we'd better do it now."

The crack of an explosion sounded in the distance. They both twisted around.

"The shack?" he asked.

"Maybe. Could be fuel tanks exploding."

Travis stood flat against the exposed wall of the pen. "Open the door and use it for cover in case anything goes wrong."

"What about you?"

"I'm sure it just wants to get away from here."

"Let's find out." She grabbed Travis and swung the door around in front, creating a small protected space for both of them. The animal bolted, heading straight for the trees. Its escape seemed certain. But then, ten yards from freedom, it halted. Its feet danced, and it dipped its head.

A figure stood outside the circle of light, only visible as a dark outline against the green leaves, blocking the animal's path. Along the person's right side, a skinny, circular shadow stuck out at an odd angle.

The barrel of a rifle.

CHAPTER TWENTY-FIVE

"Whoa." The anonymous figure spoke in a calm voice.

The creature shifted on its thick hind legs, no longer running, and yet still desperate to get away. It was stuck between the shadowy figure and the pen where Travis and Lenaia watched. Where had this guy come from? All the poachers had run down the path toward the flaming house. Unless this man was part of the perimeter patrol.

Travis pushed the door of the cage aside, then took a step in front of Lenaia, keeping his eyes on the gun. He wouldn't let her get hurt again. The person also moved closer, keeping the gun pointed at the ground, but his face still in the shadows.

From behind, Lenaia pushed into Travis's back. She slipped around his left side. "Uncle Jim?"

The man moved into the circle of light, and Travis recognized the shaggy mane of hair, the pointed chin, the glasses. *Tiernay.* At least now they knew who had set the fire.

"Lenaia? What are you doing here?" His voice sounded higher pitched than normal.

"What are *you* doing here?" Her voice rose until she was almost shouting each word. "What did you do?"

Tiernay opened his mouth, but instead of addressing her, he turned his attention back to the creature who continued to anxiously dance around. "Settle down, now, Rhea."

The creature cocked its head. It didn't settle down, but stayed put, watching and listening.

"It's okay," Tiernay said. "I thought this would be a safe place, but it's not. I'm going to take you home."

Travis stared, dumbfounded. Tiernay wanted to stick the creature back in a cage. After tasting freedom, it could never be content in a lab. "You can't lock it up again."

Tiernay looked at him, tilting his head as if he'd just noticed Travis. A wave of indignation swept across his face. "Who are you to tell me what to do with my creation? You aren't supposed to be here. Without Harmony's help, you wouldn't be here. Go home, Professor Perego."

How did he know about Harmony? It didn't matter. Travis swung around Lenaia and approached the creature. "I'm not going to let you take it."

"It's not your decision. Rhea is mine. Where were you when I created it?"

Lenaia yelled at her uncle. "Travis wouldn't have done this."

Tiernay didn't acknowledge the words, but they ripped Travis's heart into two halves. One wanted to claim her confidence for his own and agree he would never mess with God's creation in this way. But the other half knew the pitiful truth. He'd jumped on a plane to Costa Rica to test evolution, to test God. And he wanted this creature to be an evolutionary ancestor. He was willing to push his own agenda when it suited him. How was he any different?

Tiernay raised the gun to his shoulder and spoke in a smooth voice, his eyes locked on the creature. "It's okay. This will sting a bit, and then you'll sleep."

Travis sprinted for Tiernay. "Don't."

The creature let out a piercing shriek of alarm. Out of the corner of his eye, Travis saw the creature angle to face him and dig its back legs into the ground. With a sharp yelping bark, it lunged at Travis.

Tiernay shot.

And missed.

Travis dodged to his right, knowing he couldn't get out of the creature's path fast enough. His vision filled with the shiny, white teeth of a creature born only months ago. He closed his eyes, bracing for the impact.

A scream filled his ears, but it wasn't his own. A hit to the chest knocked him off his feet. Something fell on top of him.

The force of hitting the ground jarred his eyes open. Lenaia lay on his chest, her hair splayed across her face.

No sign of the creature. It must have run into the forest. Tiernay stood there, blinking rapidly, gun pointed at the ground.

Travis brushed the hair off Lenaia's cheek and felt a sticky wetness. A cranberry red stain covered his fingers. Blood.

"Lenaia?"

No answer.

He pushed to a sitting position, cradling her across his lap. He searched along her body for injuries. The bleeding seemed localized to her chest and the side of her head. She had stepped in front of him to take the brunt of the creature's attack. Why? It was his job to protect her, but he'd been worried about the creature. He swallowed down the rising panic. This was Lenaia's blood. And she'd already had one head injury today. Could she survive another?

Tiernay approached, his gun hung along the side of his left leg like a useless appendage. "Why did she do that?"

Travis shook his head, unable to answer.

The jungle stilled around them. Tiernay kept turning his head, especially conscious of the fact they couldn't hear the creature anymore. Travis took the end of his sweatshirt and began to wipe away the blood on Lenaia's cheekbone. He glanced up to see Tiernay backing toward the trees.

"Going to protect your precious scientific creation?" Travis yelled.

Confusion crashed in waves across Tiernay's face. On the edge of the forest, just before he would disappear, he opened his mouth to say something. The thick foliage swallowed him and whatever words he uttered.

"Come on, Lenaia. Wake up." Travis swallowed past the lump growing in his throat. "You have to be okay."

He pulled her close and kissed her forehead. Her eyelashes fluttered, skimming her cheeks, and then her amber eyes stared up at him. Her pupils contracted at the light. A good sign.

She tried to sit up, but moaned in pain.

"What hurts?" he asked.

One hand fluttered to the crown of her head as if searching for her missing ponytail holder, probably snapped by the force of the hit. "My head and..." She brought her fingers to her breastbone. "My chest."

"I think your chest took the biggest hit. And you have some gouges from the creature's teeth, but they don't look deep."

Down the path, he heard the distant chatter of voices. He turned to look. No one there, yet. "We can't stay here. Can you walk?"

"I don't know. Let me try."

"No time. I'll carry you."

He scooped her up. She clung to his neck as he sprinted into the jungle. The trees wrapped a blanket of foliage around them. For once, the jungle at night felt safe, or maybe just safer.

Behind them, shouts rang out from the clearing. The poachers had discovered the creature was missing.

No time to worry about trip wires or moving quietly. He needed to cover as much distance as possible and pray the poachers couldn't track them in the dark.

Branches whipped at them. He lowered his head,

thankful for his thick hair since he didn't have any hands to stop their assault. Lenaia kept her face and chest tucked against him, so at least he wouldn't add branch lashings to her list of injuries.

He moved southeast, away from the clearing, toward the village, doubling back a couple of times to make sure the poachers hadn't followed. Lenaia's wounds oozed blood onto his sweatshirt. She needed stitches and a place to rest.

About a quarter mile away, he slowed. He hadn't seen any sign of pursuit and didn't want to give the poachers extra noise to follow.

His arms ached from carrying her over the rough terrain. He'd have to take a break soon.

As he pushed his legs up the next hill, the ground shifted under his feet. He tripped and fell to the side, hitting his knee on something hard. A square stone. Balancing Lenaia on his left hip, he put a hand down to push off the ground. Instead of dirt, he discovered more stone—the crumbling part of a low wall, similar to the wall that had surrounded the old house where they'd spent the night. But if this wall had surrounded a house, it was long gone.

Crawling to the highest portion of the wall, he gently pulled her body away from his and laid her on the leaf carpet, her back supported by the stones. He sank down next to her and captured her hand in his. She didn't stir. Was she sleeping or going into shock?

CHAPTER TWENTY-SIX

Travis woke with an ache in his back from the rough stone. Lenaia's head lay on his shoulder. He rubbed the sleep out of his eyes, disgusted with himself. He shouldn't have fallen asleep. Lenaia needed help. He had to get her back to the village. A glance at his watch showed the time as after two o'clock in the morning. He'd slept for hours.

Slipping a hand around her shoulder, he felt for the pulse in her neck. Light, but fast. She stirred a little, then winced as she woke. At least, the wound in her shoulder seemed to have stopped bleeding.

"How do you feel?" he asked.

Lenaia held a finger to her lips to tell him to be quiet. She probably had a massive headache. Pushing off the stone, she tried to stand. He helped her by wrapping his arm around her waist. Once she was up, he let her go. She took a tentative step away from him before freezing in position, one ear turned to the forest.

A soft snort reached his ears. He gave her a quizzical look. She mouthed what looked like "wild pigs."

As he tried to decide if she was serious, a large brown snout broke through the leaves not far from his feet. On either side of the sniffing nostrils, two gray three-inch-long tusks protruded. The chunky body came through the curtain of leaves next. It had to be fifty pounds at a minimum.

The boar looked up, letting out a squeal of alarm that rivaled the sound of a bullhorn. More rustling and snorting sounds came from behind the animal. He gulped. There were more of them. One pig was a minor problem, a herd of pigs was a dangerous problem.

Two snouts poked through the foliage in between Lenaia and him. The original boar seemed to appreciate having backup. It dug its hoofs in the carpet of leaves, charging full speed at Travis. He jumped out of the way in time to watch the animal smack its tusks on the stone wall.

More pigs broke through the trees, lining up to attack. He felt a tug on his sleeve. "Up here." Lenaia had boosted herself up onto the four-foot-high stone wall.

He climbed up beside her just as another boar charged. The animal hit the stone wall and fell to the ground. He looked at her with raised his eyebrows. "Oh, the situations you get me into."

"Me? I think we've both had our share of issues in *this* jungle. And come to think of it, you had trouble before I came along."

He smirked. "If you're referring to my car, then you would be right."

She shook her head at him, but then shut her eyes at the pain.

He sat cross-legged on the short wall, then pulled her down to lean against him. The pigs roamed around in a circle, trying to find a way to get to them. They scratched at the wall, their tusks making noises like sandpaper on rocks.

"We'll have to wait them out," she said.

"How long will that take?"

She shrugged. "However long it takes. But I have good news."

"What's that?"

"It doesn't seem like this area is likely to erupt anytime soon." She tugged the gas meter off her belt. "It hasn't gone off once, and I'll bet the reports of smoke were from the poacher's cabin."

It was his turn to shake his head at her. Still working after what she'd been through. "Are you feeling okay?"

"Aching all over. I've got a wicked headache." She put her left hand on her upper chest. "And Rheasaurus did a number on my ribs."

"It still hurts?"

"Only if I breathe."

He put both palms up like the answer was obvious. "Well, then don't."

She scrunched her face, and he noticed her complexion had paled. He tugged her closer until she lay flat on the wall with her head in his lap. The pigs continued to grunt and stomp but they couldn't hit anything higher than three feet.

"Why did you do that?" he asked softly.

"What?"

"Jump in front of me."

"What was I going to do, let the creature attack you?"

"Yes. You've already had one head injury—"

"No lectures, please, professor. Hey, you saved me, now I saved you. We're even."

He brushed stray hairs off her face. "I know that's not why you did it. The creature could have mauled you to death."

"That did cross my mind."

"And you still did it."

"Look, it wasn't something I thought hard about. I didn't know what the creature would do, but I trust God to take care of me. Either He will work it out or He will take me home to be with Him. Both ways, I'm covered."

Shame pushed into his chest like lava pushing up from the deep. She trusted God without question, without hesitation, with her life. He couldn't even trust God with his job.

"How long have you been a Christian?" he asked.

"About six years. Since my second year of college."

"How did you come to know Jesus?"

"Well, I was dating this guy..."

"Whoa, maybe I don't want to hear this story."

She swatted at him. "It's not bad. The guy was a senior, almost ready to graduate, and a Christian. I don't know what attracted him to me."

He brushed a hand along her cheek. "I do."

She swatted at him again. "I was spunky and confident. No desire for anything to do with God. He brought me to church a couple of times. A vibrant church actually, but I remember being bored." She stared up into the leaf canopy. "I was head over heels for him, though. When he broke up with me, I thought I wouldn't survive it. And I had no idea why he did it. He said he had a piece of heaven inside of him, and I didn't. All I heard was that I wasn't good enough."

She took a shallow breath and pressed on her chest before continuing. "A few months later, a friend invited me to a different church. I'll admit, I went mostly to find out why that guy crushed my heart, why I wasn't good enough. The first couple of times confused me, so I kept going back until one day I heard a sermon on love. I found out God loved and accepted me as I am. It wasn't about being good enough." She smiled as Travis brushed a few hairs from her face. "To know God wanted me no matter what. Well, it made me want Him back."

Travis traced a finger along her lower lip, so soft and tempting. "Did you go find the guy afterward?"

"I ran into him a couple of months later. He'd already found someone else, but it didn't matter. I made my decision. I found a better love."

"And you trusted God? Just like that?"

"Yep. Living it out is harder than it sounds, but the

initial decision was easy. If God loves me, then I can trust Him. It doesn't get much simpler."

A *decision* to trust God? Somehow trust felt like something you earned, not something you decided. Which begged the question, if God couldn't earn his trust, then who could?

"You know, my head feels like it might explode. I think I'm going to ..." Her eyes rolled back just before they closed.

"Lenaia? Are you okay?"

She didn't answer. He shook her shoulder, gently at first, then harder.

No response.

He lifted one of her eyelids with his finger. Only the white part of her eye was visible. He gently touched the wound on her upper chest. Moisture came through the front of her sweatshirt again, but it didn't look like blood. He pulled down the top part of it to check. An angry red circle surrounded the bite, greenish pus oozed out.

Infection. She needed help, now.

Most of the pigs had started to move away. A lone male remained, sharpening its tusks on a rock in the stone wall. He'd have to chance it.

Her body flopped limply as he lifted her into his arms. He shifted to get his knees under her weight. Through his jeans, the rough stone dug into his skin. Using one leg, he pushed off the wall and rose to his feet.

The pig turned its head, squinting at him. He shuffled slowly sideways along the wall, ducking beneath hanging trees until he came to the corner.

The pig scratched a hoof in the dirt as it watched intently.

He inched back around the corner, placing one foot behind the other. He glanced behind with each step to make sure he didn't walk off the narrow structure.

Ten paces later, he ran out of stone. A mass of tall

ferns partially hid them from the pig, but the animal still stared warily at him. Nothing else he could do, except make a run for it.

As soon as his foot hit the leaf carpet, he heard the boar grunt and snort. Answering calls came from the jungle beyond. He had a good chance to outrun them from a distance, but first he needed to get away from this animal.

He sprinted into an area with dense leafy cover, holding Lenaia flat against his chest, to protect her from whipping branches. A thrashing sound from the vegetation behind told him the animal had given chase.

He dodged one way, then another, hoping to confuse the animal. On one zig-zag, he was too slow. The boar's tusk grazed his calf muscle.

He grunted through clenched teeth and kept moving.

The next time he pivoted, he made sure to get closer to the trees. The pig took another shot at his leg and missed. It knocked its head against a trunk. Travis paused to look back. The glancing blow slowed the pig down, but didn't stop it. He needed a new plan. He started to run again, still zig-zagging to keep the animal off balance.

Ahead, a thick wall of vines covered the space between two trees. That could work. He ran right up to it, swerving out of the way at the last second. The pig couldn't turn fast enough. It went into the tangled mess with a *thwump*. The ensnared animal bit and stabbed its tusks at the plants, but for the moment it was trapped.

Travis breathed easier and slowed the pace a bit. No need to risk falling into a ravine in the semi-darkness.

A few minutes later, he found a fallen tree trunk to rest on, one he could climb on top of if the boar came back. He pulled Lenaia away from his chest. Her head flopped limply to her shoulder, hair haphazardly tumbling from her cheek and neck.

He shifted her to a sitting position and rolled her head

onto his shoulder, smoothing her hair back. A smudge of dirt ran along her forehead. He rubbed it off with his thumb, noting that her skin had paled even more. Her coloring was almost as light as his now.

Sweat dripped into his eyes. He shifted Lenaia around so he could pull off his sweatshirt. He wiped his forehead with it while the cool night air eased the burning in his arms.

Another noise in the underbrush put him back on alert. A low snort. The branches on his left danced like puppets on strings. The boar must have gotten free.

He pulled Lenaia to his chest again and stood. As he backed away from the noise, his right heel dropped down to a lower elevation. He tripped, almost dropping her. Quickly, he recovered by stepping back.

As he tightened his hold on her, he looked around. The tree cover thinned to his left and right. He'd stumbled onto the game trail they had followed back to the village a couple of days ago. With fewer trees to block it, the moon lit up the area like a lantern in a mine shaft.

Another snort came from the trees in front of him. The branches rustled. He moved a few paces down the trail, ready to run, but still hopeful the pig would go in the other direction.

A long scaly snout with wide nostrils parted a cluster of leaves. Not a pig.

His breath caught in his throat. Rheasaurus. Definitely worse than a pig.

The creature's nose moved to the ground and began to sniff. More of its body pushed through the trees revealing the side-set eyes and thick neck. Its scattered feathers stood at attention from the base of its head past the portion he could see.

The professor in him soaked up every amazing movement. He had imagined a dinosaur would track this way—head sideways, the nostrils sweeping the ground, the eye on top scanning for prey--except this creature was tracking them. Survival instinct smacked him in the face. He backed away.

The creature pushed through the foliage until it stood at full height on the trail, slightly shorter than him. Its eyes focused on them like black laser beams. A gravelly snarl rumbled from its throat.

"Easy, boy." Or was it a female? He couldn't believe he was talking to it anyway. "We wanted to help you." Sliding his feet backward, he tried to put as much distance between them as he could. His arms shook with exertion and adrenaline, but he couldn't take a break now.

The creature crouched down, bared its teeth and let out another snarl. A crazy impulse hit. He wrapped an arm around Lenaia's back, bent at the waist, and snarled right back.

The creature shifted on its feet. Maybe this was working. He yelled in his loudest, most Viking-like voice. "Argggggghhhhh!"

Confusion flashed through its eyes, but only for a second. He had to try something else.

A wet drop hit his face, then another. Rain. He scowled up at the heavens. Of course, why not make this situation more difficult?

As the raindrops came faster, the creature also looked up at the sky and blinked, but soon refocused on him. It leaned forward, tensing its back legs. At any second, it would attack and kill them.

Lord, I need some help here. An idea came to him, but for it to work he needed another distraction. Hooking his foot around a large stick lying next to the path, he arched back and soccer-kicked it at the creature. The stick flopped end over end, causing the creature to hop backward and hunker down.

Travis turned and ran as hard as he could without

slipping. When he reached his destination, the rain might actually be a blessing in disguise.

The game trail twisted and turned like he remembered from yesterday. He heard sounds of pursuit, but didn't dare use up precious seconds to look behind. Around each curve, he searched the trail up ahead for their salvation.

After three turns, the panic burned acid into his throat. Had they come out farther down the path than he thought?

Around the next turn, the path narrowed. It seemed familiar, but he wasn't sure. The creature crashed through the bushes, not far behind. He shifted Lenaia to his shoulder and held back a large branch. Ducking below it, he held it for a second longer, then let it fly. A whack like a bursting watermelon told him he hit the mark. It would slow the creature down, but probably not stop it.

Finally, it came into view. The massive wood tree dam. He picked up his pace.

Holding Lenaia tight against his right shoulder, he swung wide toward the left side of the dam, needing a clear shot at the entrance to the blind. At the apex of the turn, he tucked Lenaia's head under his chin and did a baseball slide into the foliage. Branches tore at his shirt and bare arms, but the slippery leaves carried them several feet inside.

He froze, lying still and silent with Lenaia on top of him, trying to resist the urge to slide farther in. Any noise could draw the creature's attention. The blind had no way out except back the way he'd come. Hiding was their only option. He risked a quick glance. He'd slid in far enough to be partially hidden.

Through an open mouth, he drew short quiet breaths. As his heartbeat slowed in his ears, he heard snuffling sounds on the trail. The creature came near the opening once, its shadow causing him to hold his breath, but it didn't linger long. Just as he'd hoped, the rain hadn't yet washed away their scent from yesterday going over the tree dam, and the creature was confused by it.

Minutes of silence ticked by. No snuffling. No movement. Had it left?

He leaned back to capture Lenaia's face in his hands. Small breaths still filled her lungs. He touched her neck and found her pulse. Weak and faint.

Just as Travis was about to stir from the hiding place, the cracking sound of splintering wood froze him in place again. The noise came in staccato bursts. The creature was going over the dam.

The cracking turned to rolling, like pool balls knocking together, followed by complete silence. And yet, the silence told him the creature was still out there. No bird calls, no chattering monkeys, as if every animal in the forest showed this creature respect.

Travis continued to wait. When the songs of the birds returned, he decided to risk a peek out of the blind. Clutching her to his chest, he scooted backward and poked his head out.

The tree dam lay scattered along the trail. Logs had rolled ten yards away. A few remained in the center, but now the dam stood only two feet high.

He climbed out, pulling Lenaia with him. Beyond the ruined dam, the game trail beckoned him. Following it would be a faster way back to the village, but he turned in the other direction. Better to go the long way around than take the chance of running into the creature farther down the trail.

He prayed Lenaia could hang on a little longer.

CHAPTER TWENTY-SEVEN

Mirabel fiddled with a rock as she sat on the front porch waiting for news. Either news from Owen or from Travis and Lenaia, it didn't matter. She just wanted to know what was happening. Travis and Lenaia had been gone all night again. And Owen had come to give her the last update from their house several hours ago. A shiver streaked down her spine when she thought of Owen, Gordon, and her own father sitting in the dark, weapons ready, waiting for trouble. Maybe nothing would happen. *Please, Lord, don't let anything happen to them.*

A seed of hope blossomed in her heart. If the night passed quietly, perhaps they could go to the council today to ask for an investigation into Manuel's activities. Perhaps they could find out why a respected member of the community would be willing to pay somebody to come after Gordon and Owen. It had to be prejudice. It was so confusing how hate could live deep in the core of some people, while others barely noticed the color of skin.

Or could it be for a different reason? Manuel had said his business would improve when the doctor was gone. That implied Manuel had a business other than his position as treasurer. The only business in this area Gordon had threatened was the animal smuggling operation. Maybe Manuel's motives were financial.

A loud grunt from the tree line grabbed her attention. She jumped up from the steps, giving a gasp when Travis burst out of the jungle carrying Lenaia limp in his arms. Her heart thumped wildly in her chest.

Travis raced toward the house, but Mirabel stopped him. "Take her to the barn. The doctor stores most of his medical supplies in there. If she needs something, it will be in there or at Dr. Gordon's house."

She ran ahead of him to hold open the big wooden door, then, she directed him to a clean cot in the corner. As he laid Lenaia down, Mirabel noted her ashen face, the blood on her sweatshirt, her shallow breathing. "What..."

"The creature bit her." Travis grabbed handfuls of his hair and tugged like he would rip it all out. "I thought she was doing okay. One minute, she was talking to me, the next minute, she passed out."

Mirabel briefly placed a comforting hand on his shoulder before turning her attention back to Lenaia. She lifted the edge of Lenaia's sweatshirt and the top of her underlying shirt to peek at the wound. A ring of necrotic tissue surrounded the bite, possibly from infection, but it didn't look right. Perhaps it was something else. "She needs the doctor now. I'll go get him."

As she raced out of the barn and down the street, the first tendrils of dawn chased after her. She feared what she would find at Gordon's house. The men were going to take turns keeping watch with Owen doing the last shift. Hopefully it was all still quiet.

At the last house before theirs, she slowed her pace. Her gaze swept over the house, then the jungle in the backyard. Movement in the trees caused her feet to freeze.

She remained motionless, focusing her eyes on that part of the tree line. There it was again. A tree branch moving up and down in slow circles. It could be a bird or even a snake sliding through the trees.

She turned away, blinked a couple of times, and

refocused on the same spot. Her eyes caught a familiar shape near the forest floor. Beneath a clump of bushes, the rounded toe of a brown boot poked out.

Her heart pounding an erratic drumming beat, she closed the distance to the front door. She opened it silently, slipping into the darkness inside. "Owen, they're here," she whispered.

As her eyes adjusted, she saw Owen standing at the rear window with his back to her. He gave a small nod. He'd seen the man too.

Gordon rose from the floor, instantly wide awake. Maybe he hadn't been sleeping after all. "Positions everyone."

What did this mean for Lenaia? Gordon had to go help her.

Owen backed up until he stood in the living room near her, partly sheltered by the wall, but with a clear line of sight through the house. He trained his gun on the back door.

Her father took a position at the door of Gordon's pharmacy, housed in the laundry room right next to the back door. From there, he could surprise the intruders as they opened the rear door toward him. He picked up a sawed-off two-by-four before glancing back at her. "Mirabel, you need to get out of here."

Mirabel grabbed Gordon's arm. "Lenaia's hurt. She needs a doctor immediately."

Gordon tightened his brow and pursed his lips until it looked like his face had been shrink-wrapped. "Okay. We'll come as soon as we can. Take care of her until I can get there. But before you go, wait near the front door for a minute. Make sure they are targeting only the back before you take off and run."

Gordon ducked behind the kitchen counter, his gun within reach on the floor. In his right hand, he held a canister of pepper spray, in the left, a squirt bottle full of vinegar.

Mirabel took a shaky breath. No one would shoot, except in self-defense. The goal was to drive the intruders away without any injuries, but they didn't know what the intruders had planned.

Her eyes fell on Owen, rifle resting on his shoulder, sight trained on the back door. A damp patch of sweat darkened the back of his shirt between his shoulder blades. Surely, it made him more nervous knowing he had to protect her as well. She needed to get out as soon as she could.

The wooden boards of the house creaked in the mild wind from outside. Every noise increased her tension. If only they knew if these men were trained assassins or day laborers looking for extra money. She had no idea, and not knowing was the hardest part.

The lock on the rear door released with a click.

An eye and a man's dirty cheek peered through the crack of the door. Below it, a gun appeared. Mirabel shifted away, closer to the front door. The man's dark eyes focused on her from across the house. It was one of the poachers.

Owen shot her a glance. "Mirabel, get behind me."

As she slid over, the man pushed the door open a little farther. Her father swung the two-by-four into the man's forehead. A sickening thud. The man went down to his knees. The gun dropped to the floor, spinning toward the kitchen.

Her father shoved the door with his foot, trying to close it and push the man out, but a kick from the outside forced the fallen man's body back into the house.

Owen slid his finger onto the trigger, but kept his frozen position.

Her father raised an object toward the new intruder's face. The whoosh of a pepper spray discharge hit her ears shortly before the residual smell. She threw an arm over her mouth and nose. Several loud curses echoed through the small house, followed by stomping. Mirabel's eyes went wide. The man was forcing his way in despite their efforts.

Owen yelled at her without turning his head. "Get out of here. Now!"

She hesitated for only a heartbeat. There was nothing she could do to help them, and if Gordon couldn't come right now, then Lenaia needed her. With one last glance at Owen and her father, she threw the front door open and ran.

***

Travis knelt beside Lenaia and draped a thick horse blanket over her still form. Grabbing a handful of straw, he placed some under her head for a pillow. He shook out his arms, which burned from carrying her all the way to the village. She hadn't awakened, even once.

Her lovely face rested peacefully like a statue carved from pure marble. She was perfection, except for the angry red wound in her chest and the blood on her forehead. He brushed the matted hairs away, but then quickly pulled his hand back. She wasn't just feverish. She was burning.

Where was Mirabel with the doctor? He folded the blanket down to Lenaia's waist, fully unzipped her sweatshirt, and slipped her arms out. Feeling a bit like he was invading her privacy, he unbuttoned the front of her Henley shirt to expose more of the wound. Two slashes with a mark next to them, probably from a tooth. He could try to clean it, but whatever he found in the barn might not be sanitary. Better to wait for the doctor.

He pulled the blanket back up to her chest and tucked

it tight around her. Mirabel had said it would help with the shock.

A line of sweat dripped down Lenaia's brow. He snagged a towel from a nearby work bench and mopped it off her forehead, then he ran the rag over her hair.

Behind him, the barn door groaned on its rusty iron hinges. He jumped up, expecting the doctor or at least Mirabel. At the sight of the man standing in the doorway, his stomach clenched like he'd swallowed a bucket of rocks. "Why are *you* here?"

Tiernay looked over as if startled. He didn't answer. His gaze roamed around the barn for a minute, before falling on Lenaia.

Travis moved to block his view. "Did you lose your precious animal?"

Still no response.

Travis grunted in disgust and turned his back on the man. "You shouldn't be here anyway," he said over his shoulder.

"I was looking for supplies. I didn't know you would be here." Tiernay approached until he was standing just to the left of Travis's shoulder, staring down at Lenaia. Travis glanced up. Tiernay's face was a mixture of pity and curiosity. "Is she okay?"

"You care so much now?"

"She's my niece." Tiernay jabbed at the ground with his rifle. "I had a plan for freeing Rhea. If you two wouldn't have interfered, no one would have gotten hurt."

Of all the cold-hearted, arrogant things to say... Travis whipped around and punched Tiernay in the jaw. Tiernay crumpled to the ground. Travis stood over him, surprised that he'd punched the older man, and even more surprised that it hadn't made him feel better. "If you cared about her, why did you run off into the jungle instead of helping?"

Tiernay peered up at him, fear and defiance warring in his expression. He obviously wasn't used to being confronted. "I assumed you would get her the help she needed. Letting the animal get away would have only made her efforts worth nothing."

"Her efforts? We were trying to let the creature go."

Tiernay groped for the gun that had fallen to the ground. He picked it up, shifted his weight to his knees and stood. "Well, of course. We couldn't leave the animal in the hands of those poachers."

Now, the arrogant jerk had grouped the three of them together as "we." "Why can't you just leave the creature alone?"

"I thought I could originally. I was naïve, and you must know it pains me to say that." Tiernay ran a hand lovingly down the gun. "I lied to conceal it, Perego, and yet you still found out about it. As long it exists, people will find it. I've realized it won't be safe anywhere except my laboratory."

"You think you can control it?"

"I made it. Controlling it is my responsibility."

"You mean you want credit for creating it."

Tiernay tugged on the ends of his unruly hair. "The animal is not what you think it is."

"How do you know what I think?"

Tiernay did his best to cross his arms while still holding the rifle. "Harmony couldn't tell you what it is because she doesn't know."

Travis wrestled with the urge to punch Tiernay in the mouth again. His niece lay on the ground fighting for her life, and he only cared about the creature. And yet, Tiernay had the answers. The answers Travis wanted. No need to analyze samples, he could find out right now if this journey had been worth it.

But would learning the origin of the creature really change things? Lenaia's faith wouldn't be shaken by anything she learned about it. Travis knelt next to her again. A minute of silence ticked away, the faint noise of her shallow breaths filling the barn.

"You came to Costa Rica to find this creature, and you're not going to ask me?"

Travis didn't take his eyes off Lenaia. No, he wouldn't ask. He had the samples if he needed to know.

Tiernay came closer until he leaned over Travis's back. "Hate to disappoint your paleontologist alter-ego, but looks can be deceiving." Tiernay drew out the last word, almost like bait. Travis didn't respond. "Rhea is not an ancestral form. She's not a dinosaur."

"So a hybrid then?"

"Of a sort. I spliced in DNA from more things than you would think. Obviously, bird DNA since we used a rhea embryo, a little bit of crocodile to get the hands and tail..."

Travis looked down at Lenaia's immobile body. She had liked the name Rheasaurus, but if that thing wasn't a dinosaur, the name didn't fit. He turned to focus on the empty doorway. What was taking Mirabel so long?

"... jaguar for the teeth and long snout, and of course, a snake to get the scaling. Even a zebra to beef up the hindquarters for running. A rhea's hind legs are spindly. It took me months to figure out where to splice the DNA to get the desired results, but that's not the truly astonishing part. The creature isn't just a hybrid."

He tilted his head up to look at Tiernay. "What did you say?"

"Oh, now, I have your attention." Tiernay smiled like a five-year-old who'd finally gotten his way. "As soon as I put this particular embryo under the microscope, I knew something was different. Some of the cells had mutated. I still haven't figured out how it happened. Harmony must have done something by accident."

"Mutated? Are you saying this creature is a hybrid mutant?"

"Yes, two of the genes had mutated."

How was it possible? Mutations usually caused the embryo to be less viable. It was amazing the creature had developed at all. "But mutations are almost always harmful."

Tiernay's face fell. "And these are, as well. The mutations didn't give Rhea any new functions. Instead, the animal has a form of high blood pressure coupled with a valve problem in its heart."

"You knew." Travis sat back on his heels. "You knew the DNA had mutated, and you still let it grow. Why?"

Tiernay moved a step back. "When I saw the embryo, all divided and perfect despite the mutations, I had to know if it could keep growing. And when it did, I had to know if it could survive."

Travis turned away. He couldn't look at Tiernay any longer. The distorted image of a man desperate to know, desperate to push the envelope of science, felt a little too familiar. At the beginning of this trip, desperation drove Travis on a similar quest for knowledge, but it hadn't satisfied him. Even the answers Tiernay had given didn't penetrate Travis's heart. But he finally understood why. Knowledge itself didn't bring life. Life was a gift—a gift from the Creator.

Now, he was only desperate for God to protect the gift of life in Lenaia. He leaned over to brush a kiss on her forehead. As he pulled away, her eyes opened. They roamed the room randomly for a few seconds before settling on his face. "Travis?"

"I'm here."

She smiled at him. But when she saw Tiernay behind him, her expression hardened. "Uncle Jim, why?"

Tiernay looked blankly at them both.

Her faced pinched tight. She took a slow, shallow breath. "Why would you take God's place?"

As the last words left her mouth, her head rolled back, limp. She'd passed out again. Travis gently shook her by the shoulders. "Lenaia?"

"What did she mean?" Tiernay asked.

Travis glared up at him, making no attempt to hide his disgust. "What do you think she meant? You played God by creating a creature that shouldn't be here."

Tiernay huffed out a breath. "Well, why didn't her god stop me if he was so concerned?"

Travis didn't have a good answer for that one. "I'm sure He had His reasons."

"Oh no, you're a Bible thumper too? I thought you were a scientist."

"I am."

Tiernay shook his head. "Not a serious one if you believe some god had any part in this."

Travis sucked in a breath as he rode out another wave of anger. He believed God was in this somehow, but after all his doubts, he didn't feel like he should speak for the Almighty just now. An uncomfortable silence filled the barn.

A few moments later, Mirabel rushed through the open barn door. Travis jumped up, running to her. "Where's the doctor?"

She shook her head. "They're under attack. Owen made me leave."

"What do you mean under attack?"

Moisture darkened her eyes. "Someone in the village is trying to run them out of town."

"Why?"

"I don't know."

"But we need the doctor now."

Without asking, Travis spun around and grabbed Tiernay's rifle. To his surprise, Tiernay pulled a pistol off his waistband. "Wait. That's the tranquilizer gun. Take this one."

Travis nodded, took the pistol, then turned to face Mirabel. "Where?"

"On the main road, second house from the end, on the right."

As he ran out of the barn and down the street, the only sound came from his boots slapping the gravel. The street was too quiet. At the house Mirabel had indicated, he slowed to a walk. Muffled grunts came from the rear of the house. If they were under attack, he should sneak in the front to ambush the intruders.

Holding the pistol out, he gingerly stepped up the single stone step and eased the door open. The first person he saw was a panicked Owen aiming a rifle at his chest. Then, relief lit in Owen's eyes, and he turned the gun toward the back door.

Two men lay on the ground, a dark-bearded man who sat rubbing his eyes and another who lay flat. Travis ignored the bearded man, instead focusing on the one who was unconscious. He looked familiar. Travis took a step closer to get a clear look at the face. His chest muscles constricted. It was Christian. Were the poachers still looking for the animal? Or was this the other errand they had mentioned?

Tears drained into the sitting man's beard, but he seemed to be regaining his senses. He turned to yell out the back door. "Tanol, get in here. Christian is down."

Travis's heartbeat crashed into his ears. Not Tanol. He was the worst and the smartest of the bunch.

The bearded man jumped to a squat, lunging at Mirabel's father and thrusting them both into the laundry room. A thick crack of breaking shelves. The tinkle of glass crashing to the ground.

In the open doorway, Tanol appeared with a pistol in

his hand, his stringy hair whipping around as he scanned the hall for targets. "Jorge? Where are you?"

Tanol stepped over Christian and pushed the door open wider. His searching eyes locked onto Travis, freezing him in place. Recognition lit up Tanol's face first, then the furrowed brow of determination. He lifted the weapon in halting bursts, like a defective toy soldier.

The rifle in Owen's hands bucked. A loud boom pierced Travis's ears.

Tanol let out a scream and grabbed his thigh. He swayed on his feet for a second before he fell, managing to squeeze the trigger of his pistol on the way down. Travis ducked as a stray bullet lodged in the molding above his head.

Tanol didn't stay down for long. Dragging his injured leg, he scrambled out the door backward. Travis gulped in a breath. Two poachers down. One in the laundry room. Where was the other one?

Only crunching sounds came from the laundry room now. Gun ready, Owen moved down the hall toward the laundry room. Travis mirrored his steps as quietly as possible.

When Owen swung into the doorway, Travis peered over him. Jorge held Pedro from behind, one arm wrapped around his neck. Pedro gagged and clawed at the constricting muscles. Glass from broken vials of medicine shattered and crunched under their feet.

"Let go." Owen's commanding voice surprised Travis. This kid wasn't a typical teenager.

Jorge gave one last hard squeeze, then released his hold. Pedro slumped to the floor, gasping for air.

"Take your men and go." Owen slid the bolt on the rifle, chambering a round.

Jorge put his hands in the air, but didn't move. He squinted his eyes at the gun as if he didn't think Owen would shoot.

"Now."

Jorge walked sideways out of the laundry room with Owen's gun trained on him, almost like they were dancing. At the threshold, Jorge grabbed Christian, who had started to stir, and pulled him to his feet by the shirt collar. They took a step out the back door.

As soon as they cleared the threshold, Owen lowered his gun and raised a foot to kick the door closed. It swung halfway, then stopped, blocked by a dropped walkie-talkie. He kicked the device out of the way, then pushed the door again with the side of his boot.

The door had almost closed when Tanol jumped out from the side of the house. He kicked the door open, at the same time rotating his arm up. In less than a second, Tanol had a gun pointed at Owen.

"No!" Travis jerked his pistol sideways, pulling the trigger without thinking.

The crack of a shot split the air, echoing down the hallway.

Tanol fell to the ground outside, clutching his chest.

Travis turned from him to focus on Owen who was running his hands over his own body. No blood. No wounds.

The roar of an engine reached the house. Jorge and Christian had taken off into the jungle, leaving their partner's body in the backyard. Tires squealed in the distance.

Travis let out a relieved sigh. The fourth man must have been hiding as the getaway driver. The assault was over. His hand began to shake so he laid the gun on the kitchen table. Ignoring Tanol's body outside, he stepped in front of Owen to shut the back door.

When Travis turned back, Owen grabbed him by the shoulders. "Thank you. He would have killed me."

Travis gave a breathless nod.

Gordon walked Pedro into the living room. "You'll

be sore for a while." He tapped the skin next to a large gash in Pedro's arm. "We need to clean your cuts to make sure there's no glass in them."

Travis grabbed Gordon by the shoulders. "Doctor, Lenaia needs you. Right now."

Pedro waved his hand. "Go. I'm fine."

"I'll take care of him." Owen held up his gun as if to say he could do the job.

"Okay, come get me if you have any problems."

The doctor followed Travis out of the door and down the street. As their feet pounded the dusty gravel, the echo of that last gunshot pounded on Travis's heart. He'd shot someone. He bit down hard on his bottom lip. No, he hadn't just shot Tanol, he'd killed him.

CHAPTER TWENTY-EIGHT

Tiernay clung to the wall of the barn as if it had the power to hold him up. After Travis had gone to get the doctor, another woman had come in to help the girl named Mirabel. This woman was older, but beautiful in a long flowered dress with dark hair pulled off her face into a barrette. He tried to stay out of their way as they tended to Lenaia.

"Mom, can you get me two rags and a bucket of cool water?" Mirabel asked. "Her fever is high. We need to keep her forehead cool and clean some of this blood away. I can't see what we're dealing with or why she might have passed out." Mirabel placed her fingers on Lenaia's wrist. "Her pulse is rapid."

He should go and let the women handle this. Lenaia was young and strong. She would be fine. He looked at the door, but couldn't seem to make his feet move.

Mirabel's mother left, coming back a short time later with a sloshing bucket of water. She rushed around, doing what her daughter directed. Working quickly, Mirabel cleaned out the gouges left by the creature's teeth. The girl was a natural healer. From the awed expression on her mother's face, she must have sensed the same thing.

When the wound was dry, Mirabel covered it with a clean cloth. She held a cool rag on Lenaia's head and began to whisper softly in her ear. It took a moment before he realized she was praying. What a waste of time. Lenaia would disagree, but where was her God now while she suffered? An unexpected flash of guilt ambushed him. He couldn't blame the universe for this one. It was actually his creature that had hurt her.

Mirabel's mother came over to him. "Can I get you anything? You don't look well."

"No. I'm fine."

The woman nodded slowly. "Mirabel will do what she can. The doctor should be here soon."

A few seconds later, Travis ran in, followed by an older man who headed straight for Lenaia. Probably Dr. Gordon, Tiernay thought.

Travis closed the door, then moved to pace behind the doctor, stirring up billows of hay. Tiernay flattened himself against the wall, trying to remain invisible. No need to risk another violent confrontation.

Gordon pulled the cloth off Lenaia's forehead and tested her temperature. Next, he took her pulse with two fingers. He huffed out a breath before dipping the cloth back in the bucket and returning it to her forehead.

This was one of the few times Tiernay wished his doctorates in genetics and molecular biology had come with more medical training.

Carefully peeling back the cloth layer on Lenaia's chest, Gordon bent over to get a closer look at the bite. A few seconds later, he turned to address Mirabel. "You cleaned it?"

"Yes. Only with water."

"Good." Gordon swiveled his head to look at Travis. "When did you say the attack happened?"

"A few hours ago. Six hours at the most."

Mirabel circled a finger around the edge of the wound. "Something is not right. Her pulse if very high and this looks like decaying tissue."

"My thoughts as well," the doctor said. "This is much too fast for an infection. The only thing I know of that could cause tissue damage so quickly is poison."

Immediately, Tiernay was caught by Travis's stormy gaze. Tiernay recoiled.

They thought he knew something. But what would Rhea have to do with poison? He sucked in a quick breath as a likely possibility dawned on him. "It hadn't occurred to me until now..." Tiernay shifted his body parallel to the door. He might need a quick escape after this confession. "But there's a small chance the animal could be venomous."

"Venomous?" Travis clenched his fists.

Tiernay eyed him and took another step toward the door. "To get the correct amount of scaling, I used some coral snake DNA."

Travis covered the ground between them in one stride. He grabbed Tiernay by the arm. "You did what?"

Tiernay tried in vain to pull away. "I just said there's a chance. I'm not even sure the animal *is* venomous. The DNA was placed on a different part of the strand, far from the portion responsible for the salivary glands."

"But you never checked before releasing it into the wild." Travis stalked away, and Tiernay rubbed his aching arm.

"Let's calm down." The doctor growled from Lenaia's side. "I don't need more work caused by you two fighting. I have antivenin for the coral snake. At least, I think I do. A lot of my pharmacy was damaged in the attack. Mirabel, I'll stay with her. You go search through the damage for it. The vial should say 'Elapidae Antivenin.' Have Owen help you."

Mirabel nodded and charged out the door, leaving it open as she left. Lenaia stirred, causing Travis to drop to her side. Tiernay saw a chance to escape before they came to blows again.

Tiernay slipped out the door and closed it quickly, as if Mirabel had done it when she left. Now that Lenaia was in good hands, he could search for the animal again.

From the way it had acted earlier, he suspected it had imprinted on him. He walked to the middle of the dirt road and scanned the foliage at the edge of the village. If he stayed in one place long enough, perhaps it would find him. But he needed to be out in the open where it could catch his scent.

The midmorning mist blurred the line of trees into a single green mass. No movement. Not even a breeze.

He turned and watched as Mirabel entered a house down the street. When he turned back to the trees, he let out a little gasp. Rhea bobbed up and down just on the other side of the stone wall.

A rush of feelings pulsed through him, the sensations jumbling together. Relief. Love. Or maybe possessiveness. Definitely not fear. Even knowing the possible danger, he couldn't be afraid of his own creation. The animal had never acted aggressively toward him. She moved in a halting gait, coming slowly through the open part of the wall, inching closer to him, and closer to the ground. She kept lowering her body until she lay about ten feet away.

Soft gurgling noises came from her throat, almost like a feline purring. "Oh, good girl."

He took slow steps toward her and knelt down, so only inches separated them. She nudged his knees with her snout. He stretched a hand out and rubbed the scales above her nose, then the ridge between her eyes. He smoothed back the feathers along her spine. A magnificent creature, even if not a dinosaur.

"Last night, you thought Professor Perego would hurt me, didn't you? You were only trying to protect me." Rhea laid the tip of her snout on his lap. He listened to her fast breath, like the quick pulse of modern birds. "Well, now I get to protect you."

Rhea closed her eyes. He glanced down at his empty hands, cursing under his breath. He'd left the tranquilizer gun in the barn. If Travis came out or Mirabel came back,

Rhea would probably run away. He dug in his pocket for the strap from the gun. Maybe he could fashion a leash?

A high speed whizzing sound streaked past his ear. Then another, followed by a tiny *plink*. Rhea's head popped up, and she reared back, until she was half-standing. She gnawed at the fuzzy tip of a tranquilizer dart protruding from one of her hind legs.

The dart had come from somewhere inside the tree line. Was it the poachers?

Rhea swooned until she collapsed in a heap, barely missing his knees. He put a protective hand on her head, but it was an empty gesture. He had nothing to protect her with.

A shadowed figure stepped out of the trees, outlined by the mist. Tiernay squinted, but couldn't make out who it was. The person took a step closer. He recognized the shape of a rifle pointing out from the waist. A few more steps, and the rough features of the face came into focus. Haddock. How had he found them? The man couldn't track his way out of the local Wal-Mart.

"Looks like I gambled well. Your little pet couldn't stay away from his daddy for very long." Haddock's gruff voice spoke of the harshness of the jungle. He was probably dehydrated, and his face glowed with a nasty sunburn. "Tiernay, move away from the animal."

Tiernay lifted a knee to stand, but the dean motioned with the rifle for him to stay on the ground. Returning to a sitting position, Tiernay fisted his hands on his knees, refusing to leave Rhea's side.

"You made a big mistake running away. I deserve to be involved in what happens to this creature. It's alive because of me." A few seconds' pause, then Haddock's voice softened. "I believed in you. Even though others thought this would be impossible, I knew if anyone could make it happen, you could." The barrel of the rifle nudged toward the ground. "Why did you think you could deceive me?"

"It's you who plans to deceive everyone else."

"Perhaps, but I'm only giving the public what it wants. We all want proof that our beliefs are real. People would rather be deceived than be told they are wrong."

"At the expense of an innocent animal?" Tiernay brushed the feathers back on Rhea's neck.

Haddock raised the rifle up. "I hardly think a few library tours will do any harm." He took another step closer, then twisted the toes of his boots deep into the gravel. "I promise the fate of this animal will be better than yours."

A loud crack punctuated his last words, followed by a sudden, sharp pain slicing through Tiernay's chest.

Haddock continued to talk, his voice a muffled backdrop to the piercing sensation spreading out from Tiernay's breastbone. "You could have been famous. I would have shared the credit, but now it will just be me. The first man to prove evolution true. My face will be right next to Charles Darwin's in the history books. The father and son of evolution. And you won't even be a footnote. Merely another statistic in a dangerous country."

Tiernay felt along the front of his jacket for the protrusion of a dart, but his fingers didn't connect with anything. They came back slick. He stared down at the red sheen on his first two fingertips. Blood. *His* blood.

CHAPTER TWENTY-NINE

"That sounded like a gunshot," Gordon said.

Travis had already jumped to his feet. He gave Lenaia's hand to the doctor. "I'll go check. You stay here with her."

At the barn door, Travis hesitated. He hated to leave her, but who knew what trouble Tiernay was causing now. Travis pushed the door open a crack. Tiernay lay with his back flat on the ground and his legs folded awkwardly beneath him. A dark circle seeped onto his jacket. The creature lay unmoving next to him with its snout touching Tiernay's knees and a fuzzy dart sticking out of its back.

Travis ran outside and knelt beside Tiernay. He shook the man's shoulders, but got no response.

"This is convenient," a familiar deep voice said.

Travis whipped his head around. Haddock stood just outside the stone wall, pointing a rifle at him. Travis got to his feet, then shuffled back toward the barn, but Haddock raised the gun.

"Stay where you are. This is the gun with the bullets, in case you're wondering."

Travis stopped moving. "Why are you here?"

"Why do you think?" Haddock's thick mouth twisted into a sarcastic smile. "I certainly didn't come all this way to fire you."

Compared with looking down the barrel of a gun, getting fired didn't sound so bad.

The sound of shuffling shoes came from behind

Travis. They both turned to look. Mirabel and Owen ran straight to Travis without looking over his shoulder at Haddock. Mirabel's face was pinched into a tight frown. "I found some antivenin, but there's not much." She held up a vial about a quarter-full of clear liquid.

"Hopefully, it's enough." Lenaia had a chance, but only if he could find a way to get Mirabel past Haddock and into the barn.

"Travis, what's going on?" Owen's voice trailed off as he saw the man with the gun.

"You have perfect timing, young man. The two of you are going to help me get this creature in my vehicle over there." Haddock used the gun to point at a four-wheeled vehicle with a cage hanging out the back. The cage looked barely big enough for the animal. "Grab the folding stretcher from the vehicle, bring it over here, and put the animal on it, then put it in the cage. Simple."

Owen stared at Haddock with an open mouth.

"Do it, or I'll shoot you."

"Dean Haddock," Travis used his most appeasing tone. "I'll load the animal, no problem, but let Mirabel and Owen go back to the barn. There's a woman in there who needs medical attention."

"What's wrong with her?"

He hesitated, not sure how much to say. "She needs antivenin."

A full minute went by while Haddock pondered that. "Got bit by the creature, did she?"

"How did you know?"

"Oh, I've read the research."

"Of course. You were working with Dr. Tiernay as Fulton Pike."

"Work with that pompous man? Hardly. He worked for me, or should I say the Genesys Foundation. But the arrogant imbecile never trusted anyone. He thought I would believe he had destroyed the creature." Haddock walked to Tiernay's prone body and looked down at the fallen man. Emotion flickered across his face, but too fast for Travis to tell what it was—fondness or regret? Haddock swept his arm toward the creature. "I knew he wouldn't destroy it, but I had no idea he'd haul it way out here."

A quick clenching of the fists before Travis reined in his anger once again. "So, can they go help her?"

Haddock blinked as if he'd forgotten that was the original question. He circled the gun at Mirabel and Owen. "Once I'm gone, you two can do whatever you want. For now, Mirabel will sit on the steps over there while you two load the creature. Oh." Haddock stepped closer and threw a leather contraption at Travis's feet. "Put this on the creature first. No need for anyone else to get bit."

Travis stomped his feet in the dirt to keep from jumping at the dean. Getting himself killed wouldn't help Lenaia. Instead, he moved to the four-wheeler and found the stretcher. He walked back to the creature, unfolded it, and laid it on the ground, every second watching Haddock from the corner of his eye. The man never relaxed his guard.

Travis motioned for Owen to come help. They needed to pull the snout away from Tiernay's limp body in order to get the muzzle on. The creature's breath came in shallow gasps, like it was fighting sleep, but its eyes stayed closed. Owen bent down, ready to roll the back half of the creature at Travis's signal. Travis fought off the horror as he pushed at Tiernay's knees and managed to spin his body sideways. Once the creature's snout was free, Travis fastened the muzzle straps, then nodded to Owen. Together, they rolled the creature onto the canvas fabric.

As they lifted the stretcher by the long handles, Travis glanced down again at the man he'd punched a few minutes ago. Tiernay's pale skin hung limp on his bones, his jaw slack. So many people had already died because of this creature. Tiernay. Bob. Probably Nina. How had Travis worked with Haddock for years and seen no signs of the evil within? Maybe because Haddock killed for specific, logical reasons—like a scientist. As Travis followed that line of reasoning, his remaining hope burned to ashes. The next logical step was to eliminate all witnesses.

As Owen balanced the head end of the stretcher on the lip of the crate, Travis held the heavier end steady. Haddock kept the cage door open with one hand while his other hand followed their movements with the rifle. Owen came to Travis's side, and together they hefted the stretcher up to slide the creature in.

The head and upper shoulders slid in, but the rest refused to budge. Owen kept the stretcher high while Travis pushed on the haunches to generate some momentum. The creature made it halfway in. They lay the stretcher flat, then he and Owen pushed together to squeeze the rest of it in, forcing the thick body to curl up on itself.

"You." Haddock used the gun to point at Owen. "Go sit on the stairs with your girlfriend. I want to talk to young Professor Perego here."

Travis clenched his teeth. *Deep breaths. Relax the shoulders.* He had to keep his anger in check. Haddock was a murderer and Travis couldn't ignore that, but right now he had murderous desires of his own—if only he could get his hands around Haddock's neck.

"Now that I have the creature, the one person here who poses a threat to me is you."

"What kind of threat was Nina?"

Haddock squinted at him. "You mean that girl in the jungle?"

"The one you clubbed to death."

"Clubbed to death? Overly dramatic, don't you think. I didn't even know she was dead. I needed to stop her from telling you or Dr. Tiernay I was here." Haddock continued like Nina's death was inconsequential. "As I was saying, you're the only one who is a problem." He used the gun to point at Mirabel and Owen. "The village folk, if they talk, no one will listen. But you?" He twisted his mouth into a sideways frown. "You have the credentials. And I'm guessing you know the truth."

"Anyone who looks at the DNA will know the truth."

Haddock circled his gun in the air. "You're not that naïve. The DNA I release will say what I want it to say. It won't be any trouble persuading the public. Seeing the creature with their own eyes will convince them. And the DNA will confirm what they already believe." Haddock gestured at the creature asleep in the crate. "It looks like a dinosaur. And the whole world will believe in evolution because they'll believe we reversed it."

Travis took a step closer. Maybe he could appeal to the man's intellectual ethics, assuming he had any. "How can a lie further the cause of science?"

"Only the creature is a lie. Evolution is true. You know it. This might not be the proof of it, but that doesn't mean evolution isn't true." Haddock swung the gun around wildly as he talked. "If I use this mismatched creature to further the cause of evolution, in the end, truth wins."

Travis opened his mouth to argue, but then his mind clicked into overdrive. The pursuit of truth at all cost was the ultimate obsession of science. That philosophy had brought him to Costa Rica, cost him his job, and gravely wounded Lenaia. Most people didn't even believe in absolute truth. Somehow, he did. But whose truth did he seek? Haddock's truth or God's truth? "Doesn't it matter that you killed three people?"

"Sometimes the truth requires sacrifice." Haddock took control of the gun again and pointed it squarely at

Travis's chest. "And I might have to raise the number to four, if you don't make the right decision. Honestly, I'd rather not kill you. The death of two professors down here would be harder to explain, but, if necessary, I'll figure out how to spin it."

Travis shuddered as he imagined the news headline of his death attributed to the creature. "Paleontologist Killed by a Real-life Fossil." At this range, not much chance Haddock would miss.

"What do you say, Professor Perego? Join me in perpetuating the truth of evolution and become famous. Or die, right here, right now."

Travis ran a shaky hand through his hair. A week ago, he thought he'd die if he lost his career. Now, he had to choose between his career and death, but at the cost of a lie.

All the scientific ethics inside him rebelled at the idea of endorsing a lie. Scientists sought the truth always. But who could say what was ultimately true?

The creature was a hybrid, but that didn't mean evolution wasn't true. And if evolution was true, would it hurt to encourage that belief in others through deceit? Maybe he should take the opportunity and capitalize on it like Haddock planned. He wanted to believe in evolution anyway. The safe, easy path to success—the reason he'd come here in the first place.

But how could he live with himself when the proof was based on a lie? A pretty, university-endorsed, twisting of the facts. For what? So he could have intellectual freedom. Or maybe freedom from God.

Focus. He needed to focus. He was no closer to determining the truth than when he had started this insane crusade. And now he'd run out of time.

"I won't wait all day," Haddock tapped his finger on the trigger.

Travis tried to look in the man's eyes, but all he could

see was the black hole of the gun barrel like the gaping mouth of a snake waiting to strike.

Haddock took a step closer. Travis had to give an answer. He opened his mouth, but his tongue stuck to the roof of it.

A low rumble broke through the air. It sounded like thunder. He looked up at the cottony clouds drifting through the pastel blue sky. No sign of rain.

The trees behind Haddock shook violently. The rumble extended into a growl, growing louder until it became a deep-throated roar.

Haddock turned to look at the rain forest.

Travis seized the opportunity. He jumped for the gun, pushing it toward the ground. Haddock shoved his chest against Travis to hold him off. The man was shorter, but at least thirty pounds heavier.

They struggled for a few seconds with the gun pinned between them. Travis rammed his elbow into Haddock's face. Screaming in pain, Haddock loosened his grip. The sound of his scream was matched by a roar, right next to them.

They both froze.

Travis slowly turned his head. Before he could assess the threat, a long, brown mass jumped, barreling between them and knocking them apart.

Travis stumbled backward, but managed to stay on his feet. Haddock fell half against the taillight and half against the crate, still holding the gun.

A jaguar landed easily near the back end of the vehicle. It circled around, eyes locked on Haddock. Or maybe on the creature.

Travis backed away.

Mirabel and Owen sprinted for the barn. The jaguar swiveled its head around. It could have easily outrun the pair, but seemed more interested in the vehicle.

The jaguar reared up, placing two paws on the

crisscrossing metal bars holding the sides of the crate together. It ran its claws along the metal, creating a high pitched scraping noise. The crate shuddered, but didn't break. Curling back its lips, it let out a fierce growl, then turned to Haddock.

Travis slid his feet closer to the barn. The jaguar shifted its eyes to glance at him, but quickly returned its attention to Haddock whose face bore the look of a cornered rodent.

After a few seconds, Haddock seemed to recover his wits. He sprinted around the other side of the four-wheeler, heading for the front seat.

Travis turned and ran. At the barn, he swung the door open, turning quickly to close it. He risked a glance back. The jaguar had jumped into the back of the vehicle. It had one paw inside the cage, grasping for the creature's hind flank.

Travis pulled the heavy barn door closed, grabbed a nearby broom, and shoved the handle through the latch.

As Travis ran to Lenaia's side, the sound of another gunshot echoed through the wood plank walls.

CHAPTER THIRTY

Distant noises pulled at Lenaia's consciousness. It wasn't words, just the shuffling of people walking. Where was she? The brightness beyond her closed eyelids hurt. She opened her eyes slowly, blinking against the whiteness of the walls. A hospital room. How had she gotten here?

An IV tube ran from her arm. Wires snaked from her chest to a machine sitting next to her. Outside the open door, people walked up and down the hall.

Bits and pieces of information flashed through her head like a high speed movie, but she couldn't remember anything clearly, except talking to Travis on the stone wall.

Travis.

She lifted her head, fighting off a moment of dizziness. In a chair next to the hospital bed, Mirabel sat with her head down reading a book.

Lenaia sank back down into the pillows. He wasn't here. She wanted to smack herself for caring.

"How are you feeling?" Mirabel put her book down and leaned close.

Lenaia took a moment for a quick status check. "A pounding headache, but okay, I guess."

"What do you remember?"

"Travis and I...on top of a stone wall, avoiding some pigs."

"Nothing else?"

She searched her head for a few more seconds, but nothing more came back. "No. What happened?"

"Travis brought you to the village. The creature's bite had poisoned you." Mirabel put a hand on the bed. "But that's not why you're in the hospital. Dr. Gordon had enough antivenin to take care of the poison, but you had bleeding in your brain because of the hit you took. When Travis brought you here, the doctors induced a coma to let your brain heal. You've been asleep for three days."

Her heart fluttered like butterfly wings. Travis had cared enough to bring her here. But then he'd left. She should have known better than to get her heart involved. Life-threatening situations made people feel closer than they really were. The same thing had happened with her uncle on their jungle excursions. She hadn't really known him, and yet she still loved him. Come to think of it, they'd been looking for him. Had they ever found him? She thought so, but couldn't remember for sure.

"I have more to tell you." Mirabel looked up at the ceiling. The shadows in her eyes told Lenaia whatever she had to say would hurt.

"Just tell me."

She let Mirabel take one of her hands between both palms. "Your uncle was killed."

Nausea twisted through her stomach, followed quickly by another round of dizziness. "What? How?"

"He was shot in the village by someone from the university."

She understood Mirabel's words, but they didn't make sense. "Why?"

"The man wanted to claim the creature as his own."

She struggled to make the pieces of information fit. Her foggy mind wouldn't clear up.

"I watched from the barn door," Mirabel continued. "The man promised Travis partial credit for the creature's discovery if he would pretend the creature was a dinosaur."

"I remember..." Lenaia's words caught in her throat. "I remember my uncle saying the creature is a hybrid."

"The man said he would kill Travis if he told the truth about the creature."

She gripped Mirabel's hand tight. "But Travis brought me here, so he's not dead, right?"

"No. Travis is fine. A jaguar attacked them. It was trying to get at the creature. We all ran for the barn. When we went back out, the jaguar lay dead by the village wall, and the man was gone. An hour later, we realized you weren't waking up and needed to go to the hospital. Travis drove you here in your car. Owen and I followed later."

Lenaia nodded. Every part of what Mirabel told her made sense, except for one detail. "Your parents let you and Owen come together?"

Mirabel folded her hands in her lap and smiled the silly smile of a girl in love. "Yes. And can you believe it, he and I are going to go to university together, maybe even next year."

"Your parents support this?"

Mirabel nodded. "When Dr. Gordon couldn't help you right away, I did what I could. My mother was impressed with how I handled myself. She thinks I have the gift of healing. I know God helped her to understand."

"That's wonderful."

Lenaia twisted the end of the white sheet around her free hand. Mirabel reached out and stilled her fidgeting. "Travis stayed for two days, then he said he needed to go."

And he'd left her here with no idea what was going on in his head. "Where did he go?"

"Back home."

That meant back to the university. Had he made his decision then? "Did he say anything else?"

Mirabel nodded slowly and bit her lower lip. "Just

that you shouldn't talk about the creature to anyone, except me of course."

Lenaia squeezed her eyes tight. Uncle Jim was gone. Her heart ached for him, but there was no longer anything she could do to help him. Her stomach twisted again. She couldn't help Travis in his struggle either because he'd left. Her captured heart was forced to wait for an answer to the question that mattered most. Had Travis chosen to tell the truth or was he right now endorsing a lie?

CHAPTER THIRTY-ONE

The clacking of Travis's dress shoes echoed down the stone steps as he descended to the church basement. He brushed a hand along the cool stone banister. How odd to hold a press conference announcing a creature that proved evolution true inside St. Lucia's Chapel, one of the oldest churches on campus.

He shifted the strap of his backpack, straightened the collar of his white shirt, and continued down the arched hallway. The press conference had already started. He'd meant to be here earlier, but had spent too long working things through with Harmony. She should be coming to the press conference soon as well.

At the huge wooden double doors of the basement chapel, he stopped to listen. Nothing. The thick wood effectively smothered all sound from within. He took a deep breath. He wasn't ready for this, but he had to make his choice. No middle ground on this one.

He pushed one door with his palm. To his surprise, it opened silently, and then stuck open as he walked through. The chapel was half the size of a football field with worn wooden pews filling up each side of the room.

Haddock stood at the front on a raised platform, his large frame half-hidden behind a podium. The captivated audience hung on the dean's every word and their eyes followed his every move. Cameras angled for the best shot, reporters scribbled notes, and the air itself felt charged with excitement. At the far end of the platform sat a large, square object covered by a sheet.

"An ambitious project," Haddock said, "to retrace the footprints of evolution along its historical path through the genome. To rewind evolution if you will. The biological genius behind this project can be attributed to the late Dr. James Tiernay, professor of biological sciences. His tragic death occurred recently during a hunting trip in the jungles of Costa Rica."

Travis took a few steps down the polished wood aisle, the tap of his dress shoes drawing attention. Haddock hesitated for a second when he caught sight of Travis.

A flash of surprise crossed Haddock's face, but he recovered quickly and began a lengthy explanation of genetic markers and mutations, which probably soared over the heads of most of the people there.

Travis walked up the aisle, taking a seat in the second row behind a reporter from the local news station. He pulled out a few sheets of paper and pushed the backpack under the pew.

Haddock finished his speech with a plea for more research in this area. "The data from this project will be made available for scrutiny, but I believe the image of a creature brought back from extinction will be what resonates with the public." The members of the audience shifted in their seats, obviously still not sure what he meant. "Eventually, we will permanently house this specimen in a special habitat down by the river, but for now it will stay in the lab where it was created. Ladies and gentlemen, I would like to present to you—Rheasaurus."

Haddock walked to the other side of the stage and grabbed the corner of the sheet. He paused for dramatic effect before ripping the covering off.

The creature, which had been lying down, popped its scaly head up. Cameras and lights converged on it, along with the click of digital pictures, and the buzz of excited voices. The creature stood as much as it could in the small crate. It tried to let out a shriek, but with a muzzle over its mouth it came out sounding more like a strangled meow.

Haddock let the journalists have their fill of pictures. He worked the crowd, his face a mask of congeniality and superiority. The only crack in the mask came when he met Travis's gaze, a slight wrinkling at the corner of the dean's eyes.

After about ten minutes, he motioned for the reporters to sit down and the group quieted. "You will have many more opportunities to photograph this amazing animal. I should also let you know this project was a team effort between professors in the biological and paleontological sciences here at the university. And I want to make sure credit is given where it's due. In fact, I see another partner in this project has arrived. Professor Travis Perego, could you please stand?"

Travis clutched the papers in his hand, got to his feet, and slipped out of the pew. He moved to the front of the room, but stopped short of climbing the three steps to the platform. As he looked around at the amazed faces, he hesitated. If he followed through with this, his life would be forever different after this moment.

He glanced once at the creature. Either way, the consequences of his decision were far-reaching. He had to push ahead. Turning back to the audience, he cleared his throat. "Ladies and gentlemen, thank you for coming, but please disregard everything you heard here." He held up the five sheets of paper. "I hold in my hand proof that what this man claims is a lie. The DNA evidence shows this creature is a hybrid created by splicing DNA from other animals into the rhea bird genome. This evidence was forwarded to your news stations moments before I came into this room. I was not a part of this project. Dean Francis Haddock offered to give me credit if I kept the truth hidden. But the truth does not belong to me. It is not mine to hide."

Travis glanced over his shoulder. Haddock stood frozen with shock splashed on his face. Even so, Travis knew the man wouldn't go down quietly. He could already see Haddock's mind working, trying to figure out how to spin the situation.

The crowd sat in stunned silence until a tall, bald reporter in the second row stood up. "How do we know which one of you is telling the truth? Francis Haddock is an expert in paleontology. And you are...what's your name again?"

"Travis Perego, also a professor of paleontology. And I'm not asking you to believe me. I've already sent proof to your offices."

The reporter gave him a skeptical look. "How do we know you took the sample from this creature and not from something else?"

"Excellent question." He turned to the creature and pointed. "Good science requires repeated measurements. We have the animal in captivity. If my data is correct, further testing will reproduce my results."

He turned back to the crowd. Several reporters nodded, but they were oddly silent, probably waiting to see how this played out.

A soft shuffling of feet came from behind him. He turned his head sideways. Haddock was backing toward the crate. The creature shifted, slipping on the plastic tray under its feet. As the noise from its claws receded, Travis heard the faint click of a metal catch sliding. Haddock was playing his last card. If the creature wasn't available for repeated testing, then it would be his word against Travis's.

Moving back to the pew, Travis used his foot to pull out the backpack. He had only a few seconds to stop the chaos.

The creature slammed into the crate door, pushing it open and sending the metal grid into Haddock's legs.

Haddock fell dramatically to the floor as if it were unexpected.

Travis unzipped the pack. "Please stay in your seats. This creature doesn't want to hurt anyone, but it could."

Rheasaurus scanned the crowd frantically from the top of the platform. It took a few swipes at the muzzle with one of its back feet, but couldn't get it off. Then, it focused on the open door. Pushing off with its back legs, it sprinted down the steps and up the aisle. As it passed, Travis pulled out a white lab coat, shaking it with a snap.

The creature stopped ten feet from the door. It sniffed the air and turned around, led by its nose. It still recognized Tiernay's scent.

The hesitation gave Travis enough time to yell to Harmony. "Take your shot now, please."

Harmony stepped into the doorway. She raised a tranquilizer gun to her shoulder and fired once. The dart hit the creature squarely in the back, near the spine.

A tense moment passed while the creature shrieked and tried to nip at its back. Spinning around, it stretched toward the white lab coat again, but this time it wobbled and swayed. Finally, it dropped onto the floor with a thud. The polished wood vibrated with the impact.

Travis walked over to it, bent down and ran a hand along the feathers on the creature's neck. "We need to keep you for a little while," he whispered. "But maybe someday you can be free." He stood to address the reporters. "As I mentioned, we will be able to reproduce the results. Representatives from the local zoo are prepared to take custody of the creature and care for it until a permanent home can be found or constructed."

Harmony nodded at him, then leaned out the door. Seconds later, three men in zoo coveralls entered the room with a stretcher and began rolling the animal onto it.

Then, two police officers filed in, one young and one

an older, burly man with a beard. They nodded at Travis. He smiled as they passed him and continued up the aisle. Harmony must have done her part and given them the evidence.

Haddock jumped up. Stomping down from the podium, he evaded the young officer and strode to Travis, grabbing Travis's arm and trying to pull him away from the creature. "You can't take it. It's not yours."

Travis stood his ground. "You're right, it's not mine. But it's certainly not your ticket to fame either."

"This isn't over," Haddock hissed.

Travis looked him in the eyes. "You're right about that too. Time to answer for what you've done." He turned to the audience. "Dean Haddock will be unavailable for comment for a while."

The officers had flanked Haddock, and now the young one grabbed his arm. Haddock glared at Travis before turning to the officer with a defiant expression. "You don't have jurisdiction to arrest me for anything that happened in a foreign country."

Although Haddock was twice as wide as him, the bearded officer took over, grabbing Haddock by the shoulders and roughly turning him around. "Francis Haddock. You're under arrest for the murder of Robert Turpin Jr."

The dean's mouth fell open and the blood drained from his face. The officer clicked a set of handcuffs over the dean's wrists. At least, Bob would get justice. Travis leaned in to whisper in Haddock's ear. "Sometimes the truth requires sacrifice."

Travis savored Haddock's furious expression until the officer spun him around and pushed him down the aisle. Travis looked over at Harmony who stood with the tranquilizer gun at her side. She gulped down a breath and gave him a little salute. As the officers led their captive out the door, she followed behind.

Travis turned back to the stunned crowd. "The dean will only be answering questions for the police or maybe his lawyer." He swept a hand toward the empty platform. "This deception was planned to prove a cause. Dean Haddock thought the truth could be manipulated." He picked up the DNA results from the pew and held them in the air again. "But the truth is the truth, nothing more, nothing less. It's what we do with it that makes the difference."

He placed the sheets of paper on the top step of the platform, grabbed his backpack and walked down the aisle. As he reached the door, the crowd threw off its incredulous silence, erupting into a cacophony of voices. They shouted demanding questions at him, but he pulled the door shut, ignoring them like he would the shrill chattering of the rain forest.

CHAPTER THIRTY-TWO

Rushed travelers swarmed through the airport driven by the ticking clock attached to their flights. Normally, Travis enjoyed the airport with its mix of unusual people and the expectation of adventure at the end of a short plane ride. But today, he paced in front of the area where passengers would emerge. Every few minutes, he tried to sit patiently on one of those hot-dog-style benches, but it lasted thirty seconds before he thrust himself off the seat to pace again.

Lenaia's flight had landed twenty-five minutes ago, and yet she hadn't come out of customs. Mirabel had assured him she'd gotten on this flight, so he kept waiting...and pacing.

What if Lenaia couldn't forgive him for leaving her in Costa Rica? What if she just wanted to forget everything that happened, including him? If so, he couldn't blame her.

He rubbed a hand over his face and felt stubble. *Ugh*. He'd forgotten to shave.

Turning back to the exit, he spotted her through the narrow security hallway and understood why she'd taken so long. He'd expected, or maybe just hoped, she would run into his arms, but instead she sat in an over-sized wheelchair pushed by a young male airline employee.

The fear knotted up his chest again. Mirabel had said Lenaia was okay, but he'd left her to suffer through her recovery alone. She might want nothing to do with him now. Even so, he had to find out.

She looked stunning in a cream-colored tank top and long, flowing red skirt. As she came closer, he noticed the pout on her lips. She hadn't seen him yet, so it was probably frustration with the wheelchair. "Lenaia?"

She looked up, and their eyes locked, frozen on each other. He felt the same quickening of the pulse, the same rush of adrenaline, as when they'd first met. Hopefully, she did too.

"Travis," she whispered.

His name coming off her lips stirred up a fire in him. "Can we talk?" He moved to take the handlebars of the wheelchair.

The airline employee looked down at her. "Are you okay, ma'am?"

She nodded. "It's fine."

"Okay." The employee let Travis take over, then turned around to go back through security.

Travis pushed Lenaia for a bit before steering her to the empty back corner of a lounge. A few patrons sat watching television at the bar, but they were far enough away they wouldn't overhear anything.

He removed a chair from a nearby table, placed it in front of her wheelchair, then sat facing her. "You look beautiful."

She blushed, but didn't respond.

"How are you feeling?"

"Pretty good, considering."

He gave a half laugh. "Considering the poison and the head trauma."

She scowled. "I'm not an invalid. I can walk, but the hospital gave the airline instructions to wheel me everywhere."

He grabbed her hand, cradling it in both of his. "It wouldn't hurt to take it easy for a little while."

She relaxed her scowl a bit. "You're not the one stuck in the chair."

He took a full breath and blew it out. She might not be in the most receptive frame of mind, but he needed to get to the heart of things. "Lenaia, please forgive me for leaving you in the hospital. It tore me up to have to do that. I wanted to be there when you woke."

She nodded, but said nothing.

"For your sake, for your uncle, and for my sanity, I had to leave. I came back here to..."

She squeezed one of his hands. "I know."

"What? How do you know? I told Mirabel I wanted to talk to you about this."

"Mirabel didn't say anything." She pointed behind him. "Travis, you're all over the news. During the layover in Houston, I watched the footage from last night three times."

His eyes jumped to the television mounted on the wall of the lounge. Sure enough, the screen showed Haddock being led past Travis in handcuffs. He stared down at the ground, his whole speech forgotten. "I didn't think you would see it before I talked to you."

With her other hand, she raised his head up. "You finally made your decision." A sweet smile played across her lips. "I knew you would."

He smiled back at her, amazed by this woman yet again. She'd believed enough for both of them. "You had faith in me, even when I pushed you away." He captured her hand, gently kissing the back of it. "I heard someone say once that faith comes from love, especially in the absence of proof."

The blush deepened on her cheeks, but she didn't look away. "The creature. Is it going to stay at the university?"

He didn't want to change the subject, although he understood her curiosity. "For now, it will. I wish we could release it to the wild, but your uncle was right, somebody would find it." Her shoulders slumped slightly, and he regretted mentioning Tiernay. She would need time to grieve the loss.

"Do you know what's going to happen yet with your job?" she asked.

He shook his head. "I'm not worried. I'm putting that on God's to-do list."

"Good." She titled her head. "Funny thing about that. I might know someone who has a heart for hiring out-of-work geologists."

She was talking about her boss, Jayna. The fact that Lenaia offered to talk to her boss meant a lot. "I'm open to it as long as it's God's plan. His opinion is the only one that matters to me now." He reached up to caress her cheek. "Well, except for maybe one other person's opinion."

Leaning over, he brought his lips close to hers, waiting for a sign from her, not wanting to push. She ran her tongue over her lips, and it was all he could do to hold back. But he had to give her the choice. He needed to know if she wanted this. If she wanted him.

She tugged one of her hands free from his and reached up, her fingers brushing across his stubble. He really should have shaved. But her hand kept traveling. Over his jaw and into his hair. Every nerve tingled at her touch. When she reached the back of his neck, she pulled him to her.

Her lips tasted like sweet mint, intoxicating and innocent all at once. After a few seconds, he started to pull away, they were in an airport after all, but she tugged him back and whispered, "I'm not so fragile."

He caressed her face in both hands, and kissed her until the fire burned through his insides. Until the desire at his core churned like magma. Until he had no choice but to pull away to calm the heat. After breaking the kiss, he rested his forehead against hers. "Now *you* have a decision to make. How do you feel about spending a lot of time with me? Like maybe forever?"

She laughed, and the sound sent a cleansing wave through his soul. "Why don't we start with a real date? Like maybe a movie."

He took her hand again and rubbed the back of it with one finger. "Someplace public sounds good. I don't trust myself to be alone with you."

She gave him a teasing grin. "But you behaved yourself in the jungle, Mr. Perego."

"Yes, but there I had other things to distract me. From here on out, I plan to focus much more of my attention on you." Her light-hearted banter didn't fool him. That kiss was proof enough that her feelings ran as deep as his. It gave him hope they could create a relationship in the real world. He would do everything he could to prove that her faith in him wasn't misplaced.

ACKNOWLEDGEMENTS

No one makes it through life alone. Our family and friends impact us in ways that are essential and irreplaceable. As an author, I'm fortunate to get the chance to thank them in writing every time a book comes out, although I should really show my appreciation more often. By the way, have you thanked your loved ones recently?

To my amazing husband, Todd. Thank you for being a great example of steadfast love. I know your love for me and our kids never falters. I appreciate you more than I could ever express in words.

To my wonderful kids, Zach, Jenna and Riley. Thank you for allowing me the freedom to be an author. If you weren't such good kids, I wouldn't have the time or energy to do this. I love who you are and who you are growing up to be.

To my wonderful critique partner, Crystal Joy. I'm so glad we are partners on this writing path. Without you, the scenery on this journey wouldn't be nearly so beautiful.

To my writer friends who have been with me through it all. Jeannie Campbell, Sarah Forgrave, Katie Ganshert, Kara Hunt, Melissa Judd (thanks for the wonderful last minute critique), Jill Kemerer, Amy Leigh Simpson, and everyone in the Quad Cities Scribblers group. Other writers are the only ones who can understand the struggle to be eloquent, daring, and raw on the page. I'm blessed every time I talk to one of you and you just get it.

To my former agent, Ann Byle, who was the first professional to believe in this novel. Thank you for your encouragement and faith in my work.

To my early readers who read through the ugly first drafts of this book baby. Michele Beck, Crista DeVore,

Erin DeVore, Donna Feld, Amy Farrey, Nora Fortune, Kara Hunt, Stacey Ickes, Mary Johnson, Sue Muszalski, and Paula Rutkowski (the best sister God ever made). And to Sue Brower for her insightful developmental edit and her sweet words of encouragement. Thank you all for making my work rise to a higher standard.

To Helmut Welke, president of the Quad Cities Creation Science Association, and Dr. Gerald Bergman, professor of science at Northwest State Community College in Ohio, who read through early drafts and gave invaluable scientific advice.

To the talented professionals at WildBlue Press, Ashley Butler, Steve Jackson, and Michael Cordova for having faith in the Earth Hunters series. And thanks to Mary Kay Wayman for her inspired editing, and Kim Mesman for a cover that I adore.

To my precious reader. Your life, your time, your thoughts—they all matter to me. I'm honored you gave a portion of each to read this book. Thank you for being here. I'd love to hear from you. My email is janice@janiceboekhoff.com. And if you'd like to know when the next book in this series is coming out, plus get free goodies, you can sign up for my newsletter on my website www.janiceboekhoff.com (no spam, I promise). Also, please consider leaving a review on whichever site you purchased the book because, and I can't say it enough, your thoughts matter.

Blessings,
Janice

9 781947 290037